I0666175

Arthur Does Camelot

First Edition

Published by The Nazca Plains Corporation
Las Vegas, Nevada
2008

ISBN: 978-1-934625-72-9

Published by

The Nazca Plains Corporation ®
4640 Paradise Rd, Suite 141
Las Vegas NV 89109-8000

PUBLISHER'S NOTE
Arthur Does Camelot is a work of fiction created wholly by *Tim Desmondes'* imagination. All characters are fictional and any resemblance to any persons living or deceased is purely by accident. No portion of this book reflects any real person or events.

Cover Crest, Dan Ionut Popescu
Art Director, Blake Stephens

DEDICATION

···

This book is dedicated to my Uncle Arthur. Unlike Arthur Pendragon, the legendary king, my uncle was a quiet, kindly man, who, with his wife, raised a pair of orphan girls. His influence helped them develop into loving, caring women.

One of them was my mother and the other my aunt.

Uncle Arthur is my idea of a true hero.

Here's to you, Unkie.

Arthur Does Camelot

First Edition

Tim Desmondes

TABLE OF CONTENTS

INTRODUCTION

....

The following tales are based on sixth- and seventh- century Welsh and Latin sources. Most of the original manuscripts were written on parchment and have been preserved in abbeys, monasteries, private collections and museums.

The manuscripts were written in Latin and in Old British, a Celtic language precursory to modern Welsh. In many cases the words of the manuscripts are so archaic that their meaning must be judged from context. Occasionally time has so dulled the ink that context is the only clue to the meaning of the text.

The original documents were written or dictated by Arthur's contemporaries. After the Norman Conquest, French and Norman writers created Arthurian romances with Christian themes like those concerning the Holy Grail. Other writers added morality tales extolling a pure-hearted Christian knight named Sir Galahad. We do not find morality tales or Christian paragons in the original lusty Celtic tales.

I hope that the following tales, derived from a compilation of Celtic sources, will shed a bit of additional light on that period of time historians call the Dark Ages.

I have chosen to tell Arthur's and Myrddin's (Merlin's) stories through the eyes of their sixth-century contemporaries. I have given the characters and the locations back their original British-Celtic names.

Tim Desmondes

CHAPTER ONE

Earliest Memories

CAI SPEAKS:

One hears a fine lot of nonsense about Arthur nowadays. Mostly balderdash. I should know. You might say I've known Arthur longer than anyone. He was my brother. Well, my foster brother. And I loved him dearly, of course. But Lord knows, a great deal of the time I did not approve of the things he did. Not really. Loyal to the end. That's me. Loyal old Cai. But I must say, my brother's morals were dreadful. Not quite befitting a British Christian, if you know what I mean.

When Arthur came to my father's estate, Castrec in Powys[1], he was still in swaddling clothes. He was brought there by that old quack Myrddin[2]. I was only three years old at the time, so naturally I don't remember the occasion. In my memory Arthur was always there.

The story of the sword in the stone was trumped up by Myrddin, you know. Myrddin cast a spell on those in attendance at the sword drawing contest when he conspired to make the young Arthur High King of Britain. The trick worked. Myrddin wanted Arthur as High King so he, himself, would be the power behind the throne. From the time he convinced Uthyr to give Arthur to him, Myrddin was conspiring to run the show from behind the scenes. Myrddin had always wanted to be the real lord of Britain. And after Arthur's accession he was.

---

[1]   The site of Ector's domain was in north-central Wales near the present day city of Llanuwchllyn. The estate became known as Caer Cai during Arthur's reign.

[2]   Myrddin is also known by his Latinized name Merlinus and by his English name Merlin.

But there I go, running way ahead of myself. Damme! I wanted to start at the beginning and here I am up to that silly sword in the stone nonsense.

So, back to the beginning...

When the infant Arthur was brought to us at Castrec, father didn't know who the baby was. Myrddin only explained to him that the infant needed sanctuary. And you know father. He was a fine Christian gentleman. He couldn't refuse sanctuary to an innocent child.

Father had known and admired Myrddin for years. He had a soft spot in his heart for the old pagan. And Myrddin somehow conveyed the feeling to father that it was a matter of national security that the infant be sequestered with us at Castrec, and further that no one was to know his parentage. So all of a sudden I had a baby brother. And that event changed my life forever. As a matter of fact it changed Britain forever after as well.

For the first three years or so Arthur didn't affect my life a great deal. Most of his care was entrusted to Brigid, one of our Irish slaves. I was the apple of my parents' eye and Arthur, as an infant, was no more bother to me than one of the many puppies we kept in the kennels.

Except that he was raised in the house, and slept in my bedroom. Brigid slept in my room in those days, too. In order to take care of Arthur's needs. So, I became aware of exactly how she took care of them. Shocking!

I may have been nothing more than a child myself, but I knew that the way Brigid played with the little fellow's wee-wee thing when the adults weren't looking wasn't really proper. I wouldn't have dared to say anything to anyone about it, of course. But not only did the wench fondle the helpless little child with her hands, but with her mouth as well. And I am sorry to say he seemed to thrive on it.

As she played with that little wee-wee, Arthur cooed and smiled, and showed his appreciation in a very physical way which I certainly shall not mention. You know, I am no friend or admirer of the English[3]. But as bloodthirsty and filthy as they are, I have always found their morals superior to the Irish. And Brigid was not particularly circumspect even for an Irish girl.

Father, although British[4] to the core, had been a Roman cavalry officer, and was the finest horseman I ever knew. Thus, our estate in Powys was one of the most famous horse farms in the Western world. I can't even remember the

---

3   By English, Cai means the Angles, Saxons, Jutes, and Frisians who had settled on the East coast of Britain soon after the Roman legions left. These English raided the Celtic Britons. After battles and skirmishes with the English, the Britons usually managed to bring some English as slaves back home with them. Irish slaves were usually obtained in the same way.

4   By British, Cai refers to the Celts who controlled the Island before the Romans had arrived. The Romans occupied Britannia for some four hundred years, and during that occupation all freeborn British (Britons) were automatically Roman citizens. Ector, Cai's father, had even served in the Roman cavalry in Britannia until Rome called back her legions and Britannia became Britain.

first time I was placed on horseback. I have been able to ride since infancy.

What I do remember, though, is the day Arthur was first placed on a horse.

I was eight years old and an accomplished rider on my pony when father and one of the stable slaves placed my little brother on one of the tamer ponies all by himself.

The little redhead, with a front tooth missing, threw back his head and laughed with glee the moment he found himself in the saddle. He instinctively set the pony on a trot, to the consternation of both the slave and father. To my dismay he rode as well from that first moment as I did with my three years experience in horse riding.

Arthur immediately became my equal in equitation despite the difference in our ages. I was to discover that he was my equal or better in nearly every activity. I must admit that annoyed me somewhat. But at the same time it made it possible for us to be better boyhood companions as well as foster brothers.

By the time I was nine Arthur and I were allowed to hunt in the woods, sometimes afoot, sometimes on horseback, all by ourselves. We fished, hunted, hiked, swam, wrestled, fought, built tree forts, climbed trees, and filled the land with youthful laughter. We were always accompanied by our two hunting dogs – Arthur's hound Cabal and my faithful Clydno. Our hunting weapons consisted of pikes and swords and bows and arrows for hunting roebuck and stag. For spotted grouse, hare, ducks, and geese, we preferred nets and slings. My father, Ector, believed that hunting was the best preparation a British lad could have for battle. And he knew there would be battles aplenty if we were to save our Island from the barbaric English.

Father Byrhferth, our resident priest, taught us to read in Latin and British, to work with numbers, and even to write a bit in both the British and the Roman scripts. But such learning took up only a small part of our day. Most of our time was spent in what was a near idyllic childhood.

When Myrddin came to our estate, which he did at least twice a year while Arthur was with us, he always regaled Arthur and me with lays and legends which he sang to us, accompanying himself on his harp. He also always sang and played for the entire compound we lived in. But for us two boys he sang the Mabinogion in its entirety every time he came. I have no musical abilities at all. But in my off-key way I can sing much of the epic myself from memory because of Myrddin's performances. He sang of the heroes of our British race, Gwion, Kynan, Meriodoc, and the rest. He also sang of the times in which we lived with lively tales of Theodoric, Clovis, and the other rulers on the Continent. I was always enchanted by the old man's singing. But I could never stand the man himself. He was unpleasant to be around except when he was playing his harp. When not singing and harping he was cross, cantankerous, and just downright rude. During his interminable stays at Castrec, Myrddin took Arthur out into the woods to instruct him in the evil Old Ways of Wycha[5]. It was clear to me that Arthur was more inclined towards the pagan teachings of Myrddin than the holy teachings of Father Byrhferth. My parents seemed blind to the evil that Myrddin was stirring into Arthur's soul.

Brigid had been removed from our bedroom, of course, by the time Arthur was five years old. But, she arranged to meet him in the stables when he was about six. I know, because I secretly followed him when he sneaked away to meet her. They lay down in the hayloft and undressed. They caressed each other in most unseemly ways. How do I know? Because I found a hidden spot on the other side of the loft from which I could watch unseen. Why did I bother to watch these sinful scenes? I thought perhaps I would someday be able to explain to Arthur how wrong it was for him to submit to such odious practices. Perhaps it would help to save his soul. But, oh, my. The things they did there in that loft.

Arthur started to grow light face-hair when he was thirteen. I was sixteen that same year and I was just barely cultivating the fuzz on my own upper lip. Arthur, although younger than me, always seemed my age or older physically.

Back then, when he was thirteen, after we would go to bed, he would play with himself. He played with himself until he made a mess in his nightclothes. I did talk to him about that.

"Arthur, I see you playing with yourself at night before you go to sleep. I believe that is not a virtuous thing to do."

"Oh, come off it, Cai," he said. "I'll bet you do the same thing when I'm not looking."

"I certainly do not!" I huffed.

"How about dreams, eh, Cai? Don't you sometimes dream of girls in the night? And don't you wake up with your bedclothes as spotted as mine when I've been pleasuring myself?"

I had to admit that I had such dreams. And Arthur just laughed and said, "See. There can't be anything very wrong with that if a good Christian lad like you has experiences when his mind is asleep."

Arthur's reasoning bothered me. So, I went to Father Byrhferth to seek guidance.

"Father. I have seen my brother Arthur play with himself at night."

"Have you been guilty of lustful consideration of your brother, my son?"

"No, Father," I hastened to tell him. "It's not that. I'm concerned about whether what he's doing is likely to damn his soul to Hell."

"You are rightfully concerned, Cai," he told me. "What he is doing is a

---

5   Wycha: the religion of the Britons prior to the arrival of the Romans and Christianity. Despite the attempts of Christianity to wipe the religion out, it continued to survive among the British people.

great venal sin. The Church has a Latin name for the sin – *masturbari* – Which derives from words meaning to befoul one's hand. But, my son. It is more than the hand that is befouled. It is the very soul. You must urge your brother to come to me to confess his sin and seek absolution from Our Lord by doing an appropriate penance."

I told Arthur what Father Byrhferth had said.

"Tell you what I'll do," Arthur answered me. "Next time Myrddin comes to Castrec, I'll seek his opinion. If he says I should confess what I'm dong as a sin, I promise you I'll do so."

Well! Consulting an old pagan like Myrddin didn't seem very appropriate to me. But, I was interested in what Myrddin would say about all this anyway.

Myrddin had said he would be returning to Castrec towards the beginning of the month of An Bhealtaine, which the Romans call May. Which meant he would be with us around Arthur's birthday, since Arthur was born on the eve of Beltane[6].

We didn't have long to wait for an answer to the question of the sin of self defilement.

As always, after Myrddin was received as an honored guest by my father Ector and my mother Liv, he regaled the entire hall with epics of our people. He had the most beautiful singing voice I ever heard. And he was unequaled on his instrument. The entertainment followed a lavish dinner of meats, breads, vegetables, honeyed cakes, and plenteous mead and ale.

Myrddin brought out his harp and entertained us way into the middle of the night.

On these occasions, Arthur and I were allowed double portions of ale, which often meant we were fast asleep before the epics spun by Myrddin were completed. We would fall into a deep slumber and be carried off to our room by the burly field slaves who were allowed into the villa on festive occasions.

The second day of his visit with us, Myrddin led Arthur out into the woods for instruction in the ways of Wycha. I'm quite sure that Father Byrhferth did not approve of that arrangement. But, apparently Father had agreed to it when Arthur was first brought to us.

When Myrddin had left, I dared ask Arthur what the bard had said in response to the matter of self-defilement.

"Myrddin laughed at the question," Arthur said.

"What do you mean, 'he laughed'?" I asked.

"Just that. He said that what I was doing was the most normal thing in the world. There is no defilement at all about it. Myrddin says the Christians

---

6   Although Castrec was a Christian household, and the Roman calendar was nominally adopted by the Christians, the Celtic calendar was still followed by the majority of the people in Britain in the years 500 to 515 A.D. that Cai is describing. Arthur's birthday, Beltane Eve, would have been April 30 on the Roman Calendar. By Christian reckoning, he was born in the year 500.

have very weird ideas about our sexual selves. Some crazy notion about 'Original Sin.' I'll have to admit that when Byrhferth gets into the Original Sin story, it leaves me quite cold."

"So there's nothing wrong, according to Myrddin, to self-befoulment?"

"Myrddin says he believes old Byrhferth is doing the same to his own prick even as you are discussing the matter with him."

(Yes. That is the very word Arthur used.)

Well! I was shocked. Even today, from the viewpoint of myself as a cultured, Christian, British gentleman, I am shocked at such talk.

Father Byrhferth was a holy cleric of Mother Church. I'm sure he never engaged in such a practice himself. And behind the confession screen. The thought makes me shudder. I cannot even bring myself to think that the holy man even has a…prick.

(I hate to use Arthur's word. You can be sure it was *his* word, not mine.)

What I couldn't keep myself from doing, and what I could never bring myself to confess to Father Byrhferth was this. Whenever I spied Arthur and Brigid heading for the hayloft in the stables, I found myself drawn by a force greater than my Christian conscience to sneak off to my hiding place on the other side of the loft, where I could observe them unseen. There was no orifice of their bodies that did not manage to be met in erotic attachment.

Kissing, yes. I didn't approve of the kissing. But I could accept it. But the other actions? Forgive them Father!

Brigid was as comely a lass as I had ever seen, or indeed, as I have beheld since. Her golden hair was, as the British bard sang, "more lovely than asphodel whilst kissed by Lleu[7]." Her skin was so milk-white that she seemed as translucent as the alabaster vases brought to our shores from Egypt. And in those areas that glow pink against such coloring, no rose could ever match. She was a woman shaped for love.

But my sense of romance is intruding on common decency. I shall not describe Brigid further to you. To do so fills me with most unseemly thoughts, as her presence did in those days.

One lazy, rainy afternoon, when I had taken my viewing position of the lovers, I found my hand climbing towards my groin, unbidden by my higher consciousness. The Devil certainly had control of me.

On this particular occasion, as I watched my brother and the Irish slave-girl disport themselves, I was engaged in sinful practice myself. And as I did so, a most surprising thing happened. The knob of my member burst through the prepuce for the first time, accompanied by an odor reminiscent of the fish that was sometimes brought to the villa from the sea and had been exposed to the air for an extended period.

---

7   Lleu: Celtic sun god.

That, mixed with the smell of the hay in which I was ensconced, caused me to feel a euphoria that I sometimes cannot help but feel around the presence of over-ripe fish. May God have mercy on my soul.

Not long thereafter, I found myself engaging in the sin of self-pollution as often as Arthur had done when I had warned him of the danger to his soul. My sin of self-abuse was something that I found myself able to confess to Father Byrhferth. And, knowing I was contrite, he offered absolution after I had performed the various penances he prescribed.

The image of Brigid haunted me in various ways when I was far from the hayloft. It was her milk-white breasts with their iridescent pink aureoles blushing forth that were always present in my dreams when my nocturnal emissions awakened me. And it was of her entire body, but particularly the pubic area, that filled my fantasies when I found my antic hand exercising my own private domain.

But of none of this dared I speak to another soul, not to Arthur, and certainly not to Father Byrhferth.

Although we changed physically – hair growing on various parts of our bodies, our voices changing, and our procreative equipment now exerting a great command over us – Arthur and I followed very much the same sort of activities that had occupied us as children. We still rode, hiked, hunted, fished, swam, wrestled, squabbled, laughed, and raced each other.

However, Arthur no longer engaged in erotic play with only his previous nursemaid. He now paid amorous pursuit to every female he thought he might be able to seduce. Girls just recently flowered, mature women the age of even my mother, pretty, plain, freeborn, slave. They were all grist for his mill, so to speak. And, at night, he would brag to me of his conquests. I was shocked, and would have preferred not to hear of his sinful ways. But, after all, he was my brother, if only in a foster kind of way.

And I certainly did not wish to be rude and not listen to what he had to say at the end of the day.

Our bodies had changed, yes. And Arthur's ruttish ways became more extreme. But the idyllic life we lived remained much the same. That is, until we met Palomides one afternoon in the forest.

I believe to this day that our supposedly chance meeting with Palomides influenced Arthur's future irrevocably. As a result of that encounter my brother turned into the ruthless, merciless killer who later became the salvation of Britain. Yes, our meeting with Palomides was actually as portentous as that.

Arthur and I had happened upon a wild boar that morning as we were hunting in the woods. We had pikes and swords with us and were young and stupid enough not to be concerned about the danger posed by that fierce beast. Between the two of us we managed to subdue and slaughter it without allowing it to inflict wounds on either our persons or our horses with those vicious tusks. Arthur and I gutted the beast, butchered it, and cut out heart, liver, and testicles to roast over a fire we built in a clearing. The rest of the boar's meat we would later take back to Castrec for the kitchen slaves to prepare for a feast.

As the redolence of the sizzling organs wafted into the forest air, a tall, dark man rode out of the trees and into the clearing. We were caught unawares. Had he been bent on mischief he certainly would have made short work of us.

In a harsh, guttural accent, he addressed us.

"Hail, Britons."

"Hail, Stranger," Arthur answered as he rose from his sprawled position by the campfire. He spotted his own sword out of reach over by his horse, Eidyn.

The shrewd eyed stranger followed Arthur's glance and sidled his horse between us and our mounts, blocking access to our weapons.

"You need not be concerned about my intentions, young hunters," the intruder answered. "I approach you in peace. I know not what rules of hospitality you profess. But the scent of your cooking drew me close to observe."

I was perturbed by the intrusion of the black-eyed man. He did not look like a civilized Christian to me. Or even a British pagan. More like a heathen, if you know what I mean. But if Arthur was concerned he showed it not at all.

Stranger," he said. "These are the forests of the local brenin[8], Ector. We are of his house and welcome you to his lands. Even more, if your intentions are indeed peaceful, we are preparing more food than we can possibly eat ourselves. We would welcome you to join us at our hunters' repast. In return, all that we request is that you leave your mount and weapons by yon tree where we have left our own."

The stranger did, indeed, ride to the edge of the clearing and dismounted near our horses. The manner of his dismounting was exceedingly curious. His left foot was resting on some sort of implement hanging down at the horse's flank. Never had I or Arthur ever seen a horse so equipped. With great show, the dark man divested himself of sword, shield, bow, and dagger, and returned to the fire, extending his empty hands in evidence of disarmament.

The boar organs crackled and sizzled robustly on the greenwood spit, wafting into the sun-drenched air the scent of the boar fat with which we kept basting them. Both Arthur and I had hunting knives that we had retained to assist in the sectioning and devouring of our rustic feast. The stranger was aware of the cutlery, and evinced no concern about it.

---

8   Brenin: A title indicating a landholder, a warlord, or an acknowledged leader of a Celtic tribe.

Arthur introduced me as Cai son of Ector and himself as my brother. The stranger smiled a wide grin which revealed alarmingly white teeth.

"Young gentlemen," he said. "I thank you for your hospitality. I perceive that you are roasting delectable organs of the boar whose carcass I spy yonder. Many of my race and religion find meat from that family of beasts an abomination. Not I, young Britons. Whatever the Lord of the Universe has provided in the way of victuals for his creatures, I accept with thanks.

"My name is --- ."

He said his name. But it was absolutely incomprehensible to British ears. It was expressed in a burst of sound harsher to the ear than the screech of the banshee.

"I perceive that my name baffles you," the stranger chuckled. "Indeed, it appears to be unintelligible to all your countrymen. My native language is that of the Saracens. And of that people, I was a member of the tribe of Palomides. Thus, in this British land of yours, I answer to the name of Palomides the Saracen."

I was still quite tongue-tied but fascinated. I had heard of the Saracens and knew them to be neither Christians nor Wychans. This particular Saracen appeared to be some ten years or so older than us. But with a fellow creature of such exotic appearance it was difficult to discern such subtleties as age.

"Well, Palomides the Saracen," Arthur answered. "The meats appear to be ready for carving. We have no plates to offer you. We ourselves intend to lay the carved meat on these flat stones. More formal wear does not present itself in this rough spot."

Palomides shot us one of his astounding smiles, picked up a flat rock, and exclaimed, "If the sons of the local Brenin eat their kill on such plates, I would be most honored to join them so."

With that Arthur removed the delicacies from the spit. And behold, there was ample for the three of us.

When we had finished our feast and had wiped as much boar fat from our fingers and faces as possible without access to damp cloths, Palomides thanked us and complimented us on our food preparation. By then I had summoned enough tongue to ask him the question that had lingered in my mind since he had descended from his saddle.

"Palomides," I said. "You are our honored guest and have been most welcome at our bucolic feast."

In that, I was not entirely truthful. For though I was curious about him, I cannot in good conscience say that I found his presence welcome. But having disposed of fine British banalities, I proceeded.

"I am intrigued by the manner in which you dismounted," I told him. "I have never before seen the like. And I pride myself in knowing as much about horsemanship as any man in Britain."

Well, I was putting it on a bit, I'll admit. Yet, as you know, equitation was not foreign to my upbringing.

I continued.

"What, pray tell, good Palomides the Saracen, is the purpose of that strap you utilized to dismount?"

His answer was most enlightening. And when Arthur fully understood the scope of the device he had one of the keys that later liberated our Island from encroachments by English, Irish, Picts, and Vikings. The moment that Palomides answered our questions may have been the moment that Britain was saved from the barbarity knocking at our shores.

Palomides asked us if we had ever heard of the Scythians.

"Why yes," I answered, remembering a reference by Tacitus to a people of that name. "They are wild barbarians who dwell well beyond the Danuvius River where the Empire ends at Vindobona[9]."

"Ah," said Palomides. "A British scholar. I believe that since the Romans withdrew from Britannia there do not remain above a hundred men, save the Christian priests, who could have answered so readily."

I wondered whether the smile he exhibited when he said that was one of mockery, sarcasm, or comradeship. Was he saying that since the legions had left there were only barbarians left on our Island? I was inclined to take umbrage but I wanted to hear about the Scythians and was not aching for an argument or a fight.

Palomides flashed a beatific smile at me.

"Have I offended you in my manner of speaking, Dominus Caius?"

No one had called us Britons by our Latin names since we were abandoned by Rome. I was no longer Caius, but Cai. Father was no longer Hectorius but Ector. Mother was never addressed as Livia, but as Liv. And Arthur never had been called Arturius.

"I use your Roman name," said the stranger, "knowing you may despise it. I only sought to acknowledge how well versed you are in your Tacitus and no doubt in much of the literature of the Western world. I would not have you take offense."

As I was considering whether to pout or show interest in our guest, Arthur spoke up.

"Yes, yes, Palomides. Brenin Ector has a fine library of books at his disposal. And the priest who resides in the villa has led us through our history and geography. We know that these Scythians of whom you speak are reputed to be unrivaled horsemen who have no fixed homes. And that Rome was never able to subdue them."

"Exactly right, Lord Bear," Palomides responded with the pun that followed Arthur all his life. The British word for bear is close enough to the word "Arthur" to cause good-natured joshing. Arthur always responded to this friendly punning in good spirits.

---

9   Cai is referring to the Danube River and to Vienna.

"Yes, Master Saracen," Arthur laughed. "I am a red pelted bear indeed. But I will not go into hibernation until you regale us with your tale about the Scythians."

And regale us he did. He told us that the Scythians had managed not only to stay free from Roman rule but from Alexander's empire as well. Those nomad tribes persistently managed to sneak across the Danuvius and steal the finest horses from the stables of the Roman cavalry.

Rome, desirous of teaching the barbarians a lesson, offered the Saracens a great bounty of gold if they would put the Scythians to rout.

The Saracens were known to be extraordinary horsemen. The offer was made and accepted. And Palomides' tribe was among those dispatched beyond the Imperial border.

The Romans and Greeks were aware that the Scythian horsemen had footstrap[10] ornaments on their mounts. But with Imperial arrogance, never did the "civilized" Graeco-Romans consider adopting the contrivance themselves.

Palomides' tribe was successful in capturing three horses from the Scythians, horses that were still accoutered with footstraps. They experimented riding the beasts with the embellishments and discovered that they could wield their weapons much more expertly when their feet were thus supported. Palomides fell into a dispute with his tribal leader and was exiled from the troop. He never revealed what the source was of the dispute. And neither Arthur nor I ever attempted to pursue the point.

"And so, young hunters, I left Scythia, an exile from my people, and with only my horse and the provisions in my saddlebags. But I retained the one treasure that allowed me to overcome all obstacles. A set of Scythian footstraps.

"Against all odds I managed to ride through Roman, Gothic, and Gallic territories without being killed. When I got to Hispania, I liberated some twenty excellent horses from the residents of that province. I then paid for passage to Ireland by presenting a boat captain with two of the horses I had acquired and made my way to the Green Island. On that island I found artisans who were able to duplicate the footstraps. I paid for them by leaving one more of my horses with the workmen. Now, with footstraps for my tiny herd, I joined a group of Irish marauders, crossed the sea to Britain with them and my remaining horses, and found myself raiding your countrymen. I soon learned to admire you Britons and despise the filthy Irish."

Not long after he arrived in Britain, Palomides deserted his Irish companions. This in itself made me wonder whether he had not, in like manner, deserted his own Saracen people for base motives. I did not trust the man then. And I never did learn to trust him. But then, I don't have confidence in any foreigners.

---

10   Throughout the sixth century, and well into the seventh, there was no word in Latin, British, or English for stirrup. The only term used for the novelty was "footstrap."

"Bit by bit," Palomides continued, "with my tiny herd of seventeen horses, I began to attract a contingent of adventurous Britons. At first, three British adventurers joined me. I taught them to ride and fight, using the footstraps to advantage. The first people my new band attacked were the very Irishmen who had accompanied me to your shores. They were no match for our small group. We beheaded all twenty men. My nascent band of adventurers was enriched greatly by the bags of silver and weapons the Irish dogs had robbed from your people."

Well, anyone who had successfully attacked, robbed, and eliminated Irish marauders could not be totally reprehensible. Yet it was clear that the man was nothing more than the leader of a group of ruffians and cutthroats – an outlaw gang that preyed on invaders to our Island. Not the type of person civilized people would want to associate with.

Arthur clearly did not share my feelings.

"How many people are now in this group of yours?" he asked.

"We are now ten, including myself. As I stated, we have seventeen horses, so have room for seven more companions. If either of you fine gentlemen know of any men who are brave enough, patriotic enough, and horsemen enough to join us in ridding Britain of the filthy invaders from the West, we would welcome such bravehearted souls. There is booty to be had in the undertaking. But most of all there is good, bloody sport for the valiant."

Arthur was valiant enough, God knows. Also, he was foolhardy. The sort of person Palomides was seeking. I felt sure we would see Palomides again, and in the not too distant future.

But of all that I will tell you anon. For now, I am weary of tongue and parched of throat. Would you be so kind as to pass the cakes and ale?

CHAPTER TWO

The Young Myrddin

MORGAN SPEAKS:

Yes, I know. You came here to hear about Arthur. And you have come to the right place. For Arthur was my brother – issued from my mother's womb. However, he was not of the seed of my father, Gorlois.

But of all that I shall tell you anon. For I would speak to you now of Myrddin. You cannot really understand Arthur unless you know Myrddin – bard, warlock, magician, asshole, and fake.

I first met Myrddin the night my brother was conceived. Conceived not by the union of my mother Eigyr with her wedded husband. Sired not by my father Gorlois, warlord chief of Dyfneint[11], but conceived beneath passionate linen through my mother's fuckfest with Uthyr, High King of Britain. According to the Christian priests, that copulation was unchaste. But I do not hold with the ridiculous views of the priests of this new religion. Arthur's conception was holy in the eyes of the British religion, Wycha.

So, from a doctrinal point of view I approve of my mother fucking this stranger. Which does not mean that I necessarily had to like the creature produced by it. You will see that Arthur and I have had some differences of opinion.

Myrddin the warlock had conducted Uthyr to our ancestral castle, Tintagel, as a pimp might lead a customer – as a whoremonger might negotiate with a ruttish common soldier. The warlock used a simple trick, the oldest one

---

11   Also called Killiwic, Dumnonia and Cornwall, depending on language and dialect.

in a magician's bag of deceptions. He caused the castle guards to believe Uthyr was, in fact, my father, Gorlois. He used the ploy of misdirection. I am no mean magician myself and am well versed in the arts of misdirection.

Although I was but a child-novice in the Mysteries then, I alone, of all Tintagel's retinue, clearly perceived that the man disguised as my father was someone quite else. My twin sister, Margawse, was, of course, paying no attention whatsoever to anyone other than one of the young horsemen accompanying the visitors. Her eyes were always on the crotch of the most attractive male around. It was clear to me that my mother knew it was her lover and not her husband who had barged into Tintagel to fuck her. And I knew that the man with the bardic hat and carrying a harp was responsible for the illusion suffered by everyone other than my mother and me. The castle guards believed the man who had burst in on us with such pomp was the local warlord and master of the castle, Gorlois.

But I digress. Perhaps that is an effect of old age. I said I would tell you about this man Myrddin. And so I shall. Through my powers as a priestess of the Goddess I have gazed into the Cauldron and discovered everything that can be known about the man who fulfilled the role of Pandarus to my mother's Cressida. You see, I know the romance stories of the Roman soldiers who occupied our Island for four hundred years and who have finally left our shores. Stories like Pandarus and Cressida and Cupid and Psyche. I only hope the exeunt of the occupying Romans will eventually also remove their foul religion of the hanging carpenter from our Island.

Myrddin was a nameless bastard in his earliest youth. He answered only to such callings as "Boy!" or "Laddie!" or, as often as not, "Brat!"

His mother was a famous whore who serviced the Roman troops in Caerlleon, a town known in those days as the City of the Legion. She was called Ionna Go-to-'t by the troops. Which suggests she showed more than average enthusiasm for her profession. But her trade was not restricted to the occupying military establishment. Because of the versatility of her accomplishments she drew clients from among some of our most eminent Britons. One of those customers was none other than our most renowned and justly celebrated bard and wizard, Taliesin.

On one particular occasion Ionna was less than punctilious in her ablutions. Consequently she conceived a male child. Yes, the very "Boy-Laddie-Brat" of whom I was speaking. Who was the father of the infant? Officially he had no father. For by Roman law and Celtic tradition the child of a whore is fatherless.

However, one of Ionna's clients took a particular interest in the child. There is reason to believe this client's interest may have been paternal. Further, since this client was a wizard, he might have cast a spell on his coupling that caused the whore to conceive. My own incantations and magic visions do not reveal whether such was the case or no. You may draw your own conclusions as you listen further to my tale.

When Boy-Laddie-Brat was about five years of age our renowned bard Taliesin came from his lodge in the City of Myrddin and offered Ionna the opportunity to be rid of the lad. Since little boys serve small purpose in a whorehouse, Ionna accepted the offer with alacrity.

The boy enjoyed life in his new home at the lodge in the City of Myrddin. His treatment was vastly superior to the abuse he had been accustomed to receiving at the Caerlleon whorehouse. He was subjected by Taliesin to a rigorous course of studies from the very beginning. The lad was quick to memorize the epics, ballads, and lays of our Celtic forebears and specifically of our British bards. He learned to sing and play the harp with marked virtuosity. He was initiated into the mysteries of divination, sorcery, and magic. By the time he was ten years of age he was seen to be a prodigy.

While the boy was growing in stature and knowledge Britain was enduring the birth pangs of national tragedy. The lad had been born in the year 450, as the Christians reckon time. By that time the High King of Britain, Vortigern, had already begun the process which eventually brought disaster to our Island.

Vortigern was not the high king's given name. His actual name sounded something like Wrnach. I dare not pronounce the actual name. Nor may it be written. The tyrant so disgraced himself by his treacherous actions that King Emrys who succeeded him decreed the name may never be spoken so long as bardic tongue can sing or finger pluck. So the tyrant is only to be known by his title, Vawr-Tigherne[12] (Vortigern) so long as Britons inhabit this land.

Of Vortigern's foul decisions and the treachery he practiced on his people you may learn from the tales of our bards. Never will his infamy be forgotten so long as we have bards to sing or scribes to transcribe. Suffice it to say that in the Christian year 466 Vortigern was held as pariah by both Britons and English. With a small coterie of warriors, wenches, and wizards, he retreated to Mount Eryth[13] to build a fortified tower wherein he could defend himself.

Although the earth around Mount Eryth has supported human habitation since our people came to this Island a hundred generations ago, the specific spot chosen by Vortigern's wizards for the erection of the tower was unwise. For the earth there is unstable, a crumbly crust over an underground cavern. Vortigern chose his wizards as unwisely as he chose his allies.

A king may choose incompetent generals and survive. But if he chooses incompetent wizards or sorceresses he will surely face disaster.

Vortigern set his chief architect to work on construction of the tower. Time was a major concern since the traitor's enemies could well be in pursuit.

---

12   Vawr-Tigherne: high leader in one of the British dialects.

13   The location was subsequently named Dinas Emrys, and in modern times is called Llangollen.

While the foundations of the stone tower were being laid, a fine wooden shelter, a ty-hir[14], was constructed to house Vortigern and the wenches who had accompanied him. The remainder of the retinue, including the wizards, the builders, and the architect, had to be content contemplating the open sky day and night.

Each day, stones from the sacred precincts of nearby Plas Newydd were hauled to Mount Eryth and laid down as foundation. Each morning, when Vortigern came forth from the Mansion of Wenches where he slept, the foundation stones laid the previous day had been swallowed up by the earth.

Naturally, the bard Taliesin was aware of the problems being faced by Vortigern and his architect. He visited the site by stealth and by simple knowledge of the earth's secrets discovered the cavern beneath the location designated for the foundation. With such knowledge he developed a plan for exploiting the situation to the benefit of his young ward.

When Vortigern consulted his fat-assed wizards about how to remedy the problem of the swallowed foundation stones they told him that a magic ceremony would be needed.

"O High King of all the Britons. There is, indeed, a way in which this disaster may be overcome. Our mother, the Earth, has a thirst that must be slaked if she is to support the stones being laid upon her."

"Then, abominable wizards who have allowed this situation to develop, provide Mother Earth with the liquor she desires. Else she shall drink wizard blood on the morrow," the king warned.

He was told, "What Our Mother desires is the blood of a boy sired by no mortal man. Once we sprinkle the blood of such a lad over the foundations they will stand for as long as Britons rule this Isle."[15]

When he had stolen into the encampment at Mount Eryth Taliesin had managed to purloin the wizards' book of spells and incantations from their stash of magic materials. And he discovered this Druidic spell in their books. He saw that it would fulfill his own purposes. Once his plan was hatched he retired to his lodge in the City of Myrddin.

The tyrant was exceedingly wroth with his wizards.

"You stand there like the very stones of Plas Newydd. As we have moved those very stones, move your fat asses and locate such a lad and bring him here that we may shed his blood and get my tower built. My enemies could arrive at any moment and shed my blood instead of that of this magical youth unless you hasten. Be gone and fetch me the lad within three days. Else, all three of you shall shed blood here and shed it very slowly and painfully.

---

14   Literally a "long-house" which was built of wood, with one end reserved for human habitation and the other end for cattle. In the case of the ty-hir at Mount Eryth, the animal end was used to stable horses rather than cattle.

15   The three wizards were Derwyddon (Druids). They were here suggesting the Druidic rite of human sacrifice as propitiation to the gods.

Your king has spoken."

The wizards did, indeed, remove themselves from the sight of their king with great dispatch. And they agreed that they would need the assistance of the greatest wizard of the land to find the lad. (I wonder how in the world that idea entered their heads.) So off they hastened to the city called Myrddin where Taliesin had his lodge.

"O Bard of Britain," the chief wizard addressed Taliesin. "We are three wizards from the North who seek an apprentice to learn the ancient wisdom of the tribes who dwell at the Wall." They dared not mention that they were associated with the despised Vortigern. They were dissembling wizards, not too bright, but yet not altogether stupid either.

Taliesin had anticipated their arrival and their request.

"An apprentice, you say. Are there no lads in the North country who would serve your purpose?"

"A young man in the North Country is liege to Carl, Warlord of Northern Reged. Carl is threatened by the Tribe of Clyde to his north and will allow no sons of his people to be apprenticed other than to his own warbands. So we have come South to find an appropriate apprentice."

"And you have not found any possible candidate on your long trip from Ynyscarl to Myrddin?"

"Alas, no," the wizard replied. "For the apprentice must needs be a boy sired by no mortal man. And every tribal chief we have spoken to claims he knows of no such lad under his protection."

"A boy without mortal father," Taliesin mused. "I know of such a lad. A bright boy who plays well on the harp and who aspires to become a wizard. Perhaps I could provide you with the information you seek."

The wizards were delighted. They truly wanted the blood of such a boy to nourish the earth rather than have their own sorry blood manure the soil of Mount Eryth.

"Where can we find this child?" asked the slowest witted of the wizards.

Taliesin scratched his beard and mused a bit. "A child you say? Would a young man do?"

"A young man of what age?" asked the second slowest witted of the wizards.

"Some sixteen years or so?" Taliesin drawled.

The wizards consulted among themselves. They agreed that sixteen would be a fine age for the candidate whose blood would preclude their own from joining the earth of Mount Eryth.

"In the streets of Myrddin you will find the youth," the Druids were told. "A lad with reddish brown hair and blue eyes. Fleet of foot is he. So you must either be of sound wind or use deception to capture him. He answers to the name 'Boy,' 'Laddie,' or 'Brat.' Catch him and you will have your apprentice."

As I have told you, Taliesin had already examined the location at Mount Eryth himself and knew the source of the problem. He had shared the information with his apprentice and had told Boy to anticipate the arrival of three fat-assed wizards who would attempt to capture him. The lad was to avoid them until they were exhausted. After the wizards were wiped out physically, the young man was to allow himself to be captured and taken to the enclave of the disgraced high king. Thus, when the three wizards spotted him in the streets of the city, Boy took flight.

The three wizards followed in pursuit with nets in hand to capture the sprite who flitted through the alleyways like an elusive butterfly. They would nearly catch up with him, and he would sprint away. They would have him cornered in a building, and he would escape through a window.

The wizards huffed and puffed. They dragged their overweight bodies through windows and over fences. Perspiration drenched their bodies and clothing. They became begrimed, crawling through crannies that their prey slid through with ease. In short, they were in high pursuit for two days and a night before the young man allowed their snares to enclose him. Then, bound hand and foot, he was hauled to Mount Eryth in Powys.

The youth was presented to Vortigern by the three adipose wizards.

The warlord questioned the lad.

"What, youth, is your name?"

"I was born without a name. I have been raised in the City of Myrddin. And as is the case with many thus born, I choose to be called by the name of the city that harbored me."

"How is it that you were born without a name?"

Vortigern thought himself sly, attempting to ferret out whether the person presented to him was, indeed, a lad who had been sired by no mortal man. Myrddin, for such we may call him now that he had adopted a name, was well schooled in how to answer the tyrant.

"I had no name because I was sired by no mortal man, Your Vawr."

"Sired by no mortal man, eh? Can this indeed be proved? For, if you are indeed a youth who was sired by no mortal man, I will reward you richly."

"For proof," the young man replied, "you need only ask my mother, O great Tigherne."

"And who might this lady be who conceived you in the manner the followers of the hanging carpenter say their god was conceived?"

"She is the Great Whore of the City of the Legion, most highest Vawr Tigherne."

"And her name, son?"

"Ionna Go-to-'t, may it please your honor. She can testify to the truth of what I say."

Vortigern ordered his fat-assed wizards to hasten to Caerlleon, the City of the Legion, to find the Great Whore Ionna Go-to-'t. And off they waddled as rapidly as their stumpy little legs would carry them.

The next day they returned with the whore. She stood before Vortigern as unawed as her son had been. Ionna knew men. She knew all about men. She knew how they worked, and knew how to work them. She stood dauntless with her awesome tits proudly pointing in the direction of the tyrant.

"You are Ionna Go-to-'t?"

She did not answer Vortigern immediately. She merely let him gaze at her as she stood full-bosomed in the mist-filtered sunlight at the foot of Mount Eryth. The tyrant's weary eyes suddenly froze in admiration of the voluptuous female shape before him. His tongue refused to communicate with the world. It could be seen that there was action stirring in his groin. The tyrant began to tremble. Ionna could have that effect on men when she chose. And she enjoyed seeing the tyrant developing a hardon before her very eyes. Then she answered.

"I am she. I am known as the Great Whore of the City of the Legion. And what would you have of me here?"

Vortigern could not answer the question, though it must have been obvious to all about him from the powerful tenting in his trousers what he would have of her. Yet he remained tongue-tied and motionless except for the trembling and the pulsating of his cock.

The middle wizard took up the questioning.

"It is said that you bore a son, O Harlot."

"You speak sooth."

"And who was the father of that son?"

"The lad had no father. Everyone in the City of the Legion knows that to be the case."

"Do you see that child of yours here in this assemblage?"

"I have not seen him for many a year. He was taken off to the City of Myrddin when he was but an infant and has never returned to the City of the Legion."

"Is there any way you would be able to recognize him?"

Ionna called out, "Boy-Laddie-Brat!!".

Myrddin called back, "Coming, Mother."

Myrddin rushed into his mother's arms. She acknowledged that this was, indeed, her son. The erotic spell under which Vortigern was held had been broken by the mother-son reunion. His hard dick wilted on the spot. He had his boy-who-was-sired-by-no-mortal.

Vortigern invited Ionna to take refreshment in the Mansion of Wenches while he had a little chat with her son.

The lad had established that he would henceforth answer to the name Myrddin.

"Myrddin, my boy," Vortigern proceeded. "I have a great honor for you. You see yon rubble of stones? They were to be the foundation of a tower I am building on this spot. Every day, my masons set foundation stones in place. Every evening, the stones are swallowed up. I have brought you here to assist me. For my wizards tell me that by sprinkling the blood of a youth such as you over the foundations, the enchantment that hinders my building will be broken."

Myrddin had anticipated this moment.

Even as a young man Myrddin had the arrogant voice of a sorcerer. He was as tall as Taliesin. Which signifies that he was a very tall youth. He was also erect, self-assured, and powerful. This was the appearance of the youth whom Vortigern's wizards would sacrifice to the foundations of the tower. Myrddin looked right into the tyrant's eyes with an intensity that seemed to launch sparks through the air.

"Summon your wizards to appear before me, and I will prove them liars," the youthful sorcerer bellowed.

It was an order, and a command which suggested authority.

"Young Myrddin," Vortigern replied. "The wizards stand to my right even as you speak. Do you not recognize them?"

"Wizards?" Myrddin scoffed. "The men who stand beside your Vawrness are no wizards. They are fat-assed sons of bitches. And I shall prove this to be true. Summon your most skillful diggers to this place."

Vortigern's entire retinue was present to observe what they had believed would be the sprinkling of the youth's blood onto the foundations. In that retinue were laborers with their picks and shovels. Without so much as command from the tyrant the workmen stepped forward.

Myrddin pointed to a particular spot on the mount. Since arrogance often carries the weight of an authority beyond that of the speaker, he commanded, "Dig down three cubits from yon spot."

The crowd gathered around as the workers bent back and sinew to the task. Within minutes the crowd exhaled with one breath in wonder. "Oooooh!" For the workers had dug through the crust, the earth opened up, and the enormous cavern underneath was exposed to the rays of the sun god Lleu.

"This underground cavern was what was unknown to the three fat assholes who stand at your side, O Tigherne," the youthful wizard intoned. "No magic and no sacrifice was needed to prevent your tower's foundations from sinking into the earth. Had you sacrificed me, the earth would have cursed you and your enemies certainly would have destroyed you."

The mention of enemies, of whom Vortigern had more than any man on our Island, devastated the high king.

"Then, youth, it would be bootless to attempt to build my tower?"

"Not at all, Lord," Myrddin informed the king. "Your architects need only move the foundation location ten cubits down the hill and the cavern will be avoided. Later, another tower may be built just outside the edge of the cavern for a dungeon. The cavern will serve as prison enough for those who meet with your displeasure. But first your own tower should be built on safe, consecrated ground."

"You mean the location you named, some ten cubits down the mount."

"Nay, more must be done as well," Myrddin suggested, relishing the discomfort his pronouncement would have on the three Druids. "The earth must be fed with the fat of your treasure."

"The fat of my treasure?" Vortigern answered, perplexed. "And what may that be?"

"The earth demands that rumpfat be worked into it. Manure the earth with the lard of the butts of yon so-called wizards and your tower will stand forever."

And thus it was that the three wizards who had ordained that Myrddin's blood be sprinkled on the foundations were placed on the butcher block themselves and their broad asses were cleaved from their bodies.

The rumpfat was diced and fed to the earth. And Vortigern's tower was duly constructed.

All agreed that the wizards appeared more sightly with their asses severed. But none of those Druids ever practiced wizardry again.

Of course, the whole sequence that transpired at Mount Eryth had been conceived by Taliesin. He desired his ward (whom we all feel quite sure was his bastard son) to gain an early reputation as a great wizard. The miracle at Mount Eryth was the origin of the propaganda declaring that Myrddin was a wonder-youth. His fame spread immediately throughout Britain. Humbuggery, of course. There was no magic or wizardry involved. There was no more than the application of Taliesin's earth knowledge. Myrddin's only addition to Taliesin's plot was that of cleaving off the asses of the detestable false wizards. Myrddin had a knack for inventing such mischief.

Taliesin composed a lay about the "miracle," creating a myth of Myrddin as a great wizard. He embellished the song by telling how two great dragons, one red, the other white, rose out of the cavern. The dragons purportedly rose into the sky and battled each other in the sight of Vortigern and his retinue. In the lay, Myrddin is credited with interpreting the meaning of the duel of the dragons and prophesying Britain's future therefrom. The great lay, "The Miracle of Mount Eryth," spread though our Island from sea to sea, from The Wall to Lyonesse.

The Miracle of Mount Eryth was to be Myrddin's last act as Taliesin's apprentice. Taliesin knew that the youth needed further training at Ynyswitrin. Myrddin had memorized and could sing and play one hundred epics. To become a bard, a harpist must know two hundred epics and be able to sing and play those epics with exquisite grace. Even with two hundred epics one simply enters the first of the seven levels of barddom.

Only two men have risen to the seventh level in the past two generations, Taliesin and Aneirin.

(Myrddin turned out to be an excellent bard, but never rose above grade five.)

Taliesin felt that his ward had other things to learn before becoming more proficient in singing and chanting the Celtic songs, lays, and legends.

At age sixteen, then, after Myrddin had become the legendary Boy Wizard of Mount Eryth, he was sent off to Ynyswitrin Tor to learn to become a warlock of the Wycha religion.

You've heard of Ynyswitrin, haven't you? In the Summer Country? Have you been to the Summer Country?[16] It is home to several important religious sites. Lake Avalloc is situated there.[17] Shrouded in the mists that perpetually cushion the lake is the Isle of Avalon, home of the Lady of the Lake, a site holy to both Druidism and Wycha. On the north shore of the lake is the Christian Abbey of Saint Joseph of Arimathea[18]. A false legend states that a follower of the criminal carpenter brought relics of his religion there some four hundred years ago. We know that to be false, for we Britons were settled there way before that time and no Joseph person ever arrived with relics from the Roman province of Judea. But doleful monks and nuns have wasted their lives at that abbey for many a year. They believe in some kind of vicious god who got angry at the human race and who could not get over his anger unless his son got hanged by the Romans. I could never make much sense out of that teaching. But then I never tried very hard. The Christians are arrogant enough to claim that our Isle of Avalon, less than a league away from them out in the lake, does not exist. There is a third religious site less than a Roman mile from the abbey. It is called Ynyswitrin Tor[19].

Atop Ynyswitrin Tor stands a sacred grove dedicated to the Horned God Cerunnos. A major Wycha Coven dwells in a cave beneath the Tor and holds its festivals in the grove and around the Sacred Well called Blood Spring. The site is shared with Gwyn ap Nudd, Lord of the Fay[20] who holds revels there on Midsummer Eve. The religion of the Fay is compatible with that of the Horned god and the Great Mother.

---

16   Somerset in southwestern Britain.

17   Near the present-day town of Glastonbury. The lake was consecrated to Avalloc, a warlock who led his Wycha followers there in the early years of the Celtic invasion. The ignorant claim the lake was called Avallo, which means apple in the British language.

18   The Abbey Ruins south of the modern town of Glastonbury.

19   Glastonbury Tor, on which a Christian chapel was built after the English conquered the area and suppressed the Old Religion.

20   The Fay were a band of Pixies (Picts), sometimes called Fairies, sometimes Picts, who were dwellers on the Island before the arrival of the Celts. They adopted Morgan as an honorary member of their band when she ministered to their king, Gwyn ap Nudd, after he hurt himself in a drunken revel.

Myrddin lived for two years there at Ynyswitrin. During those two years he learned the spells, incantations, ceremonies, and beliefs of our sacred religion. He learned the magic not only of Wycha but also much of the lore of the Pixies and Druids. He participated in the ceremonies at Avalon on those occasions when we allow adult males onto the island for special feasts and revels. One thing the priestesses of Avalon never taught the youth was the art of flying. One of the major advantages I always had over Myrddin was that I can fly and he never was able to. The art is reserved for the highest ranked priestesses of the Goddess. No male has ever been known to possess the secret.

The year Myrddin turned eighteen, which by the Christian calendar is Year 468, he had learned everything he needed to know to take the first steps toward fulfilling his ambition to become the Master of Britain. And that very year, history and politics conjoined to provide the opening for him to venture out into the world of power.

Two Britons had arrived in the land to challenge Vortigern. They were Emrys and Uthyr, two British brothers who had been spirited off to Lesser Britain[21] to be raised out of the reach of Vortigern. The brothers were sons of Cystennyn Llydaw[22], the lawful high king of Britain whom Vortigern murdered in order to rule the land. Vortigern attempted to have the boys assassinated. But they were out of his reach in Lesser Britain where they were raised in the court of King Bors in Nanteos[23].

As Myrddin finished his warlock studies he became aware of the arrival of the brothers with their troops from the Continent. He decided to throw his lot in with Emrys and Uthyr and exploit any situation therefrom which would lead him to his goal.

I will tell you of his meeting with Emrys and Uthyr and how he assisted them in wreaking revenge on Vortigern. But the telling of the tale thus far has wearied me. I would rest and sip the milk of the poppy. I will retire now and dream sweet dreams of yore. However I will invite you back to hear more of Myrddin at another time. And the more you know about Myrddin, the more you will understand about Arthur.

---

21   Brittany, or Armorica: a province in current day France that is still inhabited by people who speak a modern version of the ancient British language.

22   Called Constans by the English.

23   Present day Nantes in France. There was a Nanteos (present day Cheddar) in Somerset in Britain in the sixth century as well. Each "Nanteos" claimed the distinction of being the earlier settlement.

CHAPTER THREE

Master of Britain

MORGAN SPEAKS:

So, you're back to hear about Arthur, are you? But I haven't yet finished telling you about Myrddin. Are you too slow of wit to remember I told you that you need to know about Myrddin in order to understand Arthur? Because Arthur was Myrddin's creature.

Myrddin was determined to become Master of Britain. And the instrument he used for that purpose was my brother Arthur.

Myrddin was consecrated a warlock at Ynyswitrin Tor's sacred grove at Cerunnos coven. When you hear tales of him later, you will often find Myrddin associated with a stag. That's a reference to Cerunnos. If you are not an initiate that may not mean much to you. It does have meaning to those of us who never forsook the Old Religion.

Myrddin's rise to power really began in Year 468 when Emrys and Uthyr returned to Britain. You recall that when they were infants they were smuggled to Lesser Britain to protect them from Vortigern who had murdered their father Cystennyn Llydaw, the lawful high king of Britain.

When they returned as young men, they brought an army with them. Significantly, it was an army with cavalry, which they would need not only to wrest the kingship from the tyrant, but to defeat the English to whom Vortigern had allowed a foothold on our sacred soil. Emrys Wledig is probably called Ambrosius Aurelianus in those books you've read in Latin or English. The first records about him were written by monks who wrote in Latin rather than in our British tongue. For some reason those monks used a Latin name for Emrys but never bothered to Latinize Uthyr's name other than to occasionally render it as "Uther."

When the brothers arrived, they expected to meet an army of the gwledigs[24] loyal to Vortigern. Instead, they were met by offers of welcome from all the warlords. Vortigern was sequestered at Mount Eryth with a small retinue. The gwledigs had been awaiting the arrival of the brothers from Lesser Britain in order to pledge them their allegiance against the usurper. A happy surprise and a good day for our Britain.

Myrddin was eighteen years old at the time and immediately knew that his future lay with Emrys and Uthyr. The bards of Lesser Britain had sung Taliesin's lays about the Boy Wizard of Mount Eryth so Myrddin's fame was not unknown to the sons of Cystennyn Llydaw.

The first night that the brothers appeared on Britain's shores they stood before a large campfire addressing their troops and their new allies. Myrddin used his pyrotechnic tricks to suddenly step out of the fire and appear in front of the two commanders. Reputedly, it was quite a show. I can imagine it, for I had seen Myrddin often enough both at Ynyswitrin Tor and at Avalon when he was studying to become a warlock. He was a tall, slender man with an aquiline profile and with hair down to his waist. He was, even as a young man, an imposing figure. I never did like the man. But I must admit he presented a fine figure for a wizard.

There was no real magic involved in his fire prestidigitation. I've used the illusion myself from time to time as an illustration of the power of the Goddess. But I'm sure the illusion was effective. The tall, serious youth with a harp in one hand and a sprig of mistletoe in the other emerged naked from the fire. There was a gasp on the part of the troops. The bodyguards of the two young generals immediately pointed their spears at the wizard. Myrddin was unfazed by the guards' hostility.

"Hail, Liberators of Britain," the wizard intoned. "I, Myrddin, Warlock of Britain, bring you tidings from the Horned God who protects our isle."

That title he gave himself, Warlock of Britain, sounded impressive. It had no meaning at all, though. Myrddin was a warlock. Yes. And he was British. Again, yes. But "Warlock of Britain" sounds like a title. He was just one warlock out of hundreds. But he was the most ambitious of them all.

It was Emrys who answered.

"Myrddin, Warlock of Britain, Child of the Fire. What are these tidings?"

"Victory, exaltation, and delivery from the enemies of the ancient gods."

"Is this a prophecy, Young Myrddin?" Emrys asked.

"I do not prophesy," Myrddin told them. "The gods do not give the gift of knowledge of the future to their adepts on earth merely to amuse lowly humans. I bring you a message, not a prophesy. When auguries are needed,

---

24   British for warlord.

they will be revealed. No king, no general, no varchog[25], can demand them."

"Come, then, Myrddin, warlock youth that you are," Emrys declared. "You may sit beside us and offer us such counsel as you feel is in the interests of Britain."

Myrddin sat with the two brothers, resplendent in his magnificent nudity. All his life he had an awe-inspiring physique. He sat facing the host that had gathered to save and protect our Island. He incited them to a patriotic pitch with the battle hymns he sang and played. He was not yet a bard. But his repertoire was by then approaching something like a hundred-fifty epics. And the great bards, Taliesin and Aneirin, were not around for comparison. Emrys and Uthyr perceived right away that the young warlock was an asset to their cause.

The next morning the newly appointed counselor, for that is what he was already, breakfasted with the two generals. He appeared attired in the robes of a bard. The brothers were discussing how best to begin their campaign.

"Supreme Gwledigs of Britain," Myrddin declared. "I would counsel you to destroy your greatest enemy before attacking the worms that gnaw at the carcass of the traitor."

Uthyr looked at his brother and shrugged his shoulders.

Myrddin caught the message and became immediately less cryptic. He re-explained.

"The enemy of Britain must be destroyed first. I refer to Vortigern, the former Vawr-Tigherne, who murdered your noble father, usurped the kingship, sought your own deaths, invited the enemy to dwell on our shores, and betrayed much of our beloved land into the hands of English, Irish, and Viking dogs."

Emrys replied, "This enemy of Britain must be found before we can destroy him, Myrddin."

"Have you not heard the lays of the roving minstrels?" the young warlock replied. "Did they not fill the ears of the Britons in Lesser Britain? I have listened to the songs. And I discover my own name as the person who brought forth two mighty dragons from the depths of the earth in the presence of Vortigern. I not only know where the traitor is. I know how he can be destroyed. And until he is sacrificed to the gods you will make no headway against the foreign enemies who dwell throughout the land."

Myrddin went on to convince Emrys and Uthyr that the god Lleu, the sun god, demanded Vortigern as a burnt offering if he was to assure victory over the foreign dogs who polluted his Britain.

Myrddin told the two generals he would lead them and the assembled host to Mount Eryth. Once there, they would wait, unobserved, to discover when Vortigern left his stone tower to visit the wooden whorehouse, his Mansion of Wenches. With his mastery of fire, Myrddin declared he would set

---

25   British for knight.

the mansion afire and force Vortigern out of the ty-hir into the shrine of his own immolation.

When the troops were ten leagues away from Mount Eryth a bivouac was called. During the wait, Myrddin supervised the construction of the Wicker Man. Have you seen such a shrine? No? It is a statue woven of wicker, seven times the size of a man. The Druids introduced the ceremony in our land and the priestesses and warlocks of Wycha adopted it for extreme occasions. The sacrificial victim must be induced to enter the wicker frame of his own free will. Once inside, the Wicker Man is set afire. There is no escape. The sacrifice burns to death inside the wicker statue and is accepted by Lleu as a propitiation for the evil to be expunged. The death is excruciating. Just the sort of thing that always appealed to Myrddin. And the brothers, whose father had been murdered by the tyrant, thought it had a nice ring to it as well.

Myrddin himself stole nightly to the site of Mount Eryth. On the day known as Litha[26], the omens were propitious. On that evening Vortigern left the sanctuary of his tower to visit his whores in the wooden ty-hir. There was ample time for Myrddin and a crew to haul the Wicker Man to the door of the structure. They knew Vortigern would be occupied for a long time.

When the Wicker Man was in place, Myrddin set off an explosion that began to consume all the walls of the ty-hir except the wall at the door. Myrddin, Emrys, and Uthyr crouched in the bushes to enjoy the spectacle.

Vortigern was the first one out the door, followed by a bevy of his wenches. The whole group had no choice but to run directly into the Wicker Man. As they entered, the last wall of the ty-hir burst into flames, setting the Wicker Man afire. There was no escape for any of the sacrificial victims inside the shrine. Vortigern's shrieks of pain and rage pierced through the wailings of his whores. Myrddin led the young generals out of hiding and urged them to dance around the periphery.

What a sight it must have been. Mid-Summer Night, a full moon beaming from the heavens, two generals dancing in full military regalia, Myrddin, stripped naked, painted blue with woad, wearing stag horns on his head, strumming his harp, singing and dancing. The troops were beating time to the music on their shields. In our Celtic blood, such revelries lurk, awaiting such occasions. I would have enjoyed being there myself to join the frenzy of that dance directed to Lleu and bringing the blessing of the Goddess to the occasion. All hail Lleu! All hail to the Goddess!

The gwledigs who had joined Emrys' cause led their troops to Mount Eryth to observe the charred corpse of the traitor, his flesh melted into that of the whores who died with him. Before the assembled troops, with the consumed Wicker Man as testimony to their act, the gwledigs present swore fealty to Emrys acclaiming him High King of Britain. Which made Myrddin, after Emrys and Uthyr, the most powerful man in Britain.

---

26   Alban Hefin, the Summer Solstice.

Emrys made Mount Eryth his capital. To this day the site is known as Dinas Emrys in honor of the man who liberated Britain from the shame of the tyrant. Emrys' coronation was held there at Dinas Emrys only days later. There was no time to waste. It was Myrddin who placed the golden filet on the new king's head and who announced that the gods of Britain recognized a true high king.

Standing in front of what was now his tower, Emrys addressed the gathered throng.

"Fellow Britons. Our Island has suffered many an indignity due to the usurpation of my father's throne by a man whose given name is never again to be uttered or written so long as Britain endures. That man shall be known only as Vortigern for the title he wrested from lawful authority. That title, Vawr-Tigherne, shall not be born ever again by another high king of Britain. It shall be draped with shame for evermore.

"As your high king, I assume the noble British title of Pen-Dragwn[27]. By such title would I be known – Emrys Wledig ap Cystennyn Fendigaid brawd Aldwr brenin Llydaw Pen-Dragwn."

"Hail, Emrys Pen-Dragwn," rose like an anthem over the entire plain below Mount Eryth. It has been claimed by those ignorant of our language and our traditions that Emrys' title was derived from the word "dragon" in honor of the magic dragons Myrddin allegedly brought forth from the sky on his first appearance at Dinas Emrys. Balderdash. Believe that foolish trash if you wish. Emrys chose a good British warlord tile, Pen-Dragwn.

The traitorous false king of Britain had been disposed of. The next task was to eliminate the cursed English whom Vortigern had allowed to remain in our land. The leader of those English barbarians was Hengest, a chieftain who ruled from the kingdom he had established at Cawnyt[28].

Within days of his coronation Emrys led his troops against the English enemy. Emrys' band was now swollen to many times the number he had brought from Lesser Britain, due to the allegiance of the gwledigs to their new high king.

Hengest met the approaching army with a host of a thousand wild barbaric English foot soldiers at the major ford of the Caswallan River. He was totally unprepared for the magnitude of the force facing him. He had never before had to fight an army that outnumbered his own and he was thrown into confusion. A single cavalryman from Lesser Britain was superior in killing power to thirty English foot soldiers. The ensuing battle lasted over four hours but the devastation of the English was greatly disproportionate to the losses of our own troops.

Varchog Eldol, the leader of a warband of a hundred fifty men, captured

---

27   Another popular title for the high king was Bretbrenin, which the English adapted to their language in later years when they were victorious over the Britons.

28   Cantium in Latin. Kent in modern English.

Hengest, bound him, and brought him to Emrys. When the English realized that their leader had been taken, they laid down their weapons and submitted to the British. The hated English were beaten and humiliated within weeks of the arrival of the sons of Cystennyn Fendigaid Llydaw.

When Hengest was brought before the high king, Myrddin was present at the event.

"O Pen-Dragwn of all Britain," Myrddin addressed Emrys. "If you wish to reduce the number of English dwelling in Britain, you must unman this Hengest, who years ago, by treachery, caused the death of four hundred-sixty of Britain's most noble leaders. Your varchogs are the sons of those leaders who were massacred at Ambrys Plain by the minions of this vile dog Hengest. His people, and all English in Britain, must know that vengeance belongs to Britain's gods and goddesses."

Emrys asked, "What vengeance do you propose, Counselor Myrddin?"

Myrddin was well equipped to dispense the kind of justice called for. Although I cannot abide the man I applaud the unpleasant ways he devised to humiliate our enemies.

The English soldiers who were still afoot after the battle were bound over as slaves. It took a full day before the armorers were able to forge enough chains and shackles to restrain them. After the shackling, the horse branders burned the brand of Emrys on the cheek and forehead of each one of the prisoners. Duly shackled and branded, they were rounded up in a clearing and forced to lie on the ground with a British soldier standing above each one to hold the slave by his long English hair to direct his attention to the ceremony Myrddin devised.

When the prisoners and troops were all in position, the English leader Hengest was hauled into the center of the clearing for all to see. His head and beard were shaved, he was stripped naked and painted blue on every body surface.

Emrys' butcher, a mere churl, came forth with his iron knives. While six British soldiers held the English leader immobile, the butcher proceeded to slash off the cock and balls of the captive. The guards then released him and allowed him to bleed to death from that gaping wound in the groin as his soldiers moaned and wept.

The severed cock was presented to Emrys, who attached it to his shield. That gruesome reminder of the great triumph remained on the high king's shield. However, that shield with its reminder of the great triumph was never to see battle again. Emrys, the chieftain our people had been waiting for during our years of shame under Vortigern, was destined to lead but the one battle, the one waged against Hengest and his barbaric English.

Among the English slaves who were made to witness the ignominious death of their leader was Eopa, Hengest's youngest son. Our people did not know at the time that Hengest had a son among the host. Had they known, they could have guessed that the son would vow vengeance. Would that we had known, for our great leader met his too early end because of our lack of knowledge.

Emrys and Uthyr knew about the British heroes who had been treacherously slain at Ambrys Plain[29]. The brothers now wanted to visit that site to pay homage to the dead who lay there.

Myrddin knew the place well and conducted the young commanders there. It grieved Emrys mightily to see how rudely the fallen heroes were buried in the coarse earth. It was Myrddin who suggested a memorial be built there incorporating the stones of the Giants' Circle[30], most of which at the time was in ruins.

Myrddin said to Emrys, "If you wish to sanctify the burial place of these men with a lasting monument, restore the Giants' Ring with stone from Mynydd Preslau. In that way you will have a new memorial that will last forever."

Emrys agreed immediately.

Stones had been hauled from Mynydd Preslau[31] to Ambrys Plain hundreds of years before we Celts arrived. It must have been a tremendous task for those dwellers of our Island at the dawn of civilization. In the year 469 when Emrys stood there with Myrddin, it was still an endeavor to tax the ingenuity of our architects and builders. But with his knowledge of ramps, levers and pulleys, Myrddin had the technical resources in his mind. Emrys was convinced.

So Emrys commissioned his brother Uthyr to conscript as many English slaves as he would need to quarry and transport the giant stones to Ambrys plain where Myrddin would supervise the actual reconstruction of the megaliths to enshrine the bodies of the fallen British heroes within the enclosure.

Foolish, ignorant people believe that Myrddin constructed the entire Gwaith Emrys on virgin ground by the use of magic. Nonsense. Most of the stones had been there before our people ever migrated to this Island. Myrddin simply restored it. And not by magic but by principles used for millennia in Egypt, Greece, and even way beyond in the East. But though I admit it grudgingly, I must agree that Myrddin accomplished the task wonderfully. Go visit Gwaith Emrys on Ambrys Plain for yourself. The monument stands tall and proud, a glory of our Celtic civilization.

Uthyr and Myrddin worked closely together on the enormous task of construction. Each served as foreman for his own area of responsibility. Uthyr

---

29 Salisbury Plain in English. The site of Stonehenge. It was the location where 460 British leaders were treacherously slain by the English at a peace conference by Hengest during Vortigern's reign.

30 Later called Gwaith Emrys.

31 Mynydd Preslau: A mountain in southwest Wales where the stones for the original prehistoric Stonehenge were quarried and brought to Salisbury plain.

came to know and respect Myrddin. And Myrddin used the respect he had earned from the general to further his own goal of eventually becoming the Master of Britain.

While the memorial was being built, Emrys retired to his tower at Dinas Emrys. The defeat of Hengest was just the beginning of the battles he envisioned. There were still many English tribes settled on our east coast. The Irish had many a settlement on our west coast. The Pixies and Vikings were always a threat from the North. And barbarians kept arriving in their keels and curraghs from east and west. Even the Pixies had learned to come around the Wall by boat, landing south of the patrolled area. Emrys' two most effective strategists were busy constructing Gwaith Emrys, while he was studying such maps and written documents as were available to him at the time.

While Emrys was busy planning his future battles he harbored a viper in the kitchen of his tower. Hengest's son, Eopa, still had managed to keep his identity hidden and had become a kitchen slave at Dinas Emrys. Eopa had but one goal in life. To avenge his father's shameful death at the hands of Emrys. Back in Cawnyt where he had been the son of the warlord and a favorite of the court he had learned the arts of deceit that come so readily to the English dogs. Among the mysteries that the wizards of his father's court had taught him was the fine art of poison. He knew the secret of nightshade and had gathered some of the poisonous plants from the forest when he was sent out as a slave to gather berries for the royal kitchen.

One evening he slipped a large dose of nightshade into the broth that was to be served to Emrys Pen-Dragwn. Within hours the high king was writhing in agony. A message was sent immediately to Ambrys Plain for Uthyr and Myrddin to come to Dinas Emrys as fast as possible.

When they arrived the king was still suffering massive convulsions. Myrddin knew from the symptoms that Emrys had been poisoned and that the poison was nightshade. He knew antidotes for many poisons. He also knew there was no antidote for nightshade. Poppymilk could lessen the suffering and Myrddin administered massive doses, some of which Emrys could hold down. Myrddin and Uthyr sat by the royal bedside night and day attending the king. On the third day our noble king and liberator lay dead.

Myrddin arose from the dead king's bedside determined that he would learn who had murdered Emrys. And he would avenge the treachery, slowly and painfully. It was the sort of thing Myrddin probably loved most and did best.

The most obvious suspects were the kitchen slaves. Myrddin had them brought to his interrogation room several floors up in the tower, one at a time. Perhaps "had them brought" suggests a milder procedure than Myrddin ordered. The English had been allowed to keep their barbaric long blond locks in their servitude. Myrddin sent two of the huskiest of the Viking slaves into the kitchen. One of the guardian slaves gave a mighty blow with a cudgel to the balls of one of the kitchen crew and the other one grabbed him by the hair and dragged him through the corridors and up the stairs to Myrddin's room. By the time the kitchen slave arrived for interrogation he was in a state of both pain and terror. In this state, Myrddin knew that the test of the eye-pupil response worked perfectly. He began by asking neutral questions like ""What is your race?" "What is your age?" "What is your name?"

He carefully gazed into the eyes of the person being questioned. Then he asked, "Did you put poison into the broth of the king?"

Slave after slave was thus dragged into the room and questioned. One after another, no change occurred in the size of the pupil. After questioning, the slave was thrown out the upper story window to fall in a heap on the hard ground below. Two Vikings awaited the fallen interrogated slaves and hauled them back to the kitchen in whatever state they were in. The effect on those awaiting interrogation was devastating. Finally, Eopa was tugged through the corridors and up the stairs.

"What is your race?" "Angeln."

"What is your age?" "Twenty-two."

"What is your name?" "Eopa."

"Did you put poison into the broth of the king?" "No."

Eopa was not able to control the automatic response of his pupils. They contracted to the size of pin heads. A lie always has such an effect.

Myrddin had his man.

The cavern Myrddin had revealed back when Vortigern was trying to build his tower had been fenced around and had been converted into a dungeon.

Eopa was not thrown out the second story window. A different fate was planned for him. He was brutally hauled to the dungeon and strapped to a table Myrddin had installed for the purpose of exacting justice.

The wizard had sent to Gwaith Emrys for a set of rusty iron tools. Tools from the burial place of Britain's heroes seemed justly appropriate. When slave and instruments were set up Myrddin invited Uthyr to witness the way the man who killed his brother would spend his last miserable days.

Myrddin had to restrain Uthyr during most of the operation to keep him from prematurely killing the wretch. Uthyr would get his turn, but Myrddin wanted the process to be slow and painful. Uthyr would have dispatched the murdering whelp of an English bitch too rapidly. But subtlety was called for.

And Myrddin was one of the subtlest men on the Island. Two great kings of Britain had been murdered by foul means. Cystennyn Fendigaid Llydaw had been murdered by Vortigern and his son Emrys ap Cystennyn was poisoned by Hengest's son. It fell to Myrddin to render justice. And in both cases he did so most appropriately. I'm not sure I could have done better myself.

Eopa was clamped to the execution table by heavy iron fetters. He was stripped naked and painted blue. Rusty saws, files, chisels, scissors, and knives were arranged in a rack set up next to the table.

Myrddin, as avenger of Britain, slowly dismembered the slave. The crude tools made the job particularly gruesome. Myrddin began with the toes and then proceeded to the fingers. One by one, Eopa's body parts disappeared. But with the assistance of his knowledge of ointments, herbs, potions, and tourniquets, Myrddin made sure the wretch did not bleed to death. Moreover, a special potion enhanced the pain and excruciation. Eopa had been a brave warrior. But his shrieks filled the cavernous dungeon and echoed out over the entire domain of Dinas Emrys. For three days and three nights Eopa's parts were rent from his body and tossed to a pack of ravished hounds that fought one another noisily for the choice bits. At the end of the three days Uthyr could no longer contain himself.

"Myrddin. I have enjoyed the operation you have performed. The English whelp has fed our British dogs enough. It was my brother who was sent untimely to Annwfn[32]. I can wait no longer. Allow me to dispatch the cur."

Myrddin was ready to turn the remainder of the procedure over to Uthyr. He had the necessary tools available for Uthyr. He handed the tools to Uthyr to use as he wished.

Uthyr cut off the prisoner's cock and stuffed it down his throat. Thus Eopa strangled on his own pecker. Revenge had been exacted.

Emrys had decreed that he wished to be buried within Gwaith Emrys. So, after Eopa's confession, Uthyr and Myrddin returned to the memorial, this time marching on either side of the high king's bier. Myrddin carried the golden filet that served as the crown of the High King of Britain. On the day of the inhumation all the varchogs from both above and below the Wall assembled at Ambrys Plain and were in attendance as Myrddin officiated at the burial. Then, so that all religious complexions would be satisfied, Ellyl Gwrthmwl Wledig, the Master Druid of Britain, stepped up to the altar stone.

An English warrior from among the prisoners taken at Caswallan Ford was led forth. He was, as you might expect, the strongest bravest, and fiercest of the prisoners taken at that battle. He was stripped and painted blue with woad. The prisoner was stretched out on the great altar stone of the Gwaith, the sacrificial knife was wielded, the black English heart was ripped from the body and the blood therefrom drained into the grave that was to receive the body of the deceased king.

The Druid stepped aside and Sansom, the abbot from Saint Joseph's Abbey at Ynyswitrin[33] came up to the blood-stained altar, made some peculiar signs in the air, mumbled something in Latin that perhaps the Christians present could understand, and made the sign for the closed casket to be lowered into

---

32   Annwfn: The Celtic Otherworld. Something between a Heaven and a Hell, never well
      defined in Celtic mythology.

33   The Lady Chapel from this Abbey still stands in Glastonbury. Arthur's remains were
      discovered buried there in 1278, nearly 700 years after his death.

the consecrated ground. Most of Emrys' corpse was within the casket.

Myrddin had cut off the king's head and buried it at Dinas Emrys. There it rests to this day. The head will guard our Island from the barbarians unless, in the future, it is dug up and thrown into the sea. Those of us who know the Mysteries are secure in the knowledge that our Island is safe until that day.

May the Goddess grant that the day may never come.

CHAPTER FOUR

Uthyr's Seed

GORLOIS SPEAKS:

I sense that my days are numbered. I stand with the few troops still loyal to me, besieged at Fort Dimilioc. We are surrounded by King Uthyr's troops.

How ironic. Just weeks ago I was the king's chief general. Now I am his chief enemy. Why? Lust. That's why. Uthyr's lust for my wife, Eigyr.

Just days ago the king and I were companions in arms. Emrys had defeated the English Walda[34], Hengest. But, that was merely a victory over the English settlement at Cawnyt. Uthyr had scarcely been crowned high king after his brother's death when two waldas, Octa and Eosa brought reinforcements in many keels to our Island from Anglia and Saxony through Frisia. They landed at the mouth of the River Glein[35] and swept everything before them to the stronghold of Deira[36].

A crushing defeat of these newly arrived English was necessary for Uthyr to assure his newly acclaimed leadership as Pen-Dragwn of Britain. As Gwledig of Tintagel I was a loyal liegeman of Uthyr. And, if I do say so myself, I was his best military strategist. Certainly better than that viper Myrddin. Myrddin had built up an astounding system of military intelligence that extended not only all over our Island but into Lesser Britain as well. I believe he somehow gleaned

---

34   Walda: English rough equivalent of the British Gwledig.

35   Glein means "clear" in Old British. The river bears the English name Tyne today.

36   Deira: York.

his information from fellow warlocks and bards who were everywhere. I can't be sure of that. But that fucker seemed to have eyes in every nook and cranny. According to his sources, the English dogs had arrived in fifteen keels. That meant an invading force of somewhere around a thousand warriors.

Since we wished to engage in battle as soon as possible, and we had close to a thousand British soldiers ready to fight, we set out northward with that contingent. The English enemy did not have cavalry and Uthyr's cavalry was probably the best in the western world. We thought we could eliminate the enemy in one engagement if all went well.

With Uthyr in front and Myrddin and me directly behind him we headed north to encounter the English barbarians. Officially, Myrddin was the chaplain, I was the general, and Uthyr was Commander-in-Chief.

After a four day ride we arrived close to the banks of the River Deira[37] and Myrddin's scouts informed us that the enemy was encamped just down river on the other side. Myrddin's spies infiltrated the enemy camp and brought back information that, large as our force was, the English outnumbered us two to one. Somehow the wizard's previous informants had miscounted the keels. Or a force equal to the first had landed while we were en route north. The enemy's spies undoubtedly had already surmised our strength and reported the favorable conditions to Octa and Eosa. At sunset we were close enough to the enemy to know they would attack us at dawn. Even with our excellent cavalry, the English foot soldiers would have such an advantage with their superior numbers that we had little if any expectation of victory.

We were in a serious situation. Myrddin had been badly misinformed. I'll warrant that Myrddin's great error never gets sung by the bards. That evil son of a bitch will manipulate the truth about the battle. You will no doubt hear that he came up with the solution to our problem. Lies, lies, lies. It was I who got us out of the fix and brought victory to the British. Yet scant days after our victory, that scoundrel Myrddin had connived to put Uthyr into my wife's bed, fuck the hell out of her, and make a cuckold of me. That bitter draught is difficult to swallow.

But back to our dilemma. Downstream was a ford which the English would undoubtedly cross at dawn. They would attack our position. And with their superior strength they would obliterate us. Uthyr's kingship would have lasted but days if the English had been successful.

Uthyr, Myrddin, and I held a council of war in the wicked warlock's pavilion. My two companions were in despair. Neither saw any solution. A retreat in the dark hardly seemed feasible. And to return to Lughdun[38] pursued by the English would have destroyed everything our people were expecting.

It was I, General Gorlois, who came up with a plan. I had sent one of

---

37   The Wharfe River today.

38   The town of the Celtic god, Lugh, was called Londinium by the Romans and London by the English.

my best scouts up-river and he had discovered a fine ford there. From that bit of information I conceived a plan.

"My Lord Pen-Dragwn," I said. "And My Lord Myrddin. There is one way we can defeat the English dogs and one way only if I judge the situation aright."

Myrddin scoffed. He always disdained any idea that did not originate with him. Uthyr was willing to consider any scheme that might save the day.

"Yes, Gorlois. Let's hear it."

"There is no doubt the enemy will ford the river downstream at dawn. However my most astute scout has discovered a suitable ford upriver. While the English slumber tonight, feeling assured of victory tomorrow, I propose we make a night march to the upper ford. We can sneak our entire force across the river before midnight. It is unlikely the enemy will know we are there. They will never expect us on their side of the river. Then, in the darkness of midnight, we can send our cavalry riding through their camp. Following them will be our foot soldiers. With surprise on our side we can destroy their slumbering army. That, Sirs, is my proposal as general of the British army."

Myrddin scowled. He hadn't come up with any solution. He did not want to credit me or anyone else as having a sound idea that he hadn't thought of first. It pleases me even now to remember that the bastard was, for once in his life, tongue-tied. Uthyr seized on my idea at once. Indeed, it was the only way to save the situation. And he knew it. Myrddin knew it too, but simply sat dumb.

While the English slept, with only a picket of sentries on guard, we British remained awake. We were able to move our troops so silently that no one across the river was aware of our march. The ford we found upstream was, indeed, quite adequate for both cavalry and infantry to cross.

At midnight our entire force stormed the sleeping English. The slaughter was great. At first, there was great confusion on the part of the enemy. Then they attempted to rally. By then half the English force had been transfixed by sword, lance, or pike. The remaining warriors tried to flee in an effort to get back to their keels and set sail for their German homeland. It was our horsemen who caught up with them and relieved them of their heads. By dawn we had rounded up some three hundred live English. Among them were the two waldas, Octa and Eosa. I am convinced that the Goddess was with us and had brought favor to her people.

Myrddin proposed the ceremony he had ordered for Hengest. So, in the same way, in the forced presence of their remaining band, now enslaved and branded prisoners of the British people, the two English waldas were stripped, painted blue, emasculated, and allowed to bleed to death in the presence of all. This was truly my victory. And it was so acknowledged by Uthyr at the time.

Uthyr attached Eosa's severed dong to his shield and publicly presented me with Octa's.

But Uthyr seems to have forgotten all of that now even though those pricks remain hanging on our respective shields.

We rode back to Lughdun with our branded prisoner-slaves trailing us in ignominy. We were returning for a great victory celebration and for a feast not only in honor of Uthyr's victory but of his accession to the throne.

How proud I was the day we returned to Lughdun. The crowds hailed the returning victors. They jeered the humiliated prisoners. It was a jubilant occasion.

Uthyr ordered all his varchogs to return home, prepare for the celebration, and come back with their wives. I was only too happy to ride to Tintagel and receive the loving congratulations of my wife Eigyr and my lovely daughters Morgan and Morgawse. I informed Eigyr that we would be going to Lughdun for the victory celebration. She loved the city and was truly delighted.

It was when Eigyr and I returned to Lughdun that catastrophe struck. Our high king was a fine enough warrior (although I was the better strategist). But he had other characteristics that are not uncommon among warriors. He was horny and unscrupulous. Those qualities together with Myrddin's perfidy, precipitated my fall into his disfavor.

And now I find myself camped in my own territory, several leagues from my castle at Tintagel, awaiting a conflict between my loyal troops and the troops of that vile, villainous man we chose to be our Pen-Dragwn, Uthyr.

EIGYR SPEAKS:

Life at Tintagel was usually quite dreary. So when my husband, Gorlois, returned victorious from his expedition against the English and told me we would be going to the gay city of Lughdun I was completely delighted. Since there would be varchogs coming from farther away from Lughdun than Tintagel, the celebration would not be held for another ten days. That gave me time to prepare adequately for the trip, leaving Tintagel to the care of the seneschal and porter and the girls to the care of Nurse.

It had been years since I had been to Lughdun. My heart beat faster as we approached. From well outside the city walls I caught sight of Caesar's Tower. There is nothing like it in all Britain – tall, majestic, imperial. Now, that tower was no longer a symbol of the Romans who had quit our Island. It was a symbol of Celtic Britain, the Britain of Uthyr Pen-Dragwn. My husband had fought off the English invaders who had attempted to steal our land from under us as soon as the Roman legions were called away to defend the Italian peninsula and Rome itself. I was coming to this Tower, this Lughdun, as the wife of one of the heroes who had protected our land for our people. I was very proud indeed.

Inside the city walls we passed through Cwvnyt Square on the way to our inn. The temple to Lugh impressed me as it always had. The church to the Christian goddess, Mary, seemed to me still to be somewhat of an eyesore. The architecture preferred by the new religion just never appealed to me much. The streets converging on the square were full of shops, stalls, inns, and crowds. The city was every bit as exciting as I had remembered it when I came through on my way from Linnuis to become the bride of the Brenin of Tintagel, Gorlois, years before.

The inn we stayed at was quite sumptuous. The varchogs who were particularly close to Gorlois were all there with their families. We had entertained many of them at Tintagel and had visited their castles to be entertained as well. It was a happy reunion and a convivial time for all of us. I was anxious to meet our new high king who had honored my husband, making him his chief general in the recent battle of the River Deira.

Although Gorlois had told me about his strategy of crossing the river in the dead of night and attacking the English by surprise at dawn, I somehow hadn't realized what a hero he was to the other warriors. At the inn everyone congratulated him and congratulated me as well, for as his wife, I basked in his glory. It was quite the most pleasant experience I could remember. I was honored as though I were the high queen, or the Lady of the Lake. It was so exciting.

"Is the high king staying here at the inn?" I asked Lady Anu of Tydfil.

"Uthyr Pen-Dragwn? No, Lady Eigyr. I fear this inn is far too genteel for our lusty king. He and his rowdy cohorts are at the Twrch Trwyth Inn."

"Will you be visiting him there, My Lady?" I asked in all innocence.

"Oh, my no," Lady Anu laughed. "It is not the sort of place you or I or any decent lady would come within a Roman mile of. Quite indecent, if you know what I mean. A place frequented only by men and by women of the loosest kind. You and I would never want to be seen there. Our husbands, though…" she said with a wink.

So there it was. The king was entertaining his generals at a Lughdun whorehouse. I knew the men would get drunk on mead and laid by whores.

Men!

Well, I knew what they were like before I'd even married Gorlois. So I shouldn't have been surprised.

I suspected that her husband, the Varchog Tydfil, and my own husband would be paying their respects to their liege at the whorehouse. I thought better than to ask Gorlois about it.

Just as I expected, at mid-afternoon my husband told me he and his fellow varchogs were going to go pay their respects to the king. I kissed him on the cheek and told him I did not plan to wait up for him. He seemed relieved. I knew he and the other men would return late at night drunk and noisy.

I was right. I heard them come in, laughing and singing. They had been drinking and fucking the night away at the Twrch Trwyth. When Gorlois entered our room at length he had a most unpleasant odor about him. I could tell there had been mead and maids aplenty at the high king's reception for his varchogs.

The next morning Gorlois was sullen and uncommunicative. I had been married to him long enough to know what the mornings were like after he had been carousing the night before. I repaired to the great room downstairs as soon as I could to be out of his way. Most of the other ladies were there as well for the same reason.

For the next few days we ladies would set out to visit the city midmorning. We would return to lunch with our husbands who then went off to pay their respects to their king and get drunk and laid and enjoy whatever other entertainments the wenches of the Twrch Trwyth provided for the warrior heroes. Then, when all the varchogs from the entire realm had finally arrived in the great city, the celebration at the Tower began.

It was a great feast. It was said that Uthyr's counselor, the Lord Myrddin, had organized the festivities. Whoever did so, it was magnificently done. Caesar's Tower was decorated with the insignia of every varchog who had sworn loyalty to Uthyr. I thought that we knew how to entertain beautifully at Tintagel. But never had I been able to provide the lavish broths, meats, fish, fowl, boar, venison, cheeses, and gruels that were served at the Tower that day. There was a great table in front where the king was seated in the center. Myrddin was seated at his right and Gorlois at his left. I sat to my husband's left. Yes, there were just the four of us at the head table. And I was honored to be one of the four. I was giddy with pride.

Uthyr was a fine figure of a king – unruly vigorous red hair and beard, eyes so fierce they could melt the snows of the Norsemen, and strong broad shoulders and arms. A truly magnificent body that riveted my attention. He was the most powerful person I had ever met. And he turned that virile charm directly on me.

Yes, there he was, faced by his adoring warrior chiefs and flanked by his counselor and head general. And he seemed to have eyes for none but me. It was quite remarkable.

His speech to me was all quite proper. He kept saying how much he had relied on my husband during the recent battle and what a brave man Gorlois was. Talk of that nature. He would recount some anecdote and laugh uproariously as he told it. I was caught up in his manner, his laughter, and his power. I was overwhelmed.

Gorlois became quieter and quieter as Uthyr became more and more animated. I found myself experiencing a sensation that was entirely new to me. I hope you won't find it indelicate for me to tell you about it, because it was the precursor of the love I felt for the man destined for me from the beginning of the world. It was Myrddin who later explained to me that the gods had ordained the union of Uthyr and myself. I know he was right. Myrddin was the wisest man in Britain at the time. Perhaps ever.

What I felt as Uthyr was addressing me so ardently was a sudden warm moistening in my cunt, accompanied by a tingling protrusion of my nipples. I can see that you men listening to me are beginning to smirk. You think my sensation is akin to the hardon that you so often get when you see or think of us women. But you are wrong. It was not like that at all. No man can understand this feeling for it is an accompaniment of love, not lust. You men become hotblooded, fuck us women in heat, and then abandon us in your thoughts. Not so with us. When love arrives, and it can come later in life as well as earlier, the sensation is not transitory but permanent. So it was with me. The look in Uthyr's eyes aroused this feeling of warmth and joy within me. I had never previously felt this for my husband, nor for any other man. Yet I know that I was born into this world to meet this man, and he me. I see your smirks remain. So much the worse for you. You simply do not understand.

When the feast was over Uthyr and Gorlois were surrounded by well-wishers. We ladies retired to the anteroom. The first of the men to leave the feasting hall was my husband. Although I knew that he had been roundly congratulated by his peers for his brilliance at the Deira Ford, he was scowling. He made some perfunctory remarks to the other ladies, took me by the arm, and spirited me out of the Tower. Our horses were awaiting us at the barbican and we trotted off to our inn without a word being spoken.

"Pack now. We leave immediately," Gorlois growled at me.

"But, husband. The festivities continue for days yet. You are to be further honored by the king and by the troops."

"Don't speak to me of the king. I am not blind," Gorlois growled. "I saw the looks that passed between Uthyr and you. You dishonored me before all the varchogs of Britain. You behaved like a whore. And Uthyr was treating you as such a woman with his silly tales and boisterous anecdotes. I will not be made a laughing stock before all the warriors of the Island. We leave for Tintagel within the hour. Prepare immediately."

I was shocked. I had done nothing wrong. Neither had Uthyr. I was sure that the feelings that passed between Uthyr and me could not have been discerned by anyone else. Yet… Gorlois must have detected something.

I knew there was no use protesting or arguing. My husband was determined that we should leave. And in my accommodating, wifely way, I began to make provision for our departure. I knew that everyone in Lughdun would find it strange for us to leave just as the festivities were really getting under way.

Gorlois had to go to the stables to get our pack animals loaded for the trek home. While he was gone there was a knock on the door of our room. I opened the door to find the Wizard of Britain standing there. He slipped inside the room and stealthily shut the door.

"My Lady Eigyr," Myrddin said in that smooth, convincing voice of his. "I perceive that your husband is leaving Lughdun precipitously. You may feel a bit of confusion over this evening's experiences. I have consulted the oracles of both the God Cerunnos and the Goddess, may she be praised. They tell me that at the dawn of time Uthyr was destined to become King of Britain. And you were fated to be his queen.

"The fortune has already been fulfilled for Uthyr. You, Mistress Eigyr, cannot avoid what the gods have ordained. Do what your husband demands of you at this time. But know that Uthyr will be united with you by the will of the gods. I can remain no longer. I must return to the Tower. But have faith in my words. They are sooth."

Myrddin was gone as quickly as he had appeared. Had he magically disappeared? In my confused state I could not say. But I believed his words. Somehow, Uthyr would come to me. Somehow I would be his. Not my husband Gorlois, nor my daughters Morgan and Morgawse, nor all the warlords of Britain could withstand what the gods had decreed. I would be queen. I trusted that truth with patience. And, as you know, Destiny was not to be denied.

MYRDDIN SPEAKS:

For years I had been planning how I could truly become Master of Britain. Oh, yes. As Uthyr's chief counselor I wielded great power in Britain. But I knew I would never be able to completely control Uthyr. That fool Gorlois had conceived a better plan than I could dream up back at the Battle of River Deira. Uthyr had listened to him. I needed a king who would listen to me first. Me alone. And Uthyr would never be such a king.

At the head table at the great banquet at the Tower I saw the hardon that tilted Uthyr's kilt. He was hot for Gorlois' wife. Uthyr was a great wencher, fornicator, and satyr – that was known well enough by all. And no one thought it to his discredit. One wants a leader with blood in his veins and ink in his stylus. But this lust for Eigyr was beyond the ordinary lust of man for woman. And it was my intention to see that his horniness would benefit me.

When Gorlois bolted from the Tower, taking his wife away in angry haste, I managed to get away from the festivities long enough to have a chat with Eigyr, fanning the flame that I could see had kindled in her eyes. She was not only lusting for the king's body. She felt the stirrings of power within her soul. As Uthyr's consort she would be queen of Britain. The two sensations she was experiencing, lust for the man and lust for power, could not be denied. I perceived that I could turn this to my advantage.

I told Eigyr in a quickly held meeting that the gods had ordained that she be Uthyr's and that she be queen. I could tell immediately that she swallowed the idea. I knew I had started paving the way to success for the adult who had been born the bastard of Ionna Go-to-'t. Nothing would stand in my way now. I would control a king who would be beholden to me alone. And that king would be the son of Uthyr and Eigyr.

When I returned to the Tower, I informed Uthyr that Gorlois was sneaking away in the night with his wife Eigyr. I insinuated that such a leave taking without permission of the king was more than a breach of etiquette. It was an act of treason.

The Tower was still filled with Uthyr's well-wishers, but he stormed out of the hall, assembled his guard of twenty valiant warriors, and rode as rapidly as he could to the inn where his erstwhile general had been staying. By the time he got there Gorlois and Eigyr had left. Uthyr swore a great oath and asked me what I thought.

"My Lord and Pen-Dragwn. Pursuit of the traitor would be useless at this time. You must return to the Tower and announce to all present that Gorlois has broken his oath of fealty to you and has repaired to his western demesne. Let anger at his misdeed seethe through the warriors you command. Tomorrow you must assemble an army and march on Dyfneint. The turncoat must be punished and be made an example. If this rebuff is not met with force you will lose the confidence of your loyal followers."

Uthyr heeded my advice. We did return to the Tower. And following his announcement the crowd was astounded. The effect was immediate.

"Death to the traitor! On to Dyfneint and Tintagel! War, war, war!"

The very next morning a host of a thousand marched on Dyfneint. Some of the varchogs who were neighbors of Gorlois had managed to leave Lughdun and had allied themselves with the traitor. As our troops marched through the West the fiefdoms of any varchog who had not remained loyal to the high king were torched and devastated. Uthyr was making it clear that no man dare stand against his power.

I had many spies in the West and learned that Gorlois had shut Eigyr up in Castle Tintagel and had marched north of the castle to set up a camp six Roman miles away to meet Uthyr's forces. The camp was at the fort of Dimilioc. Dimilioc had been well fortified many years before and was one of Dyfneint's traditional lines of defense. When Uthyr's troops arrived at Dimilioc they completely surrounded the fort.

While Gorlois was isolated at Dimilioc, Eigyr was waiting at Tintagel to see what the outcome would be of the events that had transpired so rapidly. It was the ideal time for the matchmaking I had been planning.

I was with Uthyr's troops. And I was constantly at his pavilion. Uthyr was not a happy man. For such a husky, strong, raucous warrior, he could be a very tiresome complainer. He was master of the situation in Dyfneint. His enemy was neutralized inside the surrounded camp. All Uthyr could do, all night long, was complain to me. His complaint? His lust for Eigyr. He had a whole litany of libidinous woes. He sniveled about his repressed love life. His hardon was driving him insane. Unless he could bed Eigyr, and soon, he might become ill and die from over-ripe balls. And on, and on, and on. The physical discomfort he felt was real enough. Every adult male knows the actual pain when we have a case of lover's nuts. Uthyr knew Eigyr was sequestered in Castle Tintagel. He had to see her. He had to fuck her. And soon. And although his complaints bored me, I fed them continually. I needed him to bed Eigyr. And the more abused he felt, the easier it would be for me to accomplish my goal.

After he had worn himself out complaining about his physical and emotional pain I told him I had a solution. He was ready to listen. This was the next important step to my becoming the Master of Britain.

I knew I could ask any price of the man, so strong was his lust.

"The magic at my command is available to you at a price, Almighty Pen-Dragwn."

"Name it." the king all but shouted. "It is yours. Just get me to her so I can get my load off."

"From your coupling, a child will be born to you and Eigyr," I told him. "I will be at Tintagel when the birth occurs. You must remove the child from the mother's breast and entrust it to me. The child will not be safe from harm if left to the wiles of the enemies of Britain. Promise me that the child will be mine to take to a place of sanctuary until it is time to reveal him to the world. Upon such promise, I will gain you access to the only person who can relieve your sad, sad suffering."

He agreed without giving the matter a second thought.

I had anticipated the situation enough to have had my armorer construct warrior attire identical to that worn by Gorlois. I had a barber trim Uthyr's beard in the exact style of Gorlois'. I made the king look as much like the traitor as human resources would permit. The rest depended on my arts as a magician – as a master of deception.

The disguised Uthyr and I set out for Tintagel with a small contingent. Through artifice I brought Uthyr into the castle disguised as Gorlois. If there was anyone at Tintagel who doubted that the man on horseback I led through the portal was the master, not a word of doubt was expressed.

So by my arts of misdirection, which were very much a part of my training as a wizard, I had convinced the guards at Tintagel that the man at the gates of the castle was their lord and master, Brenin Gorlois. Uthyr was amazed at how easily he gained access to the castle. And to the portal of the bedchamber of the lady who had been anxiously awaiting him.

Before allowing Uthyr into those chambers I addressed Eigyr privately.

"My Lady Eigyr. The fortunes of war have turned against the lord of this castle. I regret to inform you that your husband, Gorlois, has been slain in battle."

Of course, I was quite sure that Gorlois was still among the living. Uthyr and I had left Dimilioc less than an hour before and Gorlois was presumably still very much alive inside the besieged fortress. But it was important that Eigyr believe him dead.

Eigyr gasped, but did not shed a tear. I followed up immediately.

"Gorlois' death was the will of the gods and of the Goddess, My Lady. Your husband met his destiny and met it bravely. We cannot judge the will of the gods. The Goddess particularly has determined that you and Uthyr become man and wife. You are free to fulfill your destiny now. Will you consent to accept Uthyr as your lawful husband?"

The lady did not hesitate. She wanted Uthyr. She wanted to be queen. She yearned for his prick to enter her cunt. And she had never truly loved Gorlois.

I told her the gods had mysteriously brought Uthyr to Tintagel and that he awaited her permission to enter.

She gave the permission with a smile.

Uthyr entered. It was clear that the couple was ripe for fucking.

As an ordained warlock, I performed the marriage ceremony on the spot. The technicality that Gorlois was still alive, and that therefore Eigyr was not free to marry, was known to me. And it may have occurred to Uthyr. If so, he wasn't going to interrupt the process that favored getting him into bed with the lovely lady at his side.

I pronounced them man and wife and had hardly finished the consecrating prayer when they were off as fast as they could go to my lady's private chambers to consummate the holy event.

Before daybreak the next morning Uthyr joined me in the great hall of the castle. We broke our fast and were on our way back to the siege.

Within an hour of arrival back at Dimilioc, Uthyr ordered an attack on the enemy encampment. The ramparts were breached and Uthyr's troops swarmed into the fort. Uthyr encountered Gorlois and fought him in hand-to-hand battle and decapitated him. Gorlois was no match for the king. So, at that moment Eigyr was indeed both a widow and a newlywed. No one was to know that Eigyr's widowhood actually followed her second marriage.

Uthyr brought Gorlois' head back to my pavilion outside the fort. I, in turn, took that head to a swineherd of my acquaintance and had it thrown into the slop he had dumped in the trough for his pigs. A fitting end for the head of a man who had claimed he had been the strategist of the Battle of Deira. It was I, Myrddin, who had devised the dawn attack on the enemy. Let no one dispute that.

Uthyr returned to Tintagel as the conquering king. The castle was now his by rights. He and Eigyr returned to Lughdun together, where Uthyr's victory in Dyfneint and his marriage to the new queen were cause for many more days of celebration.

The marriage consummated at Tintagel bore fine fruit. Eigyr was with child. As the time for her confinement grew near she and Uthyr returned to Tintagel. On the eve of Beltane in Year 500 the child of Uthyr and Eigyr was born at Tintagel Castle in Dyfneint. I was present on that occasion.

Uthyr fulfilled his promise and handed his newborn son over to me.

I spirited the child, Arthur, away to the estate of a Briton who had been a cavalry general in the Legions before the Romans left our shore. All my hopes for the future lay with that child. I would shape him to become the instrument to lead me to my destiny as the true Master of Britain.

CHAPTER FIVE

The Brigand Gang

CAI SPEAKS:

In all Britain there was only one person who foresaw the dramatic rise in power of my foster brother Arthur. That person was that slippery rascal Myrddin. The old pagan was power mad. And his access to power was to be through control of the youth who had been brought to Castrec in swaddling clothes and raised as my brother.

I was not aware of the process until much later. But now I see that each step that led to Arthur becoming high king was planned and programmed by Myrddin. Learning about footstraps, joining the brigands, the sword in the stone trick – all of it was part of a master plan. And the plan was Myrddin's.

For instance, the footstraps. Before Palomides brought the concept of footstraps to Britain from Scythia, horsemanship was a crude matter indeed. The apparent chance meeting when Palomides just happened into the forest where Arthur and I were off hunting was designed by Myrddin. He knew that Arthur needed to learn about the "footstraps" in order, much later, to lead the victorious British cavalry to conquer the barbarians.

Back at Castrec Arthur practiced riding while using these footstraps. He practiced jousting and mounted swordplay with the guardian slave corps we had at the compound. The guardian slaves were of various races, English, Irish, and Viking. They were faithful to us, even though they had been worthy warriors before we British had defeated and enslaved them. Arthur made use of the new footstraps himself while his opponents rode in the usual bareback manner in the practice battles.

Arthur acquired gladiatorial skills sufficient to be unbeatable in his mock battles. The slaves gave him no quarter. They were a robust crew indeed, and one of them, Aethelbert, certainly could have defeated Arthur in jousting if Arthur did not have those footstraps. But Arthur had the advantage over Aethelbert because of the new Scythian technology.

One day, in the month of An Marta[39], in the five hundred fourteenth year of the Christian calendar, that bandit chief Palomides came riding into our compound. And riding right along beside him was that old rascal Myrddin. Father and Mother both came out to greet them. Had it been up to me I would have run them off the place.

Arthur and I were invited into the greathall and sat quietly as the guests and my parents were served Gawlish wine and barleycakes. Arthur and I were given honeywater to sip. It was Myrddin who began the dialogue. We were a Christian family. But unlike most Christian households, the lady of the house was not excluded from important discussions. My mother was always part of the decision making, in the Celtic manner, as opposed to the Roman Christian tradition. This is one of the few Celtic traditions I prefer over the dicta of Saint Paul. But in most matters I prefer the Roman-Christian way of doing things.

"Ector and Liv," Myrddin began. "The people of Britain will always be thankful to you for fostering Arthur here. It is still best for you not to know the origin of the lad. Nor can I reveal to you his destiny. But I entrusted his well-being to you. And you have raised him well. We can see that he has budded into a virile maturity. Under your watchful care he has grown strong and healthy. He has learned the gentle arts of reading and numbers. In addition he has also learned the manly arts of hunting, woodsmanship, sword play, and jousting. It is now important for him to learn the art of war."

My mother reacted with a start. "Oh, dear," was all she said.

Father patted her on the knee and she settled back into her chair.

The distressed look remained on her face, but she did not object further.

Father had been a cavalry master with the Legions, as you know. He was a kind-hearted man, but battle hardened. From his expression I could tell he was agreeing with the direction Myrddin's discussion was leading. I was amazed, myself. "The art of war." That sounded portentous. I started to fidget. But Arthur simply sat there, drinking his honeywater with an expression of polite interest on his face.

"Just what do you have in mind for the boy, Myrddin?" mother ventured.

"Liv, I know you are concerned for the safety of your son. And I am aware that you have taken Arthur to your bosom as fondly as if he were your own son, like Cai over there."

I fidgeted a bit more, having been mentioned in the discussion.

"And you know Palomides here," Myrddin continued. "He has met

---

39   The date of Palomides' and Myrddin's arrival at Castrec was March 8, 514.

Arthur. And, of course, Cai."

Here he looked over at me with what was intended, no doubt, to be a kindly look. The old reptile didn't fool me, though. He never cared a whit for me. And I knew it.

"But, let's let Palomides speak for himself," Myrddin suggested.

Palomides stood to speak. By doing so, he dominated the room with his presence.

"Ector Varchog and Mistress Liv. I have the honor to be captain of a warband that has the function of obliterating the foul presence of Irish and Pixies from our shores.[40] Our band is small and we need more fresh, youthful blood. The worthy bard, Myrddin, has suggested the name of your son Arthur to me. I come to petition your permission to have him learn the tactics of battle as a member of our band."

Father asked leave to withdraw with mother to the next room to discuss the matter. Again, this was his Celtic-British side showing through. Roman-Christians wouldn't think of involving a mere female in the consideration of such a matter.

While my parents were out of the room, Myrddin, Palomides, and Arthur carried on polite conversation, not mentioning the momentous matter that was at hand. I preferred to sit quietly and not open my mouth. I was flabbergasted at what seemed at stake here.

When they returned, it was my father who spoke.

"Palomides. I have known of the work your warband has been involved in for the health and safety of Britain. The Irish have been harrowing our shores ever since the Legions departed. The warlords of our people have not been able to ward off the scourge of these filthy invaders. And some of the Irish have gone so far as to form colonies on our western shores. On the eastern shores, the accursed English have gained a foothold due to the treachery of that arch villain Vortigern.

"And if that weren't enough, the Pixies have taken to boats. They sail around the Wall and attack us from the North. If it weren't for warbands like yours we would have lost our Island to the barbarians when Rome pulled her Legions back home to protect the Italian peninsula from the Vandals and Goths."

Father was quite worked up. He had served in the Legions. But when Rome called back her troops many of the Britons like my father remained on our Island to protect their homes and families.

Myrddin spoke up.

"Ector, my friend. You are a good and patriotic Briton. I take it that you and Liv will allow your son Arthur to join the warband."

---

40   The Pixies were aboriginal people of the Island, who were driven north by the Celts and Romans. It was the Pixies (Picti, Picts) who retained the habit of tattooing themselves blue with woad.

It was mother who spoke up. Stately, lovely, and with fierce determination, she answered.

"If it is Arthur's choice to join the warband, my blessing will go with him. If he should decide that his future does not lie in that direction, we will support that decision as well. But, for my other son, Cai, we desire that he remain here with us at Castrec at least for a while yet."

I knew that Myrddin and Palomides hadn't even considered having me as part of their band of brigands. I wanted no part of it, and they must have known it. But mother, bless her, had made it clear that if anyone was to leave to maraud the Irish, it was to be Arthur and not me.

Myrddin nodded at Arthur.

"Well, Arthur. It looks as if it is up to you. What is your decision?"

Arthur arose and thanked Mother and Father for their consideration. Then he thanked Myrddin and Palomides for coming and asking for his enlistment in the warband. He agreed to join and gave first a hug and a kiss to Mother, a Roman salute to Father, and a Celtic salute to Myrddin and Palomides. And at that moment the world that Arthur and I had shared for fourteen years came crashing to an end. Arthur had one destiny to follow and I had another.

For all the fine talk, I suspected then, and confirmed as time went by, that Palomides' "warband" was, in truth, a gang of ruthless British ruffians who engaged in guerilla raids against the Irish settlements. As far as I could see, they were not in it for patriotic reasons or for any other noble purpose. The young horsemen raided our locations the Irish had invaded and their goal was to murder, rape, plunder, and burn. It was loot and rape that motivated them. Oh, yes, and I truly believe that some of the raids were just for the sake of hell-raising. I certainly did not approve. It did not seem to me to be British! But since Father and Mother seemed to think it all right, I held my peace. And I must admit that Arthur's experience with that band of brigands prepared him for the warfare he later undertook to rid our land of the barbarians who were lurking at our gates even in those early days.

Arthur continued to live at Castrec part of the time. Then for weeks on end he would be constantly with the brigands. Then he would come back home for a while to be with the family. For the next two years he rode with the band to raid the Irish, and occasionally the Pixies and Vikings.

The band was small, varying between twenty and thirty members for any raid. The brigands would swoop down on a settlement, set fire to the buildings, put the men and children to the sword, and rape the women. No men were ever taken captive. It was the rare Irishman who survived on the shores of Gwynedd, Merineth, Powys, Cardigan, or Demetia during the two year span that Arthur was a brigand.

I visited the brigands' camp only once, at Arthur's invitation. I was not at all comfortable there. A circular log hall had been built for the meeting room of the gang. Outside, tents and pavilions were set up around the hall. It looked not too unlike what Father had described as the outpost camps of the Legions back during the Occupation.

Arthur and I were sitting with the boisterous gang members when Palomides came bursting in to announce that a party of Irish had just been spotted coming ashore a three hour ride away.

I was left alone in the camp while the fighters all rushed off to perform their carnage. When they returned they were all laughing and slapping each other on the back. Their tunics were blood-stained and they smelled of fresh spilled blood. Into the hall they swooped. Gwalchmai, one of the gang, went to a cupboard and brought out jars of ale and meddyglyn. They sat around a table that Myrddin had provided. This table was round and had the names of the current members inscribed on it. It was the precursor of the famous Table Round that Myrddin provided later for Camelot. Myrddin ascribed to it some mystic nonsense about equality and brotherhood. I never quite understood the concept.

The crew got to drinking heavily. Arthur didn't often drink to excess. But when he did he was a very unattractive drunk. He grew loud and boisterous, talked right into your face, and was usually belligerent. This particular evening, fortunately, he was a happy drunk, hugging his companions-in-arms and bragging about the exploits of the afternoon.

Perhaps I drank a bit more than usual myself because I referred to the warband as a gang of brigands. That made Arthur laugh.

"You've got it right, Brother. We are a jolly band of brigands who take pleasure in loot and rape. With our footstraps we are better horsemen than any Irishman who has brought his nag over from the Green Island. They loot our villages and we loot back from them. They are stupid enough to bring their womenfolk over with them, apparently so we can have the pleasure of raping them."

"Surely, Arthur, you cannot approve of raping innocent women," I huffed.

"Big Brother," he bragged. "I love rape.

"Ever since I can remember, I have enjoyed using my prick to give me pleasure. I learned from my Irish nanny that nothing in this life beats a good fuck.

"Ever since I could get it up and shoot it off, fucking is what I have lived for.

"Seduction has always been my cherished sport. I have used whatever chance I could finagle to get into the drawers of any female with a human cunt. I'm not into fucking animals, you know. At least not yet.

"But until I joined these 'brigands' as you call them, I never had the chance to discover the pleasure of using my prick as a stealth weapon. Rape is just an extension of the sport Brigit taught me and I love it.

Since I've been here, I've found a different pleasure to go along with rape. I've found the chopping off heads of Irish, Pixies, and Vikings is great sport. No man or child escapes our blades. But murder pales compared with raping their womenfolk. That is what I love best about this business."

Well I was shocked. Shocked! To my mind that was not a proper British sentiment. When I told Arthur it was not proper it just made him laugh louder. He repeated my indignation to his companions and they all howled with glee. They slapped me on the back and kept repeating "Not proper."

That tells you quite a bit about this so-called warband. A true warband is a group of good British subjects banded together under a true Celtic warlord, defending the fatherland against the incursions of the barbarians. To my way of thinking, calling Palomides' gang of ruffians a warband represents delusions of grandeur. But it must be admitted that history tells a story that perpetuates that delusion. The chroniclers of our times have inscribed in the official history of Britain that Arthur was part of a valiant warband, of which he became warlord prior to achieving the status of High King of Britain. That is the song the bards sing. That is what the chroniclers inscribe. Lies, lies, lies.

The truth was that the members of Palomides' gang scouted out the countryside to discover what British villages had been plundered by the barbarians. The Irish, English, and Pixies tended to loot the wealthiest villages of our people. Then, in lightening attacks, the warband attacked the encampments of the looters and looted the treasures back.

Do not mistake me. Arthur was my brother. And I love him. But that group of ruffians was not a proper British warband. And Arthur was not the leader of it anyway.

Myrddin later convinced Palomides to claim that he had been subject to Arthur, not the other way around. That was all part of the web of deception spread to make Arthur high king in a few more years.

That life of brigandage was exhilarating to Arthur. He loved riding wild into the enemy camps. He relished wielding the sword in his hand. But he was even more exhilarated by the baser pleasure of wielding the sword that emerged from his groin.

The idea of my brother as a rapist sits poorly with me even now. Arthur was the bear. You know the pun on his name. And when he was drunk enough he would declare how he loved to slash at intruding barbarian flesh with his bear claws and grind their barbaric bones with his bear jaws. The pun always fell flat with me.

Many of Arthur's companions in the warband or as I call it, the band of cutthroats, stayed with him up to the very end. Some of them are names you have heard because the bards have sung many a song about their valiant deeds. Two companions in particular were very close to him. I dare say closer even than me, his brother. You have heard, and posterity will forever hear, about Gwalchmai[41] and Bedwyr[42] .

Of course we didn't know it at the time but it turned out Gwalchmai was Arthur's nephew. He was the son of Arthur's sister Morgawse. It was Morgan who later told us the story of his birth. As you would expect, Morgan told it in a way that would aggrandize herself. You know Morgan.

Morgawse was never faithful to her Pixie husband, King Lot.

She spread her legs to receive the penis of any male who struck her fancy. And from what I've heard, it did not require much of a man to 'strike her fancy'.

There was a tall, blond, brawny Viking slave in Lot's court in Skara Brae whom she found special. He was often found doing what pleased her most in that welcoming trap we Christians refer to as her pudenda.

Morgawse conceived a very Norse looking child, telling Lot it was his. Lot, like all Pixies, was short and dark. The baby was blond, husky, and fair-skinned. Lot was a scurvy scoundrel. But he was not a fool.

Lot snatched the babe from Morgawse's breast and sent it to sea, in the customary way of dealing with bastards in Pixiland. A small craft was fashioned of pitch and reeds, and the child was placed in it and sent to visit Llyr[43]. The child was never expected to be seen again. Morgan claims she intervened with Llyr to have the tiny craft washed ashore near the home of some simple British fisherfolk. She is such a liar. I have never believed that she had anything to do with it. If you ever happen to meet her, don't believe a word the woman says. She hates good Christians like you and me and will tell us anything.

Whatever the reason, the baby did wash ashore and was cared for by a fisherman and his wife who raised him as their own. He grew up to be the exact image of the Viking slave – tall, strong handsome, blond, and, in my opinion, a trifle stupid. Have you ever met a Viking with the brains to fit in an acorn shell?

When Gwalchmai was barely twelve years old, Palomides visited the fishing village and spotted the strapping lad. He paid the fisherman a bezant[44] for him and Gwalchmai immediately found himself the youngest member of

---

41   Gwalchmai is called Gawain by the English and French. His given name, that given to him by his foster parents, simple fisher folk, was Gwalchmai meaning Hawk of May. His mother, Morgawse, renamed him Gwrvan gwallt-avwy when she re-found him later. But the name never stuck.

42   Called Bedivere in English and French. He was Arthur's companion at the very end, and survived him at the final battle at Camlann.

43   Llyr was the name Cai knew for the Sea God. No Briton ever seemed to know the Pixie names for anything.

44   Bezant: As the Roman Empire was disintegrating there was very little money minted and much of that was worthless. Constantinople was the one location minting coins that were universally recognized, Bezants.

the ruffian cutthroats who accompanied Palomides. Young he was, but of a personality that fit right in. The boy loved the life of plunder, loot and rape. An inheritance from his Viking forebears, no doubt. When Arthur joined the warband Gwalchmai was already a seasoned rascal. He and Arthur hit it off right away and remained close friends, drinking companions, and warriors as long as they lived.

Bedwyr was another youthful member of the gang. He was not of noble birth in any way but the son of poor British peasants. He spoke British with an uncouth accent but was clearly one of the shrewdest and most intelligent members of that band of brigands. He was always a better tactician than Palomides or Arthur as far as I could tell. But then, military exploits are hardly my field of expertise. Of other members of the group I may speak anon. For the nonce I wanted to acquaint you with Arthur's closest boon companions who were with him, in a sense, from the beginning of his blood-drenched career.

For two years Arthur and his companions were terrors to Irish, Pixie, English, and Viking. Never were the barbarians treated more ruthlessly. I must grudgingly admit that the barbarians needed to be dealt with harshly. They were a very real threat to our way of life. The earth of Britain was stained a deep red by the blood of the invaders. And many a child was born as a whelp of the rapes visited upon the widows of the would-be settlers from beyond the sea.

But, friends, my throat grows dry and my tongue is fatigued. You had asked about the beginnings of my brother's rise to power. This background will help you understand how a young man aged sixteen could become Pen-Dragwn of Britain and lead our troops to splendid victories over our many enemies. Much as I disapproved, his experience with the brigands taught him the warrior skills necessary to undergird the victories of which bards sing today, and will continue to sing as long as there is a Britain.

CHAPTER SIX

The Sword in the Stone

....

CAI SPEAKS:

You all know the story about the stone with the sword in it, don't you? Another bit of Myrddin's shenanigans. Not that I object to the outcome. Not at all. Without that bit of trickery it is unlikely that Arthur would have been elected High King and Pen-Dragwn of Britain. But since we Christians are addicted to veracity, let me tell you the true story of what happened.

Uthyr was High King and Pen-Dragwn during the years Arthur and I were growing up. Then, in Year 515, Uthyr died in battle at Camlann on Ambrys Plain[45]. Britain was left without a high king at a very precarious time. We were threatened on every side by enemies. Every warlord in the land was determined to be elected to the highest office our Island offers. None would yield to any other. Utter chaos was prevented solely because of the battles waged by brigand groups like Palomides'. I hate to admit that, because I certainly did not approve of the brigands. Yet, the fact is, without them the barbarians would have snatched our Island right away from us.

Myrddin composed many epics and lays about Palomides' warband. But, as agreed to by Palomides, Arthur was depicted as the warlord of the gang in all these rousing songs. The songs about Arthur were very popular throughout the land. The youth who was purportedly saving Britain from the marauding bands of barbarians made for exciting tales. And these stories were sung by bards, minstrels, and wandering singers all over Britain and in

---

45 Years later, Arthur also died on a battlefield near Camlann on Salisbury plain, which is called Ambrys in British.

Lesser Britain across the Sleeve[46]. Of course the lays were all lies. Arthur and his warband were portrayed as heroic patriots, motivated only by love for the fatherland. In those lays they were depicted as kind, considerate, and noble to all except the villainous bloodthirsty invaders who came to rape and pillage our land. The bards and balladeers sang that our high-minded patriots never raped, looted, or murdered. They slew warriors, yes. Of course. But when possible, they drove the hordes away from our shores with as little bloodshed as possible. Lies, lies, lies. As you know. But it made Arthur's name known. He became a romantic hero, famed in song, yet not known in person. And no mention was ever made of his parentage.

The Britons soon had to elect a high king or the English would certainly take over our Island. Yet the petty wrangling among the warlords went on and on. Myrddin had a bold plan for resolving the problem. He had waited for this moment from the time he inveigled Uthyr into turning Arthur over to him sixteen years before. This young man, known only as a leader of a group of brigands, had to be made acceptable to the warlords.

Myrddin devised a wonderful implement to thrust Arthur forth from merely the hero of bardic songs to the leadership of the warlords. The wily wizard presented the plan to Father, who had our craftsmen build a wondrous device. It looked like a large stone but was fabricated of bronze and covered with a skin of clay. So cleverly made was it that no one could distinguish it from a large granite boulder. It was hollow and of a size that a dwarf or Pixie could fit inside without discomfort. A warrior's sword of exquisite Celtic design was fitted into a slot in the mechanism and fastened within by a bolt. Unless the bolt were removed by a person inside the mock boulder, it was impossible to withdraw the sword. Until the time was ripe to display the "stone," it remained well hidden in one of the workshops of our compound.

Myrddin composed a song cycle that was sung by the bards and minstrels in every hall in the land during the month of Nollaig[47] in that crucial year of five sixteen. The songs differed, of course. But, in every case they had the following lines as the end of the lay:

"On Alban Arthuan,
The new High King
Shines forth at Caer Lludd."

Caer Lludd was the poetic, bardic way of saying Lughdun. Every warlord in Britain and Lesser Britain came to believe that it was somehow ordained that the final decision concerning the kingship would be made on Alban Arthuan Day. So all the warlords, tribal chiefs, and headmen were manipulated by Myrddin to come to Lughdun on that feast day.

---

46   The Sleeve was the name given to the English Channel by the Britons. The name persists in Celtic languages and in the French language as well. When the English finally conquered Britain they renamed the channel "English."

47   The Celtic month of Nollaig corresponds to December in the Roman calendar.

Alban Arthuan was chosen by Myrddin with good reason. It is the day of the Winter Solstice when the religions of the Druids and Wycha believe the sun god Lleu is reborn. Most of the warlords were believers in the old religion. It is also the day we Christians celebrate the birth of the Christ. And even the heathen English on the Eastern Shore celebrated a holiday then that they called "Yule." It is a joyous holiday in all the religions practiced in our land. And the name of the festival in British, Alban Arthuan, has implanted in the name… Arthur. Myrddin used every trick in the scrolls.

If you have been to Lughdun you know that the temple to Lugh stands, as it has for centuries, on the west side of Cwvnyt Square. On the east side of the square the Romans built a Christian church dedicated to the Holy Mother. In the dead of night, after the last of the holiday revelers had departed from the city center, Myrddin directed that his bronze "stone" be set up in the exact center of the square between the temple and the church. So when the first worshipers at the temple or the church arrived at dawn on Alban Arthuan, it appeared that the stone had miraculously appeared during the night.

The sword was encrusted with jewels that glistened in the morning sunlight. And above the sword these words were engraved:

"He who draws forth the sword from this stone is the rightful high king of all Britain."

Although few of my countrymen were literate, it was soon known what the words proclaimed. For every time a person who knew how to read would pass by, everyone around prevailed on him to interpret the writing. The meaning was a mystery to all. But by mid-morning all Lughdun knew of the sword in the stone, and of the mysterious message.

It was a cold, drizzly day, which, in Lughdun does not keep people indoors. The city was bustling with holiday activity and I believe everyone in the city came to see the stone that had appeared mysteriously in the square. Certainly every warlord made an appearance because the message engraved in the stone spoke of the kingly succession. A Pixie dwarf slave was hidden inside the contraption. He was enclosed in there with food, water, and an offal-bucket in which to relieve himself. He was promised a day of freedom on his release from the stone if all went well. He was promised a sound beating and flaying if he failed in the task appointed him. All he had to do was remain quiet inside the hollow stone. And at the designated word from Myrddin he had to slip the bolt away from the sword.

Word went out that the new high king would be chosen at sundown. So from noontime on, the square filled with people who were determined to stay and see what this business was all about. An hour before sundown all the warlords had crowded themselves to the front of the crowd, each one, no doubt, anticipating that he would be the one chosen. All around the square Myrddin had set up faggots for his bonfires. They were to play an important part in the proceedings. He told our slaves who were assisting him that in each bonfire there had to be wood of hazel, juniper, wormwood, and black oak. He himself added to the pile hypnotic, hallucinatory herbs brought to Britain from Anatolia by traders.

At the very moment the sun set, the Great Druidic Shield was struck from within the Temple of Lugh. The reverberation rang out over the assembled crowd. Have you ever heard the sound of Lugh's shield when struck by a Druid? It is like a summons from the other world. Eerie, mysterious, and haunting. Following the ringing of the shield the harsh bells of the Church of Saint Mary on the other side of the Square rang out. In succession the Shield of Lugh, then the Bells of Saint Mary's, rang, one calling, the other answering. And as these ominous sounds filled the misty air, Bishop Dwdrych[48] marched out of the church and Myrddin marched forth from Lleu's temple garbed in a blue gown decorated with the mystic symbols of Druidry and Wycha. He wore a blue bard's cap and carried his harp in one hand and a sprig of mistletoe in the other. But what was most remarkable, he had painted his face and hands blue with woad in the manner of the Pixies and Druids. The effect was quite awesome.

To the sounds of the shield and the bells, the two men slowly marched through the crowd that parted as the two reverend gentlemen progressed. It was quite a sight.

I was very aware that Myrddin was putting on a show for the people. I must admit he was a grand showman. All humbuggery, but a fine showman. I was disappointed that our fine bishop had agreed to play along with Myrddin. I felt he was also showing off a bit, too. But it was all for the good of Britain, so I suppose the mummery was justified by the results.

When Myrddin and Dwdrych reached the focal point of the ceremony, the stone and the sword artifice, Dwdrych raised the cross and we Christians in the crowd knelt. Dwdrych intoned prayers for the safety of Britain, to which we responded "Amen." We rose and the bishop gave a rather lengthy sermon about how we were all soldiers of Christ. He went on a bit long, I thought. But then, shortness of breath was never one of Dwdrych's weaknesses. During the bishop's lengthy exhortations I could see that Myrddin was getting exasperated. He was a man of little patience. And whether in his normal pale skin, or painted blue, his natural crankiness nearly always showed through.

At length, Dwdrych was through and Myrddin stepped forth. As he did so a large red jewel in the hilt of the Sword pulsated with an eerie light. Myrddin directed the attention of the entire audience to the glow. I had seen him involve groups in this kind of staring activity before. He caused his listeners to focus on a single point and then he would chant suggestions to

---

48   Dwdrych, or Dubricius, was actually Bishop of Caerlleon, not of London. But in 516, the bishop of Caerlleon was archbishop of all Britain, and thus came to London to officiate at the ceremony of the election of the high king. The archbishopric did not move to Canterbury until 597 when Augustine converted the English and the Celtic church diminished in power.

us, strumming quietly on his harp. He went through this procedure with the crowd. I was not immune to his suggestions. No one ever was.

"Britons," he intoned in soothing, forceful words. "You will elect today a high king to rule over you. He will drive the barbarians from our shores. You will pledge your allegiance to this leader. You will acknowledge the one who pulls the sword from this stone as Pen-Dragwn of Britain." And so on, along that line. It wasn't so much what he was saying but the way he said it that caused all of us, even those of us who knew that there was some kind of trickery involved in what he was doing, to desire to follow in action whatever he suggested.

Myrddin then began a kind of roll call. He called the warlords to come up beside him one at a time.

"Lleirwg ap Coel of Llanilltyd," Myrddin intoned.

Lleirwg approached the stone.

"Draw this sacred sword from its stony sheath," Myrddin commanded.

The sword was held in place by its bolt. And pull as he might, Lleirwg ap Coel could not separate it from its secure hold in the stone.

"Eurgain warlord of Cor Tewdws," was called next with the same result.

And thus, in sequence, every warlord in Britain was called up by Myrddin, and each failed to perform the required function to prove himself worthy to be High King of Britain.

One by one they came. From Bran ap Llyr Llediaithy of Glevissig who towered above us all by the height of two heads to Lot of Skara Brae, who came barely to my belt buckle. From the elderly Jestyn ap Gwrgan of Aber Gwaredwyr to the youngest one of all who came last and who withdrew the sword from the stone.

As Myrddin had forewarned us, Father was to be called at the end of the ceremony.

"Ector of Castrec," Myrddin called out.

Father stepped forward, grasped the sword by its shining hilt, pulled with all his strength, and acknowledged that he had not been able to budge the sword. He bowed to Myrddin and to Dwdrych, and stepped back into the crowd.

When Father had taken his place beside me and Arthur, Myrddin, still in that sing-song voice that so lulled us all, addressed him again.

"Ector of Castrec. Is your son beside you?"

"Yes, Warlock Myrddin," Father answered in the ringing voice of a Legionnaire.

"Send your son forth!"

There was a murmur from the crowd. This was an extraordinary request. Up until that time it had been the legitimate warlords, tribal chiefs, and estate masters who had been called.

"I send my son Cai," Father called out.

I went up as I had been told previously I was to do, bowed to the two holy men, and applied myself to the task of tugging at the sword. It was, indeed, secure. And I could tell that a hundred men pulling simultaneously would never be able to extract it from its position.

I returned to my place in the crowd. Myrddin called out again.

"Ector of Castrec. Have you another son?"

Father answered, "A foster son have I, named Arthur."

"Let Arthur come forth," Myrddin commanded.

The crowd gasped. Everyone had heard of the young warband leader. Few had seen him. There was a sense of expectancy.

As Arthur strode through the crowd, the thirteen bonfires that Myrddin had set up burst into flames at once, fired by the slaves who were responsible for them. The smoke from the fires wafted through the damp air. As I breathed in the smoke I could tell that it was affecting my senses. It was like having partaken of particularly good meddyglyn or cwrw. A feeling of exhilaration and euphoria began to overwhelm me. I knew the feeling was shared by all those around me. It was the effect, I could tell, of the smoke from Myrddin's hallucinatory fires. It was one of his wizard tricks.

"You are Arthur of Castrec?" Myrddin asked when my brother was there before the stone.

"I am," Arthur answered in a voice heavy with authority.

"I say you are Arthur ap Uthyr Pen-Dragwn ap Cystennyn Fendigaid Llydaw," Myrddin proclaimed.

We all, with one voice, echoed, "Arthur ap Uthyr Pen-Dragwn ap Cystennyn Fendigaid Llydaw." We had no will to do otherwise. Myrddin was directing our very souls.

"Arthur," commanded Myrddin. "Withdraw the sword from the stone."

The Pixie ensconced within knew this was the signal to withdraw the bolt. Arthur stepped up, his boyish features aglow, his muscles bulging through his tunic. He grabbed the sword with two hands and it slipped right out of the stone.

The crowd gasped. The crowd cheered. We fell to our knees.

Arthur brandished the stone above his head.

Myrddin chanted "Hail Arthur ap Uthyr Pen-Dragwn, High King of Britain."

We all with one voice repeated the formula after him.

In the euphoria of the moment the warlords approached Arthur, one by one, bent the knee and pledged fealty. It was one of the most remarkable sights I ever witnessed. These fierce men who had wrangled and fought each other for two years, each attempting to best the others in order to become high king, bent the knee. And it was all staged and arranged by Myrddin. Theatricality, intoxicating smoke, high drama. That old rascal Myrddin had accomplished a miracle. Britain had a high king again, a Pen-Dragwn.

And that king was my younger brother.

CHAPTER SEVEN

Coronation and Unrest in the North

BEDWYR SPEAKS:

Of course I remember the day Arthur joined our band. Gwalchmai and I had already been members for a while, the two youngest ones in the group. When Arthur arrived he made a third. And the three of us became the mightiest hell-raisers in all Britain. We ate, drank, wrenched, brawled, and gambled. We lived boisterously with the gusto of raw youth.

Arthur was the only one of the three of us who knew how to write or figure with numbers so he was the score-keeper in the game we engaged in for the next two years.

Here's how the game went. For every woman seduced, score three points. For every one raped, two points. For every barbarian beheaded, one point. At the end of the week we divided up the loot that we had grabbed on our raids into the settlements. We didn't divide the booty evenly. Oh, no. The more points you earned during the week, the larger your share of the plunder. We were three hot-blooded, randy youths, and we searched every British hamlet, village, and city within riding range for willing young women. We always had plenty of bezants to spend. And it was a rare outing when all three of us did not make at least the three points for seduction. In our raids on the Irish landing parties and settlements it was strictly a matter of luck how many women any of us managed to rape. If two or even all three of us raped the same woman, we each scored the same two points for the score. For the beheadings, only adult males counted. None of us actually sought to cut off the children's heads. Running them through with the sword or spear was enough. So for each adult invader decapitated, one point. It was not unusual for us to end up with even scores at the end of the week. And over the two year period I can't say that any one of us had actually outdone the other. We all ended up with about the same amount of loot.

Oh, those were the days. We rode hard, drank hard, fucked hard and slaughtered hard. It was a great life in itself and great preparation for the wars we fought against the enemy after Arthur became king.

On the day he became king, on Alban Arthuan Day, I was standing at the very back of the crowd in Cwvnyt Square. I was a nobody. My parents were churls. I was merely a member of that warband that supposedly had been led by Arthur. I was not one of the gwledigs[49] who dominated the front of the massed assemblage. But like the other members of our warband, I was invited to the feast that followed the ceremony of the sword and the stone.

The most imposing structure in Lughdun is the tower constructed by Julius Caesar four hundred years ago. There it stands in the center of the city, dominating all it surveys. Within the Tower, on the first floor, is an enormous hall. And this hall was set up for the finest banquet Britain had ever seen. Supposedly it was Myrddin who had organized the banquet. I do not know. But I do know that all the gwledigs were there with their retinues and the hall was not filled to capacity even then.

When we were living the life of brigands (yes, I admit that Cai is right when he calls us that), we had the best of everything. The spoils of our warfare made us rich. But never had we feasted as the gwledigs were feasting at the Tower of Lughdun that evening. Arthur had convinced Myrddin to include us, the companions of his warband, together at one side of the great hall. But seated there, out of the way, we were still served everything the gwledigs had on their plates. And the wenches serving us were as revealingly dressed as those waiting on the important guests. It is hard to say which was the more inviting, the luxurious viands or the lovely wenches. My own preference was for the wenches. And I had my fill of them later that evening. But that is a different story, and not part of what you have come here to listen to.

At the height of the revelries, Lot of Skara Brae stood up, seeking the attention of Myrddin, Dwdrych, or Arthur. Lot was such a short, comical appearing person, dark, tattooed, and painted blue, that no one noticed his bid for attention at first. But he was not a shy man, so he strode forward to the front table and had his henchmen pull a bench up right in front of Myrddin. The little gwledig mounted the bench and raised his arms for his fellow gwledigs to hush and listen.

At first he got a round of laughter for his efforts. Then, when Myrddin scowled, Lot got whistled at. Myrddin finally gave Lot permission to address the head table.

While this was going on Arthur continued eating and drinking, paying

---

49   After the Romans abandoned Britannia, each geographical area became the fiefdom of a warlord or tribal chief. The warlords and chiefs, known as gwledigs, elected a high king.

no attention whatever to Lot. Now as you possibly know, Lot was Arthur's brother-in-law. He was married to Arthur's sister Morgawse. But at that time Arthur probably wasn't aware of the fact. He really knew very little about his parentage or relatives until later. Myrddin had still kept most of that information secret.

"My Lord Myrddin," Lot said in his squeaky voice. "I beg clarification for the benefit of my fellow gwledigs seated here. They have all bowed the knee to the upstart sitting to your right."

Arthur spit a bit of gristle onto his plate but still took no notice of what the little blue man was saying.

"Please state your question, Lot ap Gwgawn Gleddyfrudd of Skara Brae," Myrddin commanded.

Lot's voice rose.

"At the ceremony of the drawing of the sword from the stone, you announced the champion as Arthur ap Uthyr Pen-Dragwn ap Cystennyn Fendigaid Llydaw."

"Indeed I did, Lot of Skara Brae," Myrddin intoned. "And what of that?"

"It was to the son of the late departed Uthyr that each of us bent the knee and pledged our fealty at that moment. Was it not?" Lot asked.

"You speak sooth, Blue Lord of the Pixies," Myrddin agreed.

"Yet, we know that Uthyr had no legitimate issue whatsoever," Lot insisted. "He was wed to the divine Eigyr. We all knew Uthyr and Eigyr up to the moment of our high king's lamented death on the Plain of Ambrys. No legal issue of that marriage is known to any of us. This Arthur, if he be of Uthyr's seed, can only be a bastard. We did not bend the knee or pledge our fealty to any bastard son of the land."

The effect on the hall was devastating. Shouting, brawling, and general mayhem ensued. Apparently no other gwledig had considered this point. Some now agreed. Others disagreed. But all were involved in a confusing discourse about the matter raised by Lot.

Myrddin raised his arms for quiet and attention and the riotous actions simmered and then quieted.

"Lot of Skara Brae. Your concern is understandable and I am sure that your high king, who sits at my right, takes no exception to it."

Arthur was in the process of kissing one of the serving wenches and patting her on her ass as Myrddin said this, so it was assumed that no exception had been taken nor was the challenge probably even heeded.

Myrddin continued.

"Uthyr and Eigyr did indeed produce a lawfully born son. Upon the death of the traitor Gorlois, Eigyr was left widowed. Shortly thereafter Uthyr was at Tintagel. I was with him and I myself performed the marriage ceremony that united Uthyr and Eigyr as lawfully married man and wife. I performed the ceremony as ordained warlock of the Coven of Cerunnos and in accordance with the laws that govern Britain. The newly-wed couple consummated the marriage that very evening and Eigyr conceived a son. That son was entrusted to me and I spirited him away to Castrec in order that he be saved from possible mischief by any scheming would-be usurper to the throne."

As he said this, Myrddin gave a penetrating look at Lot. The whole assemblage felt the force of that look. It was more than penetrating. It was accusatory.

Lot said to Myrddin: "My lord Myrddin. You are a very great bard and known to be an extraordinary wizard. Your word carries much weight in the land of Britain. But my people who live beyond the Wall are a skeptical folk. I fear they would need more proof than the words that flow so freely from your mouth. I ask for proof. And proof I must have before I can agree that the youth at the end of the table is the person you say he is and not a cast-off bastard of Uthyr or even of some churl."

A collective gasp went through the hall. No one had ever publicly challenged Myrddin before. And yet a low rumble through the hall indicated that many might venture agreement with Lot's position.

"I had anticipated your inquiry," Myrddin answered Lot. "And for that reason I have asked the lovely widow of Uthyr, Eigyr, the queen dowager, to attend outside the Tower."

The quiet that descended on the great hall was heavier than the British weather outside.

Myrddin called out, "Let the Dowager Queen of Britain be escorted into the hall."

A military escort that Myrddin had stationed in the antechamber marched in escorting Queen Eigyr through the assemblage. The escort accompanied her to the front table. There she stood.

I had never seen Eigyr before. But for an older woman, I found her beautiful beyond description. This was the woman who had been High Queen of Britain through most of my life. I had heard of her matchless beauty. But I felt at that moment that no previous description had ever done her justice.

As you can imagine, Myrddin had Arthur's full attention now.

Every man in the hall stood and bowed as she passed. There was no question that she was the most regal personage in the Tower of Lughdun.

When she reached the front table, Myrddin took her right hand and Dwdrych took her left. They bowed graciously before her. She acknowledged them with a queenly nod of her slender neck.

Still hand in hand with the two holy men she smiled at the gathering of gwledigs. Even those of us who were of lesser rank felt the warmth of her smile turned toward us.

"My lady, Queen Eigyr. We thank you for being present at this feast in honor of Arthur," Myrddin began.

"Indeed, Lord Myrddin, I am delighted to be present at such an august occasion," Eigyr answered graciously.

"May I ask you a series of questions which may seem impertinent, but which are nonetheless relevant to the solemnity of this occasion?" Myrddin addressed her.

"It is ever my pleasure to be catechized by you, Lord Myrddin, Bard of Britain and chief counselor of my late husband Uthyr, Pen-Dragwn of All Britain."

"Do you recognize the man who stands at my right?"

Eigyr responded, "It has been sixteen years since I set eyes on him, Lord Myrddin. He was newborn when Uthyr and I gave him over to your keeping in order that he be kept safe until this day."

"You say when you and our beloved King Uthyr rendered him into my hands. I must ask you now the impertinent question. What was your legal relationship with Uthyr at the time?"

"As you well know, Counselor Myrddin, we were married by you at Castle Tintagel according to the rites of Wycha on the afternoon our son was conceived."

Myrddin had coached those he trusted to burst out with one accord, shouting, "Hail Arthur ap Uthyr Pen-Dragwn ap Cystennyn Fendigaid Llydaw."

The shout was repeated by nearly all those present. It clearly was not repeated by Lot. And we later learned that many of the gwledigs of the North were also silent. Myrddin's ploy had won the support and eliminated the skepticism of most of the gwledigs. But hardly all of them. And the consequences of those who were not convinced had repercussions for the future.

That night I got so drunk that I couldn't tell you what happened afterwards. All I remember is food, drink, wenches, drink, wenches, wenches… I fucked myself dry…and then some.

The next morning I woke up with a head bursting with pain and a delicious naked wench on each side of me. The situation amounted to more pleasure than pain. But it took a full day for my head to clear up.

The following day we got orders from Arthur. We were to head to Caerlleon for his coronation ceremonies. They would take place on Imbolc[50] a little over a month away. Both Dwdrych and Myrddin would officiate at the ceremony so that all our people, Wycha, Druid, and Christian would recognize the legitimacy of the high king.

During the festive period leading up to the coronation itself there were two occurrences that were to have lasting consequences. First and most important: it was immediately apparent that most of the gwledigs of the North

---

50   Imbolc, a "Quarter Day" on the Celtic calendar. It falls halfway between Alban Arthuan (Winter Solstice) and Alban Eilir (Vernal Equinox). It is sacred to the Fire Goddess Brighde, celebrating midwinter and the return of the sun. The Christians also celebrate it as Candlemas or Saint Bridget's (Saint Bride's) day. An auspicious day for a coronation.

were not present at Caerlleon. Word reached us through Myrddin's spies that most of those northern gwledigs were forming an alliance against Arthur, declaring that Arthur was not lawful king of the land. Lot and Mynyddog were the apparent leaders of the revolt. But we also had allies in the North. We heard that Gogyrvan Gawr of Agned had refused to join the revolt, although his lands were adjacent to Mynyddog's. Apparently the evil alliance was leaving our ally Gogyrvan Gawr alone. There seemed to be confusion on the part of the gwledigs beyond the Wall about what action to take, if any.

The other matter of consequence during those days at Caerlleon prior to the coronation was that we made regular excursions to Camelot Hill in the Summer Country[51]. Arthur declared that his chief castle would be built there. Myrddin's people were surveying the land and making preliminary plans for the construction. Work was already in progress before the coronation on Imbolc Day.

On the day of the coronation it was rainy in Caerlleon. But rain is never allowed to be an impediment on our Island. Festivities proceed, drizzle or flood. The Romans had built a major church in Caerlleon after the conversion of the empire to the worship of the hanging carpenter. Caerlleon was the City of the Legion and the legionnaires converted to their emperor's religion in large numbers. This church was called by them a cathedral. And it was the church that Archbishop Dwdrych considered his home base. The ceremonies began at this cathedral. Dwdrych presided over the events within the cathedral's walls. The ceremonies included the chanting of long, tiresome poems in Latin followed by a longer, more tiresome sermon by old Dwdrych. Then, for some reason I never quite understood, the bishop poured water over Arthur's head. Silliest thing I ever saw. Then he rubbed some oil on Arthur's chest. You tell me what that was all about. He held a cross in front of Arthur's mouth and Arthur proceeded to kiss the foolish thing.

Next thing I knew we were all processioning out of that dark, depressing building and were being led by Myrddin and Arthur to the Sacred Grove of the Goddess atop a hill just beyond the city walls. I noticed that Dwdrych did not accompany us.

Once within the Sacred Grove a lady dressed in a silvery-blue robe appeared from among the trees. I did not know who she was at the time. But it was Arthur's sister Morgan, who is a priestess of the Goddess. But what did we know of Arthur's family? I'm not positive that Arthur himself knew the lady was his sister.

Myrddin encircled Arthur's head with a wreath of holly and mistletoe. Morgan presented him with an exquisite sword. Myrddin bid us all kneel. And as we did so the warlock removed the wreath from Arthur's head. Then Morgan placed a golden fillet in its place and Myrddin replaced the wreath over the fillet. None of this made any more sense to me than the mournful chanting in

---

51   Near present day Chard.

the Christian church.

But I enjoyed it more.

Arthur stood with that splendid sword held before him and called upon each of the loyal gwledigs present to come forth and kiss the sword. I found that to be the most impressive bit of the whole ceremonial folderol. Then, when the gwledigs had thus re-sworn fealty to him, Arthur summoned his foster father Ector and his foster brother Cai. Myrddin asked them each to declare whether they wished to acknowledge undying fealty to Arthur as Pen-Dragwn. They answered affirmatively of course. Arthur then tapped his foster father and foster brother on the head and shoulders with his newly acquired sword and declared them his varchogs.

Then Arthur called Gwalchmai and me to come forth. This I did not expect or anticipate. The two of us strode up to the front of the crowd to stand before Arthur. We were told to kneel before him. Myrddin asked us if we acknowledged undying fealty to Arthur as Pen-Dragwn. I was proud to do so, as was Gwalchmai. Arthur tapped each of us on the head and shoulders with that awesome blade and we arose varchogs of the high king.

When I returned to my place in the crowd Arthur was performing the same ceremony with the other members of our warband. We were now not only a group of companions but also a consecrated band of brothers.

That evening Arthur presented gifts to each of us who had been with him in the warband. To me he presented a spear and a dagger, which I carry to this day. The spear is called Ron-cymminiad and the dagger Carnwennan.

The next day we received confirmed word from Myrddin's spies that there were five Northern Gwledigs who still did not acknowledge Arthur as high king. They were Lot. Gwgawn Gleddyfrudd, Gwythyr, Mynyddog Mwynfawr and Meirchion. Of these, three were Pixies – Lot, Gwgawn Gleddyfrudd, and Mynyddog Mwynfawr. The other two were of mixed Pixie, Viking, and British blood. They would make an interesting host if we had to confront them in battle one day.

Gwalchmai and I had no doubts about the outcome if it should come to war against the five Northern Gwledigs. None of the northerners had learned yet to use footstraps. Their troops were more barbaric than civilized. That is to say, they were known to be a disorganized group of tiny warriors. So we felt we had nothing to worry about.

However, many of the gwledigs were frankly nervous about the conflict that was sure to take place eventually. They wanted assurances about the results of such a conflict. It was Myrddin who came up with a solution to satisfy the concerns of our warrior chiefs. The auguries of the Druids were more acceptable to the gwledigs than those of the priestesses of the Goddess. The Master Druid of Britain was Ellyl Gurthmwl Wledig[52], and it was he whom

---

52   Ellyl Gurthmwl Wledig was clearly not the Druid's given name. It was a priestly name given to him when he became Master Druid. The words, in British, signify Demon of the Earth.

Myrddin prevailed upon to read the auguries.

The first requisite demanded by the Druid was a sacrificial victim for the ceremony. The Druidic auguries are read only in the entrails of an enemy. So Arthur called on Gwalchmai, me, and the other companions (now varchogs) to raid an English settlement in Cawnyt. We were commissioned to come back to Caerlleon with three healthy English warriors. The fiercer the better.

What a delightful task.

Our band rode immediately to Cawnyt and scouted out an English settlement near the Roman lighthouse.[53] The English had built a rough wooden wall flanked by a ditch round their settlement. We had attacked such primitive fortifications many times before and knew what to do. Our tactic was to set the wall on fire, which would bring the bravest of the English out to fight us. All we needed to do was snatch three of the fiercest of the fools and haul them back to Caerlleon. We could take delight in beheading those we didn't take back with us. It had been too many months since we had entertainment like that. I was itching to get the engagement under way.

The campaign went pretty much as expected. The force that came charging out of the compound to meet us when the wall caught fire didn't amount to more than twenty men. At least, there were seventeen headless corpses left behind when we slung three brave warriors, well bound up, over their horses' backs and led them to civilization.

I had never attended a Druid augury and looked forward to it. Two days after turning our prisoners over to the Druids to perform their ritual cleansing of the sacrifices, the ceremonies were ready to begin. I thought perhaps the ceremonies would be held at Gwaith Emrys. But I learned that the Stone Circle there has nothing to do with Druids. Strange. I had always been told it was a Druidic site.

All the gwledigs and varchogs rode out of town, up the river Usk past Caerusk, to a hilltop grove dedicated to the Druidic deities. There was a clearing in the oak and shrub copse. Ellyl Gurthmwl Wledig was already there, his body painted blue as a Pixie. He was wearing a blue gown with mystic symbols on it. The appearance was very similar to that of Myrddin at the sword drawing ceremony in Lughdun on Alban Arthuan. The tall, heavily bearded Druid was standing behind a large rough stone block. I believe the stone altar had once been white, but it was covered with dried blood. So I can't be absolutely sure what its original color was. There were twelve fellow Druids flanking the Master Druid, six on each side.

The three English captives were hauled to the front of the crowd and caused to stand before the Druids. The long blond hair had been shaved from the prisoners' scalps. They were naked and painted with woad from shaven head to soles of feet. I will have to credit all three prisoners. They held contempt

---

53   Roman lighthouse: The best known of such lighthouses in Kent at the time was at Dover. It is likely that the raid was there.

on their faces in place of fear. They appeared worthy of the task ahead.

Ellyl Gurthmwl Wledig held a lance-like object in his hand. He pricked each of the victims in the chest. Just enough to draw blood. None of the three flinched. The Druid then lowered the pike and drew blood from each one's navel. Again, not a flinch.

He then lowered it further and pressed slowly on the each one's prick. This time, two flinched. The tallest one, whose blue eyes blazed defiance, stood rigidly at attention.

Ellyl Gurthmwl Wledig commanded that the shorter of the victims who had flinched should be led to the altar. The Druids on his left and right stepped around the altar and led the short English warrior forward. He did not resist. He stood manly proud.

The first sacrificial offering was stretched out on the altar facing the heavens. The Master Druid held up a bronze knife inscribed with the mystic symbols the Druids seem to relish so. He chanted in a language that was not British. It was as harsh as the language of Pixiland. But I knew it was not Pixie. I believe I had, by that time, heard every dialect spoken by the people who inhabited our Island and those who were its invaders. This chant was in none of those tongues.

Slowly, then, the Druid priest lowered the knife and cut into the area called by the Romans the solar plexus. He made an incision down to the pelvic bone. The victim's jaw quivered, his body shook, but he did not cry out. It was a good sign.

Ellyl Gurthmwl Wledig then made a transverse cut at the area of the navel. He parted the skin revealing the live internal organs of the English warrior. Blood was streaming from the sacrifice's body. The Master Druid grabbed hold of the intestines and began extracting them. He pulled slowly and surely, extracting additional organs as he did so. When he was satisfied that he had enough he passed the organs to one of his fellow Druids who cast them onto the earth. One by one those organs were removed from the body on the altar. Each time, the extracted organ was passed to a different waiting Druid and cast upon the ground.

The Master Druid checked regularly to make sure the sacrifice was still breathing. When the breathing stopped, the corpse was turned over so its blood would drain onto the sacred altar-stone. When the body was sufficiently drained the Druid made a sign for the corpse to be removed and cast into the surrounding woods.

It was the most delightful religious service I had ever attended. I wanted to laugh aloud but propriety forbade such an outbreak.

The two remaining English captives were witnesses to the procedure, so knew pretty much what to expect when their turn came. The second victim, the one who had flinched slightly, was led to the altar next. He did not step as confidently as did his lately departed comrade. Yet, considering the circumstances, he seemed a good enough sport about the whole thing.

Again, he was stretched out on the stone, which was now blood soaked.

I will not amuse you by repeating the process with the second sacrifice. It was close enough in most particulars to the previous one to warrant skipping the details. The main difference was that during the sacrificial procedure the remaining victim, the one who had shown the most restraint, who did not flinch, was seized with a severe vomiting fit. His guards held him over the entrails of his companions, so he sprayed the contents of his stomach over the offal. This was an added amusement but hardly worth mentioning.

When this bravest of the brave had his turn under the knife, his body shook with mad vibrations. However never a word or shriek of pain did he utter. It was quite a show. Gwalchmai and I kept nudging each other during the entire proceeding. We were just enjoying it all so much.

When this last corpse had been drained of its blood and tossed into the copse, the thirteen Druids gathered around the entrails that littered the ground. The offal steamed in the cool, damp air. The odor was intoxicating, nearly as pleasant as battle perfume. The reverend gentlemen consulted each other, pointing to this bit of liver, that pancreas, a spleen. They commented at some length and finally seemed to come to a common agreement.

Ellyl Gurthmwl Wledig invited Arthur and Myrddin to join the blue-clad Druids in front of the altar. He then addressed Arthur and Myrddin in loud, stentorian tones that echoed over the entire warrior-filled clearing.

"Your Highness, Your Worship. We have read the omens and are all agreed on the meaning contained therein. You, Most Exalted Pen-Dragwn, will face five enemies who will bring evil forces against the Sun that shines over Holy Britain. The auguries inform us that the Bear who wears a crown will humble the Bear who circles the ice floes. Eleven times more will the Crowned Bear consume the Lice that would feast on his coat. Then peace shall ensue until the Cursed Cub strikes out and destroys the seed that produced him."

Yes, friends. That was it. Did it make sense? Not to me it didn't. I didn't believe it meant anything then. I still don't. Arthur explained to us later that the gwledigs interpreted this nonsense to mean there would be success in any battle led by him. Well, what does a poor churl like me know?

Arthur was king. The loyal gwledigs were reassured. Life was sweet. I looked forward to the morrow, and the next day, and all the tomorrows stretching as far as my imagination could extend. Perhaps there would be bloody battle ahead.

I hoped so with all my heart.

CHAPTER EIGHT

Rumors of War

MORGAWSE SPEAKS:

My twin sister Morgan and I were step-daughters of the high king Uthyr Pen-Dragwn. After he married my mother and assumed the throne of Britain we were embarrassments to him. After all, we were the daughters of the man he claimed was a traitor to him. In actuality we were the daughters of the man he murdered so he could marry and fuck my mother. He arranged for Morgan to be sent to Avalon to study with the Lady of the Lake. That suited Morgan just fine. She was always the religious kind.

Then he married me off to a gwledig from as far away from him as could be – to Lot of Skara Brae.

Lot's main seat was Baledur Castle on the Skara Brae Islands[54]. All freeborn inhabitants of his domain were Pixies, as Lot was himself. You may never have seen a Pixie. There are very few of them down here in the South. They inhabited these islands before we Celts who call ourselves British arrived here. And the Pixies have told me they intend to dwell on these Isles long after the British, English, Irish, and Vikings have gone back to wherever we all came from. These tiny people were called Picti, "painted people," by the Romans and the name stuck as Pixie among the people south of the wall the Romans built to contain them. To this day the Pixies still tattoo themselves blue and then paint their entire bodies blue with woad prior to battle or religious ceremony.

The Druids adopted the use of woad from them.

Pixies have always preferred to live naked. But when the weather

---

54   The Skara Brae Islands are called Orkney in English and Orkneyjar in Norse.

becomes particularly harsh they put on animal pelts. I learned that what they call fair weather, that is, nice weather in which to go about stark naked, my people at Tintagel would call beastly. Life in the Skara Brae Islands is very harsh indeed. The tiny people who live there ride on very small ponies that are bred in the islands to the north, the Skelda Isles[55].

Lot himself was a Pixie, and a wild man. He was tiny, blue, and ugly. But I devised pleasures enough to make life bearable in that cold, windswept, icy wasteland. Lot surrounded himself with Viking slaves who were tall, blond, and handsome. My Pixie husband took pleasure in wenching all over he lands north of the Wall, in riding his horses, and in warfare against the Norsemen and Irish. I took my pleasure in fucking his Norse slaves.

When my half-brother Arthur was chosen High King of Britain, my tiny husband and his companion gwledigs north of the Wall were not happy. Lot wanted to be high king himself, or if not himself, he would have been content if our oldest son Gaheris ruled Britain. I say our oldest because we believed him to be so at the time. We did not yet know that a son I had born previously was still alive. But I will tell you that story some other time if you wish.

Although my husband had shown the forces south of the Wall that he did not accept Arthur's leadership, he was not yet ready to lead the Gwledigs of the North against the greater armies he knew could be raised by Arthur. Lot needed to buy time. He needed at least a year to negotiate with his erstwhile enemies in Thule and the Green Island to join rather than fight him. He believed he could convince the Vikings and the Irish to quit pestering our north shores and join him against Arthur.

In order to keep Arthur from attacking the North while he was assembling a large armed force, Lot hit on a scheme. Since Arthur was my brother, Lot thought that I would be just the person to go to Caerlleon and convince him not to send a force north to attack. So Lot dispatched me to Caerlleon to convince Arthur to keep his forces from advancing north.

I traveled practically the whole length of our Island with my sons Gaheris, Agravain, and Gareth. Our ploy was to inform Arthur that although Lot was not ready yet to bend the knee to him, the boys wanted to meet their famous uncle who was now High King of Britain-below-the-Wall.

When we arrived at the castle at Caerlleon we were greeted by the porter. He was a little man, not much taller than my husband. He was not a Pixie. Not by any means. His features were unmistakably Celtic, but packed together in a miniscule manner. His name was Glewlwyd Gavaelvawr.

I knew that Arthur's seneschal was his foster brother Cai, whom, of course, I had never met. So I assumed that this Glewlwyd Gavaelvawr was Cai.

"How do you do, Varchog Cai," I said in my sweetest tones. "I am the high king's sister, Morgawse. And these three strapping lads here are his nephews. I come from the court of Gwledig Lot of Skara Brae and bring loving

---

55   Called the Shetland Islands in English.

greetings to the court of my brother from that of my husband."

"Queen Margawse," the little man said, with utmost flattery. For I am certainly no queen. "I regret to inform you that I am not Varchog Cai.

"Varchog Cai, the seneschal, would have been delighted to greet you but he has other duties this morning. We had word that you and your handsome sons would be arriving today. Allow me the honor of escorting you to the quarters we have reserved for you and your noble family."

I met seneschal Cai later in the day. I was glad that it was the porter who received me on my arrival for he was not as great a fool as that stupid Christian Cai. But then, few men are.

Glewlwyd Gavaelvawr called to a bevy of gorgeous young pages to assist us with our belongings. I could see that I would be able to keep myself amused there at Caerlleon with so many good-looking boys at my disposal. I might just stay for a while and enjoy myself a bit. Each and every one of them was as cute and as fuckable and suckable as could be.

The pages unloaded our belongings, conducted the slaves who had accompanied us to the kitchens, stabled our horses, and, in fact, took care of all our needs. Well, nearly all. I planned to choose one or two of them to attend me personally after I had bathed, eaten, and relaxed. My cunt was dripping wet just looking at them.

My sons were led to a suite on the other side of the castle from my chambers. I thought that was excellent foresight on the part of Glewlwyd Gavaelvawr. I can't stand to have my sons around me all the time. They're a noisy, bothersome bunch, not really suited to being inside for very long. And I can't have them bouncing into my quarters while I'm fucking a darling page... or two...or three. Can I?

After a couple of hours I was quite refreshed from my journey, and was considering wandering through the castle in search of a pretty boy or two when I was startled by a knock at my door. Who could it be? Certainly none of the castle staff would interrupt me without my summoning them. But as I was alone I answered the door myself.

And there stood my twin sister, Morgan. What a surprise!

"Morgan, my dear, dear sister. How nice to see you looking so well," I enthused.

It was a lie of course. She looked haggard and her priestess gowns did not become her at all.

"Morgawse!" She gave me one of those little puckish kisses that always annoy me. "I was told you had arrived. And you brought your lovely, noisy boys with you. How charming."

"How is it," I asked, "that you are not at Avalon[56] weaving one of your

---

56   Avalon: An isle in the Lake of Avalloc in the Summer Country. It is the home of the Lady of the Lake, and the central shrine of the Goddess.

spells, or flying about Cambo[57] on your broom?"

"Come, come, Sister. None of your wicked jests about brooms, eh?" my sweet sister simpered. "I have come to greet you. Our brother is in the throne room and would welcome you and his nephews to his castle."

"I would be most happy to see our brother," I answered her with an insincere smile. "But might he not greet my sons at another time? I have spent the last week traveling the length of the Island with them. And I must admit, I have had quite enough of their company for a while."

"Of course, dear sister," Morgan replied with her simper. "I understand perfectly. Come, let me accompany you to the throne room."

Morgan led me through a series of corridors and into an open courtyard. In the courtyard I came to a dead stop. For there, playing at dice, was what appeared to be a ghost. The man casting the dice looked exactly like my dead Viking lover Leif. I'm certain I turned pale. The blond giant looked up at me, smiled a sweet innocent smile, and then returned his gaze to the game.

Morgan laughed that annoying cackle that she had even when we were little girls. It was clear she knew something I didn't know and that she was enjoying every minute of my discomfort.

"Seeing ghosts, Dearie?" she asked.

"Apparently so, Sister," I answered. "Is this some of your Avalon magic you're practicing on your dear, sweet sister?"

"Come into this side parlor, Dearie," my sister cooed. "Before we go farther there is a tale I would tell you.

"There once was a queen in a far northern land who was married to an ogre. She would have been a very unhappy queen, except that she had a recreation that kept her from becoming wretched. Can you guess what that recreation was?"

"I think I begin to catch your drift, Morgan," I replied. "Did it have anything to do with Viking slaves?"

"Oh, you are so clever, my dear," Morgan exulted. "Indeed it did. While the Ogre King went riding over the wild desert lands, the queen disported herself with the handsome Norse slaves who guarded the castle. And our mother, the Goddess of Nature, paid a visit to the queen and rendered her womb fertile."

"I see you know many things about what goes on in the Northlands, Sister," I told her.

"You know I dwell among the Fay, who have eyes everywhere above the Wall," Morgan continued. "They report to me much of what happens in Pixiland, clear up past Skara Brae, past Skelda, even into the wastes of Thule."

"You have spies, Sister?"

---

57   Cambo: Kingdom of the Fay people north of the Wall and northwest of present day Newcastle-upon-Tyne. A band of Pixies living there reputedly had magic powers. Morgan dwelt among them from time to time.

"Let us just say I have friends in hidden places. Shall I continue my story?"

"I know you will," I said resignedly.

"In the course of time," Morgan went on, "a very robust, very blond baby was delivered to this frisky queen. She informed the dark skinned ogre king that the child was his first born son. But the ogre king was no fool. In the manner of his people, he had a wicker boat constructed and coated with pitch. The infant was taken from the queen's breast, placed in the boat, and sent out to sea to be received into the loving arms of Llyr. Do you follow the story so far?"

"Of course. Please go on."

"The Fay were aware of all this. They miss very little that takes place in Pixiland. By the intervention of your loving sister, the tiny wicker craft was directed not to the destruction of the waves but to the shore where a fisherman found the boy, conducted him to his wife, and the two fine folk raised the child.

"When the lad grew up and began to sprout a beard, a Saracen riding through the North Country saw him, offered the fisherfolk a sum of money, bought the boy, and lo! He became a member of a famous warband reputed to have been led by a man who later became the high king of a great land."

"Don't tell me," I said. "I would wager that the little lad grew up to be the exact image of his Viking father."

"You are so clever, Sister," Morgan chuckled. "Yes, he did. His name is Gwalchmai and he is one of our brother's closest companions. You have seen no ghost. You have seen the fruit of one of your early frolics."

"May the Goddess be praised," I intoned ironically.

"All glory to the Goddess," Morgan answered piously.

We returned to the courtyard following our conversation in the side parlor. Gwalchmai, my son, my first-born, was still gambling with his companions. I was delighted to observe that he seemed to be winning. I gazed at him with the eyes not only of a mother but with recollections of his father, Leif, who had been sent out by my husband Lot to fight the Irish on our western shore. Leif never returned. Which was not so strange. None of my gorgeous Nordic lovers ever returned from the campaigns Lot sent them on. How I miss those scrumptious men.

Morgan and I continued down another set of corridors, and, at length reached the throne room. I had no idea what to expect. The throne room at Baledur Castle up in Skara Brae is a simple enough affair. The Pixies do not go in for elaborate show. I thought that perhaps down in the South, the high king would have an elaborate throne, perhaps a seat of solid gold flanked by giant dragons breathing fire. I entered and saw my brother sitting on a seat in the rear of the room. I had last seen him as a tiny, squalling brat being whisked away by that fool Myrddin, back years and years ago. Now there he was, a ruddy, brawny, redheaded young man in simple tunic and trousers, seated on a throne. And the throne amounted to nothing more than a seat of green rushes covered by flame-colored satin. It was just as my step-father Uthyr had decreed his throne should be. It followed the dictates of the laws of the Druids and Wycha. I was happy to see that Arthur had not taken on the Christian custom of elaborate trappings.

I approached the throne and bowed my head in greeting. Arthur arose, strode forward with graceful steps, kissed my hand, looked into my eyes, and kissed my cheek.

"Sister, you are most welcome at our court. I hope that you come with tidings of peace from the Northlands."

"Brother. Arthur. It delights my heart to see you," I responded. "Yes, my lord and husband Lot sends you greetings and desires me to tell you he holds you in esteem and brotherly love. He is in hopes you will allow him and his brother gwledigs north of the Wall time to consider your claim to the high kingship."

"You may tell your husband I am pleased to give him all the time he needs."

With that Arthur kissed me on the mouth. What surprised both of us, I believe, is that the kiss, which started out as a brotherly-sisterly embrace soon took on a different character altogether. Our tongues were intertwining and playing games of push-pull that sent spasms of delight throughout my body.

I could tell he was feeling the same pleasure. How could I tell? I had a nice hard prick pressed against my cunt as Arthur pulled me tightly against him. That's how I could tell.

So! My brother was a randy little bastard. I just knew it ran in the family.

I wondered if anyone else in the room could tell what was going on. It must have appeared to be a bit extreme for a family greeting. Morgan, I was sure, could tell that little brother was giving me a dry fuck right there in the throne room.

But who cared what Morgan might think?

Thoughts of a night accompanied by young pages left my head after that embrace. My brother and I had given a signal to each other. And there was, I know, no doubt in the minds of either of us who would be my bed companion that night.

A lazy afternoon passed with Morgan introducing me to the wonders of Caerlleon. Evening settled in and a welcoming feast was provided for me and the boys. At last, blessed night fell.

I had hurried to my room knowing I would not have to wait long for

Arthur's arrival.

I left the bedroom door unlocked and unlatched.

When Arthur stepped quietly into the room, I was scantily clad.

He was fully dressed, but was quite adept at getting out of his outer garments with haste.

There we stood, facing each other. Me attired only in a flimsy robe. Arthur in his small clothes.

Me with a moist dripping cunt.

Him with a hardon protruding from his small clothes.

Clearly neither of us was in the least surprised at what was happening.

"Shall we just stand here ogling each other…" I asked.

"…Or should we hop in bed and get better acquainted?" he finished for me. "It's been a long time."

"And, we have a lot of catching up to do." I concluded.

We were in that bed in a trice.

We had discarded the minimal clothes we had on and resumed the kiss that had started in the throne room and that we knew would continue in the boudoir.

His hands had to set about getting to know my tits. My hands hastily began feeling his cock and balls.

Not bad! Firm, hot, vibrant prick. A worthy handful of balls.

I could tell we were a good match.

His hands had learned enough about my tits, and his lips slipped down to suck my nipples. Both of his hands were exploring my cunt. The finger of one hand was flicking my clit. A finger on the other was slipping up my hole.

I didn't know which hand or finger was doing which. I didn't care.

I bade him desist for a few moments so I could take the measure of his cock with my salivating mouth.

Aah, good. I could get it swallowed to about half way down the pole without hitting the gag response.

Just the right size. Just the right circumference. Just the way I like them.

Without having to tell one another, we stretched out in the bed on our sides, our heads aimed in opposite directions so we could lick and suck each other's love havens.

As it happened, we both came before we had a chance to fuck.

But the night was young. There would be time enough to fondle, suck, and fuck the night away.

While we were recuperating from the suckfest we had just enjoyed, Arthur asked me, "How can I trust you, Morgawse, when you say Lot is not preparing to attack me?"

"I'm your sister, Arthur. Of course you can trust me."

"I love my sister dearly, of course," Arthur answered.

"You certainly have a wonderful way of showing that, Brother Dear."

"But," Arthur countered. "I am not sure my advisors will be as easily convinced as I am. I really must insist on you leaving a hostage with us to assure that your husband Lot will not be persuaded by the other gwledigs of the North to surprise me with an attack."

"A hostage?" I asked, as though surprised. "Who might you have in mind?"

"I must ask you to leave one of your sons here at Caerlleon with me."

I tried to sound shocked and dismayed.

"One of my darling boys? A hostage? Oh, Arthur. What a cruel idea," I protested.

"Let me re-state it, Dear Sister," Arthur said diplomatically. "I would be delighted if you would leave one of my beloved nephews here in the South to enjoy the pleasures of the court of the High King of Britain."

Of course I was thrilled. Nothing could please me more than to be rid of one of the brats. Oh, I loved them as a mother, of course. But I certainly did not need them hanging around Baledur Castle. However, Arthur did not need to know that. So I put on a fine act of feeling put upon. I finally agreed that Gareth could stay on after I left and we returned to our lovemaking.

Hour after hour after hour we fucked, we sucked, we fondled.

I can say this for my little brother. He certainly had stamina.

I certainly enjoyed having a little brother.

Gareth was just thirteen years old and was a nuisance to me and to his older brothers. But he was all boy as they say, and would certainly enjoy the life at Caerlleon. Arthur and I agreed that Gareth should be disguised, lest any of Lot's enemies harm him. In this disguise, he had some interesting adventures. You might ask that fool Cai about them if you're interested.

I remained at Caerlleon for a week. The three boys, Gaheris, Agravain, and Gareth enjoyed the time spent there. I noticed they became acquainted with Gwalchmai, having no idea he was their brother. Arthur visited my bed one more time before I left. Which left me time to enjoy a few of the more delicious looking pages.

The darling pages were a delight. No matter how I took each one on, he was grateful. I particularly like to suck them off at that age. But there were a couple who, while I fondled their pricks, were so absolutely fuckable that I took them right into my cunt.

It was the kind of vacation I just relish.

Gareth was delighted by the idea of remaining at his uncle's castle, hidden behind a false identity. It sounded like an adventure to him. And as I have indicated, for me it was a week to remember.

At the end of the week, Gaheris, Agravain, and I made the long voyage back to Pixiland. Lot was happy that I had arranged to reassure Arthur that he was in no danger from the North by leaving Gareth as a friendly hostage. It gave him time to make allies for the battle he planned in the future.

The next month, I knew that there was a quickening in my womb. Was the child Arthur's or Lot's. Or perhaps from the seed of one of my Caerlleon page boys? Time would tell.

In due course, at the end of the allotted time, I bore a son. And, behold! He was the very image I carried in my mind of Arthur before he was spirited away from Tintagel by that crafty Myrddin. A pink little bundle with red fuzz sprouting from his skull. There was no longer any question as to the source of the seed.

Sometime during the period of nine months I carried the child, Myrddin must have discovered that I had conceived and the manner in which it occurred. I'm sure he had spies both in Caerlleon and among the Pixies of the North as well. His calculations must have informed him that Arthur's child was conceived on Lughnasadh[58], so would be born around Beltane, Arthur's own birthday. At any rate, as the time neared, a decree was sent out from Arthur that all babies born within two weeks of Beltane were to be put to death. Arthur had no need of a bastard son born to his sister.

Now Arthur's various decrees were never carried out in the lands Lot controlled. However, Lot made a point of obeying this particular decree from Caerlleon. And the little red-haired infant was placed in a tiny wicker boat and sent to Llyr.

The first child I had born had been sent to sea and had been retrieved. The Fay were at work again with the last child I bore. For Medrawd's[59] tiny boat did come ashore. It also was retrieved by fisherfolk. But I did not know that at the time. I did wonder if the tot might have been saved. I found out years later. And the result of Medrawd being rescued boded no good for Arthur, who was both the child's father and his uncle.

But that is a tale for someone other than me to tell.

---

58   August 1.

59   In languages other than British, the boy's name appears as Mordred among other spellings.

CHAPTER NINE

Fairhand

AUTHOR'S NOTE:

Most of the tales re-told here were first recorded in the sixth and seventh centuries in Old British (Celtic) or Latin.

Gareth's story, which follows, was originally transcribed in a curious mixture of both Old British and Latin, probably by a literate Briton who had forsaken the monastic life. How else to explain his sometimes crude language in the Latin original.

I have attempted to render the tale into the English vernacular a Celtic thirteen year old might use today.

T. D.

GARETH SPEAKS:

Mum left me at Uncle Arthur's court when I was thirteen years old. I thought that was just about the neatest thing that ever happened to me.

Caerlleon was a lot more fun than dreary, drafty old Baledur Castle up home in Skara Brae. The thing about Caerlleon Castle, particularly, was that it was swarming with beautiful girls. I mean it. Gorgeous chicks.

Mum had left me in Heaven.

You might say that at age thirteen I had an awful lot to learn about women. I discovered that they can be unpredictable, flighty, and moody.

But most of all what I found out was that they are absolutely super.

Mum and Uncle Arthur (he's the king you know) decided that during my stay down South here, it would be more fun for me if no one knew I was the king's nephew. I'd have to act all dignified and grownup and stuff if people thought that about me. So I was just going to pretend I was a nobody. I'd be like a scullion in the kitchen crew. I don't think Mum and Uncle thought about it, but there are lots and lots of chicks working in the kitchen. I figured that out right away. I was thirteen and girls were about all I did think about then.

So Mum and Gaheris and Agravain went back to Da's castle after we'd been in Caerlleon for a little while. I bet Gaheris and Agravain didn't want to go back up there into the cold and damp. But they didn't say so. And I sure didn't want them hanging around while I was having my big adventure.

I was given some kind of raggedy old clothes to wear, and that suited me just fine. I was the youngest one in the kitchen crew, and that was great, too. I got to wash pots and pans, scrub floors, carry out garbage, and peel vegetables. But I was doing it with the other scullions and they were not all that much older than me. And it was not like anything I'd ever done before.

Since I was never introduced by my real name, which was part of my disguise, everyone called me "Brat." That was at first. I got another nickname from Cai the Seneschal later. But hang on. I'll tell you about that in a moment, all right? Did you know the seneschal was Uncle Arthur's brother? That made him one of my uncles, if he only knew it. But he wasn't supposed to know. No one was.

Cai was in charge of the kitchen, all right. And he always gave me a hard time. What he really did was make fun of me. All the time he'd say things that were kind of mean but that made the others laugh. I laughed right along with them. If someone else spilled something on the floor no one said much about it. They just cleaned it up and that was that. But if I dropped something, Cai would say stuff like "The brat made a splat." Everyone then would think that was real funny and I pretended I did too. I think Cai would have liked it better if I got pissed. But what was there to get pissed off about? I had made a splat, hadn't I?

Naturally the best part about being in the kitchen was the girls. I tried to get it on with the wenches every chance I got. I didn't have any success. They always said I was too young for them. But then a few of them would admit, "But you're a cute little brat, anyway." I kept right on trying.

One day I was in the pantry and I got some good hog grease on my hand and got to jacking off. And who should look in where I was? Cai. But he didn't let on. He sneaked back into the kitchen and brought all the girls to the pantry door. Then he swung the door open and there I was for all them to see, whacking away big time. You never heard so much laughter at one time. It was really embarrassing. But, then, I just joined in the laughter with the rest of them. I guess it *was* really pretty funny.

That was when Uncle Cai, who didn't know he was my uncle, gave me a nickname that stuck. That nickname was Heirddllaw[60]. So at least I wasn't "Brat" any more.

Part of my job was to bring food and drink into the great dining hall to serve to the varchogs and ladies. Most of them didn't pay much attention to me. Gwalchmai, though, was nice to me. He'd been nice to me and my brothers when we first got to Caerlleon, but in my disguise he didn't recognize me. And he didn't know he was my brother. None of us knew that at the time. All of that got revealed a lot later. But when I had time off Gwalchmai would give me pointers about handling a sword and a lance. The Viking slaves up in Skara Brae had taught all us boys a lot about fighting. And Gwalchmai looked a whole lot like those Vikings. But he had some fighting tricks to show me that I hadn't known about before. Gwalchmai enjoyed helping me and some of the other kitchen boys and pages with swordplay and stuff like that. I was better at the sword play than any of the pages. And I guess that's part of the reason Gwalchmai was especially nice to me.

Life in the kitchen was fun for me most of the time. I could usually get away from my chores for at least part of the time when they had jousting matches and sword games out in the lists and in the field of honor. Cai was always out there on those days, so not much was happening in the kitchen anyway. Most of the pages and scullions were allowed to watch. And the varchogs I knew who were there participating or just watching would wave to me or greet me with a merry "Halloo!"

Well, one day, when there was a really good jousting tournament, Gwalchmai saw me there. I considered him a good friend, like an older brother (which, as you know, it turned out he was). I was feeling pretty confident of myself so I said to him:

"Varchog Gwalchmai. I've been watching those blokes out here in the lists. I can do better than any of them. You know I can. How about you arrange it so I can enter and show them what I can do?"

Gwalchmai had taught me jousting and knew I could take pretty good care of myself. He was way cool. He gave it a moment's thought, flashed those bright white teeth at me with a twisted smile, and said, "O.K., young man. I'll see what I can do."

That made my heart beat faster than ever.

I saw him go over to where Uncle Arthur was sitting. I could tell he was urging the king to let me go into the lists. He pointed over at me. I waved at my uncle and smiled what I hoped was a very mature smile. Uncle Arthur looked back at Gwalchmai and shook his head. It looked like the answer was "no." Gwalchmai addressed the king more animatedly and finally Uncle Arthur laughed right out loud. I could see that. And he nodded his head. Gods damn! The answer was "yes!"

Gwalchmai came striding over to me. He was laughing. Blimy but it

---

60   In English that translates as Fairhand. The French call him Gareth Beaumains.

made me feel great.

"Well, Heirddllaw," he greeted me. "I have convinced the king to let you enter the lists to show off what you can do. But are you absolutely sure that's what you want to do? These are the big boys you'll be playing with and they play rough, you know."

"Just let me at them," I answered.

Gwalchmai said he knew where he could find a suit of armor to fit me, along with a horse, a shield, and a lance. I could hardly believe my ears. This was going to be my lucky day.

Gwalchmai came through with all the equipment he'd promised. So at the lists the next day I was ready to participate. When I rode into the lists all the pages and the scullions cheered.

My friend Fforgall that I palled around with shouted out:

"Hey, Heirddllaw! Use that fair hand of yours and you'll knock the stuffing out of those varchogs."

Everyone at the tournament heard what he shouted and the place was rocking with laughter.

I guess the story of me being caught jacking off in the pantry had been told around the palace.

Well, I planned to show them something that would knock those laughs right off their faces. Because I was good and I knew I was good.

Everyone watching the jousts was really amazed at how well I did. I must have been a little nervous because I didn't win any contest. But I didn't lose any, either. They let me joust against Dagonawt and Dynydawn. Maybe they weren't the brightest lights in the kingdom's candelabra but they were seasoned warriors in their own way. Even Uncle Arthur congratulated me after my matches.

Gwalchmai gave me a horn of mead in the dining chamber that night when I was serving the varchogs and proposed a toast to me. Everyone joined in. It was kind of embarrassing, but neat anyway. Know what I mean?

Every time there was a jousting match or a sword fight at Caerlleon after that they let me participate a bit. And I always did just fine. Each time they matched me against bigger and stronger varchogs. And I got to be a real favorite, particularly with the other scullions and pages. But it wasn't getting me any action with the chicks. They'd smile at me, and didn't complain too much when I'd grab a pat at their asses. But no action. Not even a good feel. But I knew if I bided my time, a good opportunity would present itself. Because I kept getting better and better with horsemanship, lance, and sword. I figured that was how to make points with the ladies.

Six months went by and I still hadn't been defeated in the lists or the field of honor even once. I even managed to outdo some of the varchogs who were well known for their fighting ability. I guess you could say I was riding high. But, like I say – still no action with the wenches. And I was still

Heirddllaw, scrubbing grease out of pots and serving the important folks in the dining chamber.

Then, one day, when Uncle Arthur and a score of his varchogs were sitting at the Table Round I was on serving duty. I brought in horns of mead and baskets of fruit and made sure everyone was well served. I was as good at being a serving vassal as I was at being a fighter with lance and sword. I was good at everything. Except getting a chick into my bed. I was about halfway through serving the king and the varchogs when Cadfan the Butler approached the head table.

"My lords," he said. "A lady has come to court with a strange tale to relate and would like to tell you her story."

"Is the lady attractive?" Uncle asked.

"Very beautiful indeed," said Cadfan.

"Is she in distress?"

"It does appear so, Your Majesty."

"Then what are you waiting for?" my uncle roared. "Bring in the damsel-in-distress."

I was still in the room when the lady was ushered in. A knock-out! It came to me out of the blue. I promised myself right then that if there were any way in the Gods' green earth that I could nail that beauty, she would be my first conquest.

The lady was dressed in red velvet and showed enough of her tits to reveal that she was built like a stone privy. There were some shapely wenches in Caerlleon. But this one had a shape that made my eyes bulge out and my pecker rise. Yes indeed. I wanted her bad.

She approached the head table in a most saucy, even pouty way.

"Your Majesty and Gentle Varchogs," she began. "I have traveled many a day to seek the help that I am certain this great court can provide."

"All our ears are at your disposal, fair lady," Uncle Arthur responded.

"I have a sister, my elder by a year, who has been held captive for two years by an audacious tyrant of a warrior," the beauty explained. "He not only keeps her locked within her own castle, he profits by the land's use for his own purposes. That is, he robs her of what is rightfully hers under your majesty's laws. I seek relief for my sister's situation."

"And what would that relief be, my dear?" quizzed Arthur.

"I demand that you send a warrior from your court here in Caerlleon to overcome the tyrant, restore my sister to freedom, and return her lands back into her own keeping."

With a quirky smile, Uncle Arthur said, "Tell us, lovely lady. What is your name? What is your sister's name? Where is she being kept? And who is keeping her prisoner?"

The lady's pout had disappeared for a while but back it came. Her lips puffed out. Great Gods! What kissable lips they were.

"My name, an it please Your Majesty, is Llynn ap Coblynaw. I am simply not permitted to tell who my sister is or where she may be found. But I can tell you who the tyrant is who holds her captive and benefits from the use of her lands and vassals. He is called the Red Warrior of the Red Lands."

Gwalchmai addressed the king.

"Your Majesty. I met this Red Warrior once and dueled with him. We fought to a draw. He is a very powerful and dangerous opponent."

"Just let me at him," I thought. But I had to hold my tongue.

Uncle Arthur's voice took on its harsh, official tone. He looked at the lady with his coldest stare.

"Lady Llynn. If you cannot tell us your sister's name, nor where she lives, you can forget about any assistance from this court. If you cannot be frank and open with us, I am afraid you will have to solve your problem any way you can. Good day."

I just couldn't let my big chance slip by. I spoke up.

"Please allow me a word, Your Majesty."

The king and all the varchogs looked over at me in surprise. I was standing there with an empty fruit basket in one hand and an empty mead bucket in the other. I had never spoken up when serving them before. I could see they were shocked. Best of all, the bitch was shocked too.

"Yes, server," Arthur said. I thought maybe he had forgotten my name or something. I didn't know. But anyway, I was invited to speak my piece.

"I have been here six months, Lord Pen-Dragwn. I have proven myself in the lists and in the field of honor. Varchog Gwalchmai can vouch for my courage in jousting and my bravery in sword play. I request leave to accompany the lady to wherever her sister is held captive and secure her release."

Uncle Arthur looked at Gwalchmai and the two of them burst out laughing. I didn't know whether that was a good sign or not. I certainly hoped it was good. The bitch looked uncomfortable.

At length Arthur cleared his throat and answered.

"So, my young Heirddllaw. You would go forth to assist the damsel in distress, would you?"

He did remember the name I was called by everyone in Caerlleon Castle after all.

"Yes, an it please Your Majesty."

"Well, young man. As it happens, it does please my majesty. This is a most novel and amusing idea. I can see that my varchogs are taken with the concept."

The bitch looked uncomfortable. Uncle Arthur went on.

"Not only will I allow you to accompany the lady, I will supply you with a horse."

"And I will give the lad the armor I loaned him for jousting," Gwalchmai added.

There was no mention of weapons or a shield. Oh, well. You take what you can get. I knew I shouldn't push it.

"Your Majesty and his varchogs are most gracious," I enthused. "I will be a credit to your court in this adventure, if it so please the gods."

I threw in that last bit of religiosity to make me sound like it was for the highest ideals that I had asked this. Actually I did it, as you know, to get a chance to get it on with the lady.

Llynn spoke right up.

"Oh, no you don't! I didn't come here to go back with some filthy youngster. What did you call him? Heirddllaw? No, never. I won't have it. I simply will not have it."

I looked that bitch right in the eye. "Try and stop me," I said. Just like that.

She turned red in the face and then broke into a fierce rage. I thought it made her look even more beautiful than ever.

"We'll see about that," she snarled and sashayed out of there wiggling her ass after the barest curtsy to the king. The little lady had spunk. I liked that.

Later that day Gwalchmai brought me the suit of armor I'd used in the lists, and helped me into it. He led me out of the castle gates as though I were a real somebody. And there at the barbican was the well-caparisoned charger that my uncle had promised. It seemed that all Caerlleon knew about what had happened in the dining hall. And they were there to cheer me. Just about then Llynn came out the gates to mount her palfrey and damned if Cai didn't come riding round the corner just behind her on his stallion. It looked like we were going to have a party or something.

Cai and Llynn and I were all sitting on our horses in front of a big crowd. Cai said, "Well, Heirddllaw. Don't you think you should toddle back to the kitchen where you belong?"

Llynn said, "Heirddllaw? Kitchen? This insignificant hobbledehoy? There is no way that I will allow him to come along with me and create an embarrassing mess."

I said to Cai, "Sorry, Fat Ass. I'm going. And with the king's permission. What are you going to do about it?"

"If you're going, I'm coming too," Cai responded.

"Bad idea," Gwalchmai said.

He was right. Cai would just really get in the way and muddle things up. Who needed him?

"You stay here, Seneschal," I said. "The lady doesn't want you. And I certainly don't either."

"I don't want either of you," Llynn retorted.

Arthur chimed in. "Heirddllaw can certainly accompany the lady as far as I'm concerned. Cai can go along if he wants. It's entirely up to him. But you need a valet, Heirddllaw. (He was still calling me that). I am sending a skillful dwarf by the name of Cywyllog along with you."

And at that moment a dwarf appeared, mounted on one of the tiny horses that come from the Skelda Islands up home. He saluted the king, then Llynn, then Cai, then me. The effect somehow was comical and Gwalchmai burst out laughing. Llynn was not amused.

She turned red as a sunset, glared at her king, then spouted, "Shame on you, Your Majesty. What a foul decision for a king. Fie on you. Fie on all of you. I will not have a filthy scullion accompanying me. I simply will not have it, do you hear?"

And off she rode, in a huff.

That seemed to really amuse Uncle Arthur. I could see he wanted me to dismount and I did so. He embraced me and said, so no one else could hear, "You have my blessing, Gareth."

I knelt in front of him and said in a loud, clear voice, "I thank Your Pen-Dragwnship. I promise to do your court proud."

Everyone cheered.

Then Uncle said to Cai, "Cai, it's up to you if you really want to go too. Cywyllog can be valet for all three of you."

Llynn had a head start. So without further ado I hopped on my horse, saluted everyone and trotted my steed after her.

Well, as soon as we got into the surrounding forest where no one back at court could see us and I had almost caught up with Llynn, old Cai shouted, "Well, Heirddllaw. I hope you still know who your master is."

I turned my horse around to face him directly.

"What I know is that you stink as master or as anything else. Watch your fat ass, Cai."

That really got to him. He couched his lance and charged directly at me. I think he would have killed me if he could have. I didn't have lance, shield, or spear. But I managed to grab that lance of his as I pulled my charger over to the side. I gave a push to the lance. And damned if Cai didn't fall right off his horse and onto his fat ass.

I dismounted and picked up his sword, shield and spear while he was dazed and whimpering.

Llynn had stopped her palfrey. She turned around to watch the conflict, and came riding back to take it all in better.

I gave Cai's weapons and shield to my dwarf to carry for me and saluted Llynn with a big smile. She snorted and huffed and turned her back on me. Well, at least I'd caught up with her. Or she with me. And I was now armed.

Things looked pretty rosy to me.

"What did you think of that?" I asked her.

"I think you stink of tallow and grease, Scullion. And you have that ridiculous name, Heirddllaw. Go back to your smelly kitchen. I don't need you anywhere around me."

"But didn't you see how I overcame Cai, the king's own brother? And I won those weapons from him." I pointed to the weapons Cywyllog was carrying.

Llynn would have none of it.

"Pure trickery on your part, little churl. Cai is a real varchog. You're just a Heirddllaw. Your trickery doesn't count. That was not a true joust."

"Look, Llynn, Love," I said. "I've come to serve you. And serve you I shall. Nothing can change that."

"We'll see about that," she huffed. "The first ruffian we run into will chase you back to the kitchen where you belong."

But I was determined she was going to be the first woman I was going to win. I felt sure that my persistence would pay off.

Just about then a man came running out of the forest and into our path. He was dressed in the garb of a varlet or groom. And he was clearly one very upset dude. Of the three of us, he spoke to me.

"Help! Help! Three thieves have attacked my master. They have him bound and will probably kill him any moment now."

Now this promised a little adventure. I would get to show this Llynn babe what I was made of. So, with great confidence, I said, "Lead us to him."

I called Cywyllog to me, took my shield and hung it around my neck and decided on the sword as my weapon of choice for whatever was to come.

I rode after the varlet. Llynn followed along to see me get it in the neck. The dwarf rode along on his pony to be of whatever help he could.

There was nothing to it. The three thieves, or whatever they were, were a bunch of cowards. I simply rode into the clearing where they had the dude tied up, approached the first villain I saw, and cut off his head. Just like that. The other two, when they saw the blood spurting out of their mate's neck, high-tailed it for the woods and were out of there. So I had Cywyllog untie the chap on the ground. The victim was, to say the least, quite happy to see me.

"Oh, thank you, sir," he said. "How can I ever show you my appreciation?"

"Well," I replied. "It's beginning to get a bit dark out here. Have you any place you can put us up for the night?

He was happy enough to accommodate us. He had a very nice big villa not too far away which he led us to. Llynn wanted to spend the night someplace comfortable, so she didn't object at all.

As we were riding along to the villa I said to her, "What did you think of the way I handled those rough blokes, eh, Sweetheart?"

She said, "Don't call me that, Kitchen Boy. I thought you looked ridiculous. That's what I thought. You cut up that first man probably about the way you cut the heads off ducks and geese in your kitchen. And that's where you belong. I just wish you would go away and leave me alone."

I could see she wasn't softening up much yet. But I was still confident she'd be mine before all this was over and just smiled to myself. I thought Cywyllog got kind of a charge out of her waspishness too. But he didn't say anything.

The bloke I'd rescued had plenty of servants at his villa and they took real good care of us. There were good baths in his place like the Romans had at their nicer villas here in Britain. So we got cleaned up. There were fresh clothes provided for us and I was feeling great.

At dinner time I went into the dining room and Llynn was sitting there at the main table waiting to be served. I drew up a chair and was greeted with, "Don't you dare sit at the table with a lady like me, Scum. I do not eat with the kitchen help."

The villa owner whose hide I'd saved was just entering, and he indicated a table over by the kitchen door. "Over here then, good sir. You and I can take our meals apart if you wish."

Of course I wished. Llynn ate proudly alone, served nearly reluctantly by the servants. The owner and I were served lavishly with great meats, fruit, even wine. And service was just about as good as it gets. Everything was up to what they get at Uncle's court. After all, I have an eye for food and service. I kept smacking my lips, which I could see annoyed the hell out of Llynn. I was having myself a grand old time.

Next morning, we got up and had a real British breakfast. The cooks had prepared loads of everything. Llynn chose to eat by herself again, as I figured she would. But she didn't eat much for breakfast anyway. I learned over time that a lot of cunts are like that. Eat like birds. Particularly early in the morning.

We said goodbye to our host who wanted to give me some bezants. I didn't need them. But I did accept a batch of food for us to eat along the road if we should get hungry. Cywyllog loaded bread, cheese, and a couple of fowl into his saddlebags for later. And off we went heading for wherever Llynn's sister was holed up.

There wasn't much to do except admire the scenery for a couple of hours. Then we came to a ford in a river. On the other side of the river there were two warriors. Llynn looked at them, then at me, and scoffed.

"Now you're in over your head for a change, Sonny. I can see those are *real* men over there. If you turn tail and go back to your kitchen now you can get to scrubbing pots and pans instead of humiliating me by getting drubbed by those warriors."

"Stick around, Sweetheart," I said. "You're going to love the show."

The first warrior couched his lance and headed into the stream towards me. Cywyllog brought me my lance, my sword, and my shield. I spurred my courser and met the challenger half way. It was no contest at all. I simply gave him a blow to the helmet. He fell off his horse and drowned right there. I got to the other bank and the warrior there was waiting for me.

I charged at him with my lance and broke it on his shield. He looked surprised from the shock. While he sat there dumbfounded on his horse I whipped out my sword and ran him through the gizzard. Cywyllog rode along behind and scavenged the weapons from the drowned warrior. Then he gathered up those of the one I ran through. We had added to our armaments. And now I had a couple of extra horses, too. This was getting to be fun.

"Well, what did you think of that, my fair lady?" I asked.

"I think you're a worthless clod, Heirddllaw. The first warrior's horse stumbled so the warrior fell off and drowned. With the second one, you slipped your sword in when he wasn't looking. Pure luck and foul play. Now will you just get lost?"

I was going to get lost, all right. But with her underneath me and my prick in her cunt. I just smiled and saluted.

"Shall we be on our way to save your sister?" I asked.

"Scumbag," was her gentle reply.

It wasn't as though she shut up after that. No, she kept blabbing and blabbing all morning long. And there was only one subject – me. She was dissing me every minute. Yap, yap, yap. It didn't bother me, though, because I was sure where it would all end up. In the end. If you know what I mean. I just let her complaining all run off my back.

I guess I wasn't too surprised when we came upon a warrior up the road who was sitting on his horse watching us approach. And this blighter didn't look very welcoming at all. It seemed our way was loaded with unpleasant characters. This one was all suited up in black. His horse was black, his shield was black, everything was black. The whole outfit looked quite nice, I thought. The fellow seemed to know Llynn because instead of talking to me he started right out asking her a question like he'd seen her before.

"Still trying to do something about your sister, are you?"

"Of course," she said, rather peeved.

"And *this* is some champion you've brought back from King Arthur's court to help you do it?" he asked with a sneer.

"It certainly isn't," Llynn snipped. "This is just a pest who attached himself to me like a bloodsucker or a flea. He's only a filthy scullion from the kitchen in Caerlleon. I would appreciate it if you could get rid of him for me."

"Bloodsucker or flea?" I think to myself. "I wouldn't mind being a flea jumping all over your bush, Sweetheart."

But I chose to keep my trap shut.

The black warrior spat on the ground. Cywyllog brought me my spear and lance. I belted on my sword. It didn't seem to impress the fellow very much.

"I wouldn't sully myself jousting with that callow youth," the Black Warrior scoffed. "I think I'll just take his armor and weapons and send him scurrying back to his kitchen with his dong and ass hanging out to amuse the peasantry."

I couched my lance, aimed it right at him, and said, "I'd just as soon run you through like a sitting duck, if that's what you want. Or, if you'd care to, you could defend yourself."

He looked rather surprised but he could see I was serious and that he'd have to either fight me or get run through. He decided to fight so as I charged him he charged right back at me.

My lance hit his shield and his hit mine. The impact broke both our lances and knocked us off our horses. So out came our swords. He hacked at me. I hacked at him. Damn, this warrior was good. Best fight I'd had since we'd hit the trail and I had that little bout with old Cai.

Blackie got in some good whacks and I was bleeding a little myself. But I gave as good as I got. This battle lasted a lot longer than the others, and we both got bloody and tired. But I was younger, had more stamina, and was quicker with my sword. I got in a good swing to his neck and damn near cut his whole head off, like that first combatant I got before. He fell to the ground, gurgling away as the blood came pouring out his mouth and neck.

I unlaced his helmet and finished the job of slicing off his head. I was pretty exhausted but not enough to let Llynn see it. I sauntered over to her, carrying the dude's head.

"Here you are, Llynn Baby. This head's for you."

"Ugh," she said. "How coarse. About what I'd expect from a scullion. You're so uncouth. Take that dreadful thing away."

So I wound up real good and tossed the head off into a clump of bushes.

"How do you think I did on that one?" I asked her.

"The poor man was blinded by the sun and you took unfair advantage of him. You cannot even fight fair. You cannot do anything right. I doubt you were even much good in your kitchen. You're absolutely worthless."

"You'll see whether I'm worthless or not," I said under my breath, "when I've got you in bed."

But she didn't hear me. I didn't mean for her to.

I said to my dwarf, "I say, Cywyllog. That armor the headless corpse is wearing. What do you think of it?'

"I think it would fit you perfectly, Master. And very becomingly, too."

"That's what I think," I answered. "Strip the body and bring me the black armor. From now on I'll wear black armor, carry a black shield, and ride a black horse. I'll be quite a sight, won't I?"

"Yes Master," the little fellow said, jumping down off his pony and getting right to work on the job.

Cywyllog and I stepped into the brush so I could get dressed up in my new suit. I could tell I really looked terrific in it. While my valet was about it he bandaged up my wounds so I wasn't bleeding any more and I was feeling pretty good.

When I came back onto the trail, Llynn was sitting there on her horse ogling my opponent's headless nude body. I could see from her look at the corpse's prick that she was randy, even though what she was looking at was dead. The vixen would be mine one of these days soon. I was pretty sure.

When she saw me approaching in my new outfit she said sarcastically, "The kitchen cockroach managed to survive. The better man perished."

I smiled at her to show that her bad manners did not faze me one bit.

Back on the trail again. Same old story. Yack, yack, yack. All about how put-upon she was to have a lowly kitchen boy messing up her ride back to where her sister was. About how I never won any of my battles fair and square. About how uncouth I was.

I just kept smiling along, making jokes, conversing with my dwarf, happy-go-lucky as I could be.

Then, what do you know? There in our path, in another clearing, there was a green warrior. Yes, just like the other one was all in black, this one was in green. Well, his horse wasn't green. But the horse's trappings all were.

"Look," I said. "Would you get a load of this? A real nut case. All decked out in green. What do you make of that?"

Well, I don't want to go through telling you all about how that went because it was pretty much a repeat performance of what had gone on before. Only this time, when we jousted, I knocked the green asshole off his courser.

Llynn piped right up at the fallen warrior:

"You should be ashamed of yourself. Letting a kitchen scullion knock you off your horse. What kind of warrior are you? Shame, shame, shame on you. Get up and give the little jerkoff a lesson."

To even things up I got off my horse and met him on foot. He got in a good blow and cut right through my shield. So I had to kind of dance around to avoid his sword while he had his shield up deflecting my blows. But then I got in a good blow to his helmet, knocking him silly. He reeled around a bit and then bit the dust. He lay there, flat out, his sword knocked away from him. And he couldn't get up. So I unlaced his helmet and got ready to chop off his head.

"Please don't hurt me," he whimpered.

"It won't hurt at all," I told him. "I'll just chop off your fucking head. You won't feel a thing."

"Oh, please," he cried. "Mercy, mercy, mercy, mercy." And on and on like that until it almost made me sick.

"It's mercy you want, is it?" I snarled. "You'll get no mercy from me unless the nice lady over there pleads for you."

Llynn got all huffy. "Plead with a scullion? A Heirddllaw? That will be the day."

I looked down at the terrified warrior at my feet. "All right, Fucker. You heard the lady. So say your prayers, you green villain. Here goes!"

The warrior shouted out, "Just a minute, there. Hold it! If you spare me, I'll be your boy. I have a warband of fifty men. I'll turn them all over to you. You can have anything you want."

That really annoyed little Miss Prissy.

"What do you mean, you'll be his boy? Turn over your warband? To a youngster who washes pots and pans? Are you fucking out of your mind?"

So I raised my sword again to cut off his head. I had a pretty good backswing going when Llynn changed her mind, I guess.

"Wait a minute, there, Heirddllaw. You win this time," she snarled. "Spare the green warrior's life."

I had to smirk. It was the first real good win I'd had from her yet. It seemed a hopeful sign.

I said, "Anything you say, Sweetheart. All right, Greenie. Get up. But your life is in my hands from now on. Say 'thank you' to the nice lady."

Greenie staggered to his feet and couldn't look me in the eye. He ambled over to Llynn and muttered, "Oh, thank you, thank you, thank you."

She sniffed in response.

The fellow was really kind of a bloody mess. I guess I must have got in a few strokes that I hadn't realized. He looked terrible.

Llynn asked him if there wasn't some place near-by where we could freshen up. Cywyllog gathered up the man's sword and shield to add to our collection. I let Greenie have his horse back and he led us to his castle. All the way there, though, there were nothing but complaints from Llynn.

I can say this for the bitch. Up to this point she was pretty consistent.

The green castle was a very nice place – big barbican and portcullis, turrets, moat, everything. I led the group in and Greenie told everyone I was in charge there from then on and to treat me with respect. It was all very pleasurable.

After we got nice and cleaned up it was dinner time. As usual Llynn wouldn't eat at the same table with me. So Greenie and I sat together and had a nice meal. Llynn sat alone with her nose in the air. Meanwhile the servants groveled around me. It was just neat.

Greenie went over to where Llynn was sitting.

"Why are you such a bitch?" he asked. "This gentleman you're with is very nice. You have bad manners, lady."

Llynn shot back at him, "You make me sick. You're as bad as he is."

What are you going to do? She had her mind made up. But I thought I was perhaps on the verge of changing it.

The next morning after breakfast, Greenie and his warband were with us as we went down the road. But I didn't want his fifty men, well, my fifty men now, coming along to fuck up the works. I was going to get in the bitch's drawers on my own. So after we'd gone on for a while I sent Greenie and my boys back to the castle. Llynn, Cywyllog, and I continued on pretty much as before. With the same jabbering by the lady. To cut off the sound of her sharp tongue my dwarf and I sang some of the raucous songs we both knew from having been in Caerlleon. That annoyed her, too.

One of the things she'd managed to tell me on our trip was that her sister was being held at a place called Castle Dangerous. And that it was by the seashore. We were definitely approaching the ocean now and she let me know that Castle Dangerous wasn't very far away. This was a new turn of events.

I concluded I wasn't getting very far with the tack I'd been taking with her. It was time to change strategy. So, I decided on a whole new approach.

"Look Llynn," I said. "You came to King Arthur's court because you needed someone to free your sister."

"So?"

"So you've seen I can fight better than anyone we've encountered."

She had to agree.

"And you're such a snob, you can't get past the fact that you think of me as being of the lower classes."

She was beginning to melt. I could see it.

"Suppose I were to tell you who I really am," I challenged.

"Who are you?" she asked.

I told her how I was the youngest son of Brenin Lot of Skara Brae, and that Arthur was my uncle, and about the game Mum and Uncle Arthur thought up for me to pretend to be a servant. And damned if she didn't buy the whole bag of shit. She even kissed me on the cheek.

Now I knew it would be only a matter of time before I got her in bed.

It was getting dark by then and Cywyllog set up three pavilions, cooked up a pretty fair meal, and we each went to our respective pavilion.

I was just settling down towards a nice snooze when I heard a rustle at the pavilion entry flap. I sneaked a peek and could see that it was Llynn sidling into my tent.

I breathed deep as though asleep. I even made a little snore sound for effect. I felt her snuggling down into my blankets. She kissed me on the cheek and left. All I got out of it was a raging hardon. But it was at least a beginning.

The next morning Cywyllog had our breakfast all ready for us when we came out of our respective pavilions. I just said, "Good morning," to Llynn and she responded as if nothing had happened the night before. So I just pretended I didn't know she had kissed me. After all, I had become pretty good at pretending back at court.

Cywyllog got the campsite all cleaned up and our gear packed on our horses and we were off to take on Castle Dangerous. I could tell we were just about at the shore from the smell of the air. I hadn't been close to the ocean since I'd left Skara Brae and I'd really missed that tangy smell of the breezes. We rounded a curve and there it was. Castle Dangerous. It must have been nearly as big as my uncle's castle. It was quite a sight. Its moats were formed by two dikes that ran down to the sea. There were several ships at anchor just off the coast. They looked Irish to me. That meant they were probably pirates or smugglers. So the evil warrior who was holding Llynn's sister was probably dealing with the enemy. A real traitor and scoundrel. He needed to be shown a thing or two.

Nearby was a copse of tall trees with something weird hanging from the branches. I went up to see what that was all about. I counted forty men hanging there nude with their eyes plucked out by the ravens that were all around the area. These men hanging there had to be the ones who had attempted to help Llynn rescue her sister before I came along. No wonder she had come to Caerlleon to get a better champion.

On a sycamore tree near the barbican, an elephant horn was hanging. I blew on it. And before long the Red Warrior came riding out of the castle armed for a tussle. As he rode out, warriors and ladies appeared at the castle windows and walls to see the fight.

Red rode into the field of honor. Llynn was waving like mad at someone standing up on the parapet.

"Who's that?" I asked her.

"That's my sister. My sister Dwynwen."

I got a good look at the figure up there. Oh my gods! Tits, ass, the whole works. I was in love. Forget that bitch Llynn. Dwynwen was for me. What a beautiful damsel. What a lovely name. What hooters. I waved up at her. She smiled down at me and waved back. Hot damn!

The Red warrior woke me out of my dream of love.

"Who do you think you're ogling, Boy?"

"My own true love, Dwynwen, that's who," I replied jauntily.

Red huffed, "See those corpses hanging in the trees? Those fools thought they were Dwynwen's beaux too. It looks as if you are going to join the throng. You'll look very attractive up there with your bare ass hanging out in the breeze and your eyes pecked out by the ravens."

That didn't faze me one bit. I shot right back at him, "We'll see about that. Did you ride out here to talk or to fight?"

He had definitely decided on fight, because that's what we did.

He couched his lance. I couched mine. And we rode as fierce as we could toward each other.

My lance hit his shield. His hit mine. Both were direct, lance-splitting blows. The impact of that first lunge at each other was so strong that we were both knocked off our horses onto the ground. So for all the cheering going on from the bulwarks, windows, and parapets there was nothing going on down on the field, because we were both just lying there dazed.

Lucky for me we both came to at about the same time and managed to get back up on our feet in a wobbly way. We drew our swords and had at each other as soon as some of the dizziness cleared out of our heads. At the first blow on my shield I was focused again and was flailing my sword vigorously. I would catch him a good blow and he would stagger. Then he would make a good jab. I would ward it off with my shield and stumble. And so it went, back and forth, blow by blow. I gave as good as I received. But so did he. Neither of us could attain an advantage.

About noontime we had to stop for a moment to catch our breath. We rested on our shields and glared at each other. Our shields were chipped and our mail and armor were tattered. I knew I was bleeding from some of the cuts he'd managed to land on me. But I could see he was bleeding too. The red color he wore disguised the blood some. But I could make out that I'd drawn as much blood from him as he had from me. During our scuffles we had exchanged swords a few times. I looked down while I was resting and saw that I had my own sword back. Glancing at him I could tell he had his as well.

Before long I thought we'd rested long enough. I wanted to get back at him. So we came at each other angrier even than before. We kept stabbing, feinting, swinging, and pounding on each other until mid-afternoon. This was the toughest fight I'd ever been in. He was a good match for me. But we were wearing down and agreed to rest again. During this time out, Cywyllog came up to me and unlaced my helmet so I could catch the cool sea breezes. He gave me some water to drink, too. That helped a lot. I looked up at the ramparts and there she still was – Dwynwen, the lady of my dreams, beautiful ass and all. I was re-inspired.

Cywyllog got me back into my helmet and I was ready to go at it again.

"Back into the fray!" I shouted and charged Red.

We now fought even harder than before. We both looked like red warriors because now we were both drenched from helmet to spur in blood and sweat. Nothing would slow us down. Then Red came at me with two skillful blows and knocked the sword right out of my hand. The impact knocked me to the ground. Red jumped on top of me and began to unlace my helmet for the final thrust when a voice came down from the parapet. It was my new-found love.

"O warrior, arise. My heart longs for you."

That did it. If her heart longed for me I had to rise to the occasion, right?

Thrusting up with all my strength I flipped Red over and with a deft reach retrieved my sword. We both managed to get off the ground and back onto our feet and the battle continued. This time, I sent Red's sword flying and followed up with blows to his helmet. It knocked him silly, it did. Now

I jumped right on him and knocked the rest of the wind out of him. He was gasping as I unlaced his helmet to relieve him of his head. Before I could do the deed he got enough breath back to do some begging.

"Most powerful of warriors. Mercy, mercy, mercy!"

Now where had I heard *that* before?

"Mercy? You've got to be kidding. How much mercy did you show to those birds you hung up on that tree over there?"

"Oh, them," he stuttered. "I can explain that, if you'll just listen a tad."

I had the sword raised up for that slice that I so wanted to cut through his sweaty, bloody neck.

"All right, then. Let's hear your story. But it better be good. Or you'll find yourself hanging up in that tree with the others. But without a head you'll be upside down and hanging from your feet with your miserable cock pointing down at your bellybutton."

(I thought that was a pretty nifty line, myself.)

"Here's what happened," he gasped. "I loved a lady whose brother was killed by Varchog Gwalchmai. I found Gwalchmai and fought him myself to avenge my lady. But we fought to a draw. Since then I've fought every varchog who came this way so I could lure Gwalchmai back and fight him to the death. It was all because the lady I love asked me to avenge a great wrong done to her by a varchog of King Arthur's court."

That story didn't convince me much. But as he was spinning that shit out, his warband came out of the castle and surrounded us. I could chop off Red's head, all right. But if I did, the fifty or so ruffians would make short work of me. It was time for negotiation.

"All right," I said. "I guess I can forgive you this time, since you did it for a lady."

That was the best excuse I could come up with to back off and save my own skin and yet seem to be winning at this game.

So I told him, "I'll spare your neck on condition that you release Lady Dwynwen from bondage, restore her holdings to her, and leave this part of the country with your whole warband by dark."

I brandished my sword a bit more to make myself look good. He agreed to my terms. I released Red. He dusted himself off, went into the castle, packed his bags, and headed off toward the North with his band of cutthroats. I have never heard any word about him since.

Llynn and I rode into Castle Dangerous in triumph, me as dignified as a varchog, with my faithful dwarf following right along.

We were met by the castle staff, which was now at our disposal. I was bathed, my wounds were bound, and I was dressed in regal splendor. So now I was ready to go to Dwynwen's chamber to get my reward. I envisioned that she would lead me to her bed and we would fuck the rest of the day away.

Dwynwen opened her door to me. She stood very stiff and started to thank me formally. While she was saying her fine words I was hustling her towards the bed with a terrific hardon, telling her how much I loved her and that she was the only woman in the world for me. She managed to push me away and hold me at arm's length. I was stupefied. I didn't want to stand there and talk. I wanted to fuck.

"I thank you, Heirddllaw, for fighting that dreadful Red Warrior for me," were her disappointing words.

"You're welcome," I answered, starting to pull her towards the bed again.

"Slow down, Boy, slow down. Not so fast there," she protested.

What a blow! I was tongue-tied.

"That bit down there on the field was nicely done," she went on. "And don't think I don't appreciate it. But, you'll have to prove yourself better than that if you expect to get my ass into bed."

"Prove myself better than what?" I protested.

"You stood up quite well to the Red Warrior. I cannot deny that. However, you did not manage to cut off his head. And it would have pleased me if you could have strung him up on the tree. But all in all, it was not too shabby a job on your part."

"Not too shabby a…"

"Right. But, if you want to get between my legs, you're going to have to do better than that."

"Better than…," I stammered.

"Yes, you had better go out and have more adventures. Win more fame. That sort of thing. Perhaps grow up a bit more. You really are a bit young for me. Then you can come back here when you are more mature and we will see."

Females! Try to figure them out!

I left her chambers mightily disappointed and went off to my own room – the master room that used to be Red's before I came along.

Cywyllog came and set out some soft nightclothes for me that Red had left behind and I climbed into bed.

I didn't have to sleep alone though. I was just settling in, thinking of how I'd been deflected by Dwynwen, when Llynn came tiptoeing into my room in her nightgown. She snuggled into bed with me and my lips were sucking her tits. Just a few minutes of that and I couldn't wait any longer and nailed her on the spot.

And that, boys, is how I got my first real fuck. Yet it wasn't with the lady I'd fallen in love with so it still wasn't as perfect as I would have liked.

But, man. It wasn't bad, either

The next morning, after breakfast, Cywyllog and I set out from the castle in search of adventure. I had to convince Dwynwen of my valor. And this time it was different. I was really in love.

We rode all day long without a single adventure along the way. We stopped at a hermitage where a kindly hermit gave us gruel and a night's lodging in exchange for a hefty contribution. I was pretty tired and was off to sleep on the hard cot he made available. I was just well settled into a nice snooze when I was awakened by screams.

"Master! Master! Help! I'm being kidnapped!"

It was Cywyllog. I jumped out of that cot and saw a hefty man heading out the door with my dwarf tucked underneath his arm. It took me a while to get into my mail, armor, and helmet, grab my weapons, and get on my horse. By then the kidnapper had a good head start on me. But I could tell he was on the trail back towards Castle Dangerous. I could hear Cywyllog's screams and knew I was catching up with him.

As I was pulling up in front of Castle Dangerous I saw the kidnapper ride through the gates and into the courtyard. I was right behind him.

Imagine my surprise when I got to the courtyard and there Dwynwen was standing, holding my dwarf in her arms like a baby. I wasn't too surprised that Cywyllog was cuddled up contentedly with his little head resting snuggly against her tits. I would have liked that myself. Wouldn't you?

Dwynwen set my dwarf down on the ground very gently and held out her arms to me.

"Oh, Heirddllaw," she cooed. "I got to thinking about those fair hands of yours. I've been driven mad just thinking about them."

We left Cywyllog standing there smiling in the courtyard. I followed my true love up to her chambers.

I ran my fair hands all over her tits, her ass, her bush, and gave her cunt the best handjob she said she'd ever had. And then I aimed my pecker at that fragrant cunt of hers and nailed her good.

Believe me, Boys. If you know what you want, and are really persistent, even the merest broth of a lad, a heirddllaw, can attain his heart's desire.

Would I lie to you?

Trust me.

CHAPTER TEN

The Battle of Arderydd Ford

GWALCHLMAI SPEAKS:

All of us at Caerlleon knew that the unrest in the North would eventually lead to war. Arthur decided it would be to our advantage to wait for the northern gwledigs to invade our territory rather than us striking first. So we waited.

Myrddin's spies were watching and reporting to him the events above the Wall. The five Northern Gwledigs continued to refuse any acknowledgement of Arthur as High King. Along with Lot there were Gwgawn Gleddyfrudd, Gwythyr, Mynyddog Mwynfawr, and Meirchion. Gogyrvan Gawr of Agned had refused to join the evil alliance. So we had friends in the midst of the dissatisfied warlords. That was to our advantage.

One day early in the month of Feabhra, Myrddin called a closed council meeting consisting of Arthur, Myrddin, Bedwyr and me. Myrddin had news for us.

"Arthur, Varchogs, greeting," Myrddin began in his abrupt manner. "I have an intelligence report that war with the North is likely before the end of the month. Brenin Lot wants to mobilize all the warlords north of the Wall. He is having trouble convincing his fellow brenins that war is necessary. But he himself is very ruffled and has his Pixie warband ready to march any moment."

Arthur asked, "What is Lot so roiled up about?"

"Lot's wife, your dear sister Morgawse, gave birth to a son in Skara Brae last week," Myrddin informed him. "It is said that the child bears an uncanny resemblance to you. At least Lot believes so. He claims you fathered it."

Arthur commented, "So our fears were justified when we ordered the infanticide."

I was surprised. I had no idea that Arthur had fucked his sister. But the implications were immediately clear. Not only could the child's birth precipitate immediate war with Lot. It could jeopardize the future lineage of the Pen-Dragwnship. But the immediate concern was the possibility of Lot starting a war before we were ready to respond. That was Arthur's thought as well. He wondered how strong Lot's position was at the moment.

He asked, "We really can't be certain how many troops Lot will be able to get to join him, can we, Myrddin?"

"There's no way of knowing with those people," the wizard replied. "Today they can be on a rampage to go to war. Tomorrow they might decide to go off fishing, or have a party, or just sit round painting each other blue."

Arthur said, "I don't want them to come south of the Wall until we have troops enough to withstand them. Lot needs to be taught a lesson once and for all. Myrddin, what do you say we tap the Continent?"

Over on the Continent Arthur had two cousins who were impressive warlords. Gwledig Bors was warlord of Lesser Britain. Gwledig Ban was warlord of Bawn. They were brothers and were grandsons of Cystennyn Fendigaid Llydaw, as was Arthur. It was clear that if they could release some troops to help us fight the folk from beyond the Wall our chances of squashing the foe would be enhanced greatly.

Myrddin acted as though that was his idea in the first place.

"Exactly what I was thinking, Arthur. The sooner we contact them the better."

Arthur looked at Bedwyr and me.

"I am sending you two to the Continent to convince my cousins that we need help. I'll send Meigawse and Brastaws with you. They're good men and have ample reason to keep gwledigs like Lot from overrunning their families' lands.

"Bors is going to have to fight that barbarian Clovis one of these days and will need our help. And Ban must be aware that the Burgunds are eyeing his bailiwick. Tell my cousins that if they come to our aid now we will come to theirs when the need arises."

The four of us headed for the coast that very afternoon. We crossed the Sleeve and were well received by both of Arthur's cousins. Bors was at his capital in Nanteos and Ban at his castle in Avallon.

We, too, have a Nanteos and an Avalon (one "l" in Britain). But how different our cities are from their Continental namesakes.

Bors and Ban could see the advantage of supporting Arthur at that time. The barbarians from the North, the Franks, Burgunds, Goths, Visigoths, and Vandals were making inroads in their rampages through the vestiges of the Roman Empire. Nanteos and Avallon were right on the path to Rome itself. Help from Britain could be of great value to our Continental allies when the need arose.

Within ten days we were back at Caerlleon with the happy news that Bors and Ban were on their way with some eight hundred warriors each to fight off the threat from Pixiland. When they were threatened by Franks and Burgunds in the future, they knew they would be able to count on our help.

We never knew what it was exactly that caused Lot to begin his sudden, precipitous march south. Perhaps he was aware of our contacts with our Continental allies and hoped to force an engagement with Arthur before the allied troops reached Britain. Perhaps he simply could not contain his vehement anger at Arthur for the insult of cuckolding him. But, whatever it was, we received word before the month was up that the Pixies were on the move.

If Lot was hoping to make a preemptive move before our allies arrived, his sources of information were deficient. As he was bringing his troops down below the Wall, sixteen hundred troops arrived from Europe to help us. Added to our fifteen hundred, we were a sizable army.

On Feabhra 20, 518, Arthur led our massive troops north toward the Wall. We were as strong in cavalry as in infantry. The troops advanced with the confidence of knowing they were led by the Pen-Dragwn of Britain and the greatest warlords of Europe. Arthur was eighteen years old and was as respected by his men as his father and uncle had been before him.

When we arrived at Mocetawc Plain our scouts informed us that the enemy was within striking distance. The moment had come. An army of true Britons against a rag-tag bunch of Pixies. That was the way we saw it. A well-armed infantry and the finest cavalry in the world were about to enter conflict with a people who were tattooed, painted themselves blue, fought naked, and whose chief weapons were slings and spears. Gwledigs Bors and Ban brought accomplished infantry and cavalry with them as well. If Lot wanted war he would get war.

We were justifiably confident.

As would be true for most of our battles over the next three years, Arthur managed to engage the enemy at the ford of the river.

Lot's Pixies attacked us at the ford. They streamed across the river, beating drums, howling, and wailing. I thought I knew what the people beyond the Wall were like in battle. I was wrong. This was the most unnerving sound I had ever heard. It disconcerted Arthur, Bors, Ban, and the troops. Arthur was confused and bedazzled enough to withdraw his troops a bit. Then, accommodating to the weird battle situation, he regrouped the cavalry and charged into the naked, blue, barefoot army.

Lot's cavalry consisted of one person – himself. He came riding across the ford painted blue, bare-ass naked, and mounted on a Skelda pony. The tiny blue man on the tiny horse was like an apparition from Annwfn. Again, our people were stunned for a moment.

Arthur rode forth to meet Lot. Troops on both sides, as convention decrees, ceased hostilities as the two chiefs approached to decide the battle by hand-to-hand combat. Our people stopped their killing spree. The Pixies gave respite to their slings and spears.

Arthur was on his mighty charger Eidyn. The Pixie Gwledig rode his tiny pony. It was too bizarre. The armies were mismatched. We had twice as many troops as they and a cavalry which they had not. Our general was tall, well armored, and majestic. Theirs, tiny and naked. Was ever there such a war as this? I decided that Lot must indeed be a madman.

Lot shouted insults at Arthur in a voice filled with rage. Then the assembled Pixies began to make a low, wailing sound that must be a battle technique above the Wall. Whether they were calling on spirits from the Otherworld or just involved in some war magic, I never did figure out. But it did hold all of Arthur's people spellbound.

The two generals met in this uneven hand-to-hand conflict. It was no contest at all. I was a burlesque of combat. The battle was over in five minutes. Arthur simply rode up to the little blue man, deflected a spear lunge aimed at him from below. Arthur then sliced with his mighty sword, and Lot's headless corpse lay on the ground.

The wail of the Pixies rose to a keen. The sound must have reached the ends of our Island. Then, all their voices quieted simultaneously and the blue troop turned its back on us and silently headed back to its homeland.

We did not follow or harass that blue army. Just as silently, Arthur motioned our troops to turn south, and we returned to Caerlleon.

We had won the battle, and presumably the war. But we did not have a feeling of victory. The whole engagement was pathetic.

Arthur had Lot's body brought back to Caerlleon. Camelot was the ceremonial hall but Arthur's military capital was still at the old City of the Legions. Arthur ordered that Lot be given the funeral of a fallen chief. And preparations were made for that ceremony.

The Master Druid of Britain was called upon to conduct the services. It was felt that neither Warlock Myrddin nor Bishop Dwdrych was the appropriate officiant. The surprise of the event was the arrival of one hundred naked, unarmed, painted Pixies who came to attend the immolation of their leader. As the Master Druid conducted the funeral services appropriate for a great warrior, a ceremony as ancient as our people, the Pixies keened at the top of their voices in the most mournful farewell ever heard below the Wall. When their gwledig was set on his funeral pyre their voices raised to a pitch that caused shivers to run down my spine. When the last ember had burned out, the tiny blue people silently turned their backs on Caerlleon and headed back to walk the entire length of our Island to their northern abode.

After the battle in the North, the Gwledigs who had not bent the knee to Arthur at his coronation did not give us any more trouble. They had their hands full with incursions of Vikings and Irish and did not need conflict with Arthur's kingdom.

We no longer felt Pixiland to be a threat. However there were still the English settlements on our eastern shore. The settlements that Vortigern had yielded to the Angles, Saxons, Jutes, Frisians, and Danes. We called those settlements England. As long as England didn't threaten us, Britain would leave it in peace. So there was a peace. But a tenuous peace.

I, for one, did not trust the English to stay behind the artificial borders Vortigern had set for them. I foresaw more war ahead. I believed that Britain and England could not long co-exist on our Island.

CHAPTER ELEVEN

Accolon and the Wrath of Morgan

MORGAN SPEAKS:

Once Uthyr married Mum, he had no need for me or my sister Morgawse to be around. So he sent us away. We were fourteen, we were adults, and we were ready to get on with our lives.

Morgawse was married off to that dreadful little Pixie, Lot, the gwledig of Skara Brae.

I was more fortunate. I was sent to the Isle of Avalon to study to become a priestess of the Goddess. Avalon must be the most beautiful spot on earth. And being a priestess of the Goddess is the highest calling a human can undertake.

I was not restricted to Avalon. The Magic Isle is certainly not a prison. Among other places, I spent time north of the Wall with the Fay. Do you know the Fay? They are a band of Pixies who dwell in Cambo under the kingship of Gwyn ap Nudd. Although racially I am not at all of the Fay-folk, they adopted me into their fellowship when I ministered to their king at Ynyswitrin Tor. He got very drunk one evening and fell into a thorn bush. With my healing art I was able to sooth his pain. As a result his people adopted me as reward for my assistance.

Up in Cambo the Fay live in souterrains which include miles and miles of underground passages. Since the Fay can slip into souterrains while being pursued they have the reputation of being able to make themselves invisible.

The Fay are all much smaller than I am and are dark-skinned and tattooed. They paint themselves blue with woad like all Pixies. But they practice a magic not known by the other Pixies. Many of the Fay women can fly, like I can.

I often go to dwell among those delightful little blue folks. When I am there, I live naked too. And I paint myself with woad. But I have never subjected myself to being tattooed. I am a British princess as well as being an adopted Fay. Like all Britons, I have a fierce sense of what is proper and what is not. And tattooing would not be proper for the daughter of Gorlois and Eigyr. But aside from that I fit right into the revels of the Kingdom of Cambo.

Why do I tell you all that? Partly to explain why I am often called Morgan the Fay. And also, because you need to know that I have a place I can always escape to when things get uncomfortable for me south of the Wall. You will see as my tale progresses why that can be very important for me.

I was a full-fledged priestess of the Goddess and an honorary member of the Fay at the time my brother Arthur's castle at Camelot was completed. I came to Camelot during the castle's opening celebrations. I wanted to be near the seat of power.

To be more than just an occasional guest I needed a legitimate reason for dwelling there. So I managed to marry that old fool Gwledig Urien, a regular member of that band of idiots Arthur keeps with him at the Table Round. Of course our marriage was never officially consummated. But Urien did not know that. He thought he was having marital relations with me from our wedding night on. In reality, by the administration of the potions I have mastered, I caused him to dream that we were engaged in matrimonial pleasures while I was jacking off that tepid dick of his. He thought it was the real thing. I couldn't stand to have the old fool assault me in bed, so I simply put my training in magic and my adept right fist to work on him.

With my husband disposed of in that manner I was free to play with the handsome young men who were readily available at Camelot.

But you came here to ask me about that dear boy Accolon. I suppose what I just told you fits in with the tale. As I continue you can decide for yourself.

Anyway. When Arthur was working out strategies for his upcoming battle with Brenin Lot, his cousin Ban of Bawn came to Britain with some troops to help out. He brought two of his sons with him – Llenlleawc and Accolon. It was Accolon who caught my eye. What a stunning lad he was. Fair of hair, broad of shoulder, gentle of face, and wildly ruttish as only a boy can be. It may have been his skin that first attracted me. He was nearly bare of body hair other than a very soft beard on his face and wispy tufts beneath the arms and on the pubis. His eyes were the blue of the lakes of Reged. And that laddie was blessed with a shy smile that totally engaged me. He had a complexion that was reminiscent of a perfect peach – just delectable. His white teeth suggested the sweetest kiss imaginable. And his prick – adorable. He was eighteen but had the stamina of a fifteen year old.

About the time Accolon came into my life I was growing quite peeved with my young brother. I flooded him with good advice which he ignored. Myrddin gave him advice at every step which he followed. I loosened my charms on Arthur to lure him to my bed. He had fucked nearly every other female at Camelot. Yet he never so much as responded to my lures with a glimmer.

When my sister Morgawse came to his court in Caerlleon, my brother was aroused by her, fucked her, and knocked her up. Yet he never showed any amatory interest in me whatsoever.

So, since I would never be his paramour or advisor I decided to play Myrddin's game and create a king to my own liking. One I could control.

I decided I would make Accolon High King of Britain and would rule the kingdom through him.

So I told Accolon he would be my king. I dared not tell him the wiles by which I would rid the kingdom of the two obstacles to this – namely husband Urien and brother Arthur. Accolon was too naïve to have a hand in eliminating the necessary people. At least knowingly. So I just told him I had read the future and in it he was to be king and I was to be his queen. He, youngster that he was, never seemed to sense the implications.

The first step in my plan was to arrange for Arthur, Urien, and Accolon to go hunting together. That was simple enough since all three loved killing animals. Men! So, with my connivance, one fine day, the three of them went out a-hunting. We priestesses of the Goddess have acquired some of the Druidic lore. I certainly know how to direct horned wild creatures. Using my enchantments I brought a hart into the woods and the three hunters set out in pursuit. The hart led them to the banks of the River Yeo where a young priestess of the Goddess, Nimue by name, had brought a gaily colored elegant barge. On the barge with her were eleven of the Goddess' acolytes, ravishingly beautiful young ladies all.

The three dauntless hunters were exhausted and famished by the time they arrived at the river. Nimue stood on the bank and greeted the hunters.

"Gentle hunters all, I greet you. And beg of you a boon."

Accolon was the first to respond.

"Fair maiden. We honor all women, but most specially those of such beauty as is possessed by yourself. Ask and it shall be granted unto you."

Because of his youth, perhaps, Accolon was not aware that it was his liege, Arthur, who should have responded. Accolon was a darling boy and so naïve. How I loved his youthful ignorance.

Nimue gave Arthur her most artful smile as though it were he who had answered cleverly and eloquently.

"I truly have two requests. First, cease your pursuit of the hart that has disappeared into the woods. It would please me to have its life saved."

"Granted," Accolon answered.

He was beginning to annoy both Arthur and Urien. But they nodded agreement anyway.

"And second, I would have you partake of our hospitality on yon painted barge. By we, I mean the eleven other lovely young maidens whose sole happiness in life is to pleasure such valiants as yourselves."

At this, the eleven acolytes came out on deck in a state of deshabille that quickened the pulses of the three riders. With one voice the three responded, "Agreed!"

The young ladies came ashore and escorted the men aboard.

"First, a soothing bath before dinner," Nimue suggested.

The men were very receptive.

Each was escorted by three lovely acolytes to a separate tepidarium. There, each was disrobed and bathed by his three escorts.

They were soaked in warm water. Their bodies were lathered from head to toe, with very special attention given to peters and scrotums.

Indeed, every one of them spurted his jism into the pool before re-emerging into it.

Following the bath, fresh clothing in the Roman style was placed on the men and they were led to the lavish dining room where they were served all manner of delicate meats, cheeses and breads accompanied by fine Samian wines.

The three men ate to satiety and drank to inebriation. Each was led to a separate richly appointed cabin furnished with an enormous bed of downy comfort. There, they enjoyed the pleasure of the fair nymphs' hands and lips on their erect cocks. Those who managed to remain awake and responsive after that got a royal fucking.

Each of the hunters then sank into the most contented sleep a man can know.

But on the morrow, what a rude awakening I had planned for them.

That old fool Urien awoke in my arms back at Camelot. I had flown to the River Yeo and carried him back in my arms. He awoke expecting three nubile damsels ministering to his cock. When he found himself with his wife, the silly old fool didn't know what to say. I let him stew for days.

Arthur was not as fortunate as Urien. No, not at all. He awoke in a dungeon with twenty fellow prisoners. He asked his unhappy companions where he was.

"You are in the dungeon of Castle Drogo. You were most unceremoniously dumped here at midnight by three horrible, foulmouthed dwarves. Your condition was that of a man drugged by potions fiercer than wine."

"And what is the nature of this dungeon?" Arthur asked.

"Alas," answered a prisoner. "Some of us have been here for years and years. One loses track of time. Since I have been imprisoned here eighteen fellow prisoners have perished of neglect, starvation, disease, and dehydration."

"And there is no escape?" Arthur asked.

"Oh, aye. There is indeed," a prisoner answered the king. "The lord of Castle Drogo is as evil a caitiff as any who dishonors King Arthur's kingdom. The lord of Castle Drogo is the evil Damas. Yet the castle is not rightfully his. His older brother Ontzlakis is the lawful master of the castle and the countryside. Ontzlak is a noble, honest subject of Arthur who challenges Damas to single combat to settle their differences."

"Such is the code of the realm," Arthur answered.

"But," the prisoner continued, "Damas is a craven coward and refused to meet his brother in battle. For this reason he has enlisted evil sorceresses and loathsome dwarves to waylay such as you and us. He offers his captives the choice of championing him or durance vile. We all hate Damas with such passion that each of us has refused to fight on his behalf."

Arthur pondered the choice which would be offered him. And, I knew my baby brother's heart well enough to predict the path he would take when confronted with the choice.

Before long, a filthy, begrimed wench came to the dungeon bars and offered Arthur the choice that had been proposed to each of the other prisoners. Her clothes were in rags and her hands and face were covered with soot. She told Arthur the conditions for being freed.

Arthur addressed her: "I have been expecting that one of your master's people would come here and offer me exactly this choice. I have considered it well and have decided that I prefer to die with sword in hand rather than languish here to die of starvation, disease, and neglect. But I have two conditions which must be met if I am to engage in hand-to-hand combat."

"And what may they be?" asked the wench.

"I must be provided with a noble mount, an adequate suit of armor, and a trusty blade."

"That much Lord Damas will agree to," the wench responded.

"And secondly, whether I succeed or fail to best my opponent, all my fellow prisoners are to be released."

"I can certainly promise you that also," she answered.

Now I must tell you that the wench was not some lowly servant of Damas. She was none other than Nimue, that priestess of the Great Goddess who had welcomed Arthur onto the barge. Yes, Nimue herself. But, disguised in the costume of a slovenly serving wench. And with her face begrimed, Arthur did not recognize her. I do not leave such matters to chance, you know.

Nimue informed Damas of Arthur's decision and Damas called for the new prisoner to be brought before him.

You well know that Arthur was an imposing figure. Damas was delighted to have him as his champion. It struck him at once that the red-haired prisoner would easily defeat his brother.

"O prisoner. I understand the conditions you have set for being my champion. I have kept a great charger in readiness for the event. My armorer will outfit both you and the horse with as splendid protection as any seen even at Camelot. And for sword and lance you will be supplied with the best in the land."

"And about my fellow prisoners?" Arthur asked.

"Regardless of the outcome, the doors of the dungeon will be flung open and all those within will be free to wander whither they will," Damas assured him.

This was the outcome I had planned. And when Nimue reported it to me, I rejoiced.

The third part of my plan involved my dear beloved Accolon. He awoke the morning after his experience on the barge, his head throbbing with pain. He found himself next to a sacred well near Caerllydd. Struggling through his painful morning-after, he discerned a hideous dwarf ambling up to him. The dwarf addressed Accolon but his voice was heard only through the buzzing that rattled through the young man's skull.

"Young lord," said the dwarf. "I bear greetings from your lady-love and future queen, Morgan. She bids you know that the day of your coronation approaches with the speed of a burst of light."

The words "burst" and "light" caused discomfort to Accolon's hung-over condition. He groaned but the dwarf continued.

"At the rising of the morrow's sun you will meet the champion of an evil pretender to a vast domain. You will overcome this so-called champion and with your victory win the crown as High King of Britain. And your mistress, Morgan, will sit at your right hand as your loving queen."

You might think that Accolon would have considered that Britain already had a high king of whom he was subject. And thus he might have raised a question or two. But then, I did not love Accolon for his quickness of wit or perspicacity. My love had more to do with his good looks and his cute cock. And the youth's stupidity never seemed a hindrance to my plans to seize power from the upstart who emerged from the womb of my mother but was not of the seed of my father.

Accolon's tongue was heavy and faltering. But he managed to say to the dwarf:

"Inform your mistress, who is my lady and my love, that I will meet and vanquish this dastard who fights for an unworthy lord. With those words convey my love and inform her that I shall not fail her in this heroic battle I undertake."

No, it's true. Those were his very words. Silly boy, he. Magnificent body. Weak intellect.

"Follow me, then," said the dwarf. And Accolon accompanied him up a path that led to an attractive villa of Roman design. It was a pleasant enough abode but clearly humble compared to Castle Drogo where Arthur was being accoutered. At the villa entrance the dwarf left my sweet boy with Ontzlak, who had come out to meet his guest. Ontzlak had his arm in a sling, was limping, and walked with a cane.

Those were all props, of course. They covered the cowardice of the son of a bitch.

(But, remember. He was *my* son of a bitch.)

"Welcome to Villa Ontzlak, noble youth," his host said. "The esteemed Lady Morgan informed me through a messenger that you would come forward to be my champion."

Accolon murmured some acknowledgment that such was indeed the case. But he was still feeling unwell and was a bit nonplused by the rapidity with which matters were shaping up.

"I have been seeking to meet my brother in hand-to-hand combat to settle a grievance I have with him concerning family property," Ontzlak told Accolon. "He has refused to accept my challenge until now. But he has sent word to me that he has secured a fighter to champion his cause. Alas, as ill-fortune would have it, while riding to the hounds yesterday I was thrown from my horse and broke my right arm and left leg. Just as I despaired at not being able to engage my brother's champion on the field of honor, the gracious Lady Morgan apparently got word of my predicament. And as a result, here you are to substitute your valor for my honor."

In his painful condition from overindulgence the night before, poor Accolon could only nod his head and wish his host would use less words and speak softer.

Ontzlak escorted the dear boy into the villa and had refreshing liquid refreshments brought. After imbibing the welcome drinks Accolon's head cleared and he was soon as lucid as it was possible for him to be.

Now that he felt better he could appreciate the armor, weapons, and charger that Ontzlak showed him.

"This sword," Ontzlak told my love, "Is none other than that of the high king. Your lady, the king's sister, borrowed Excalibur from Arthur in order that you might have the very best at your disposal when fighting my brother's champion."

Accolon was quite pleased to have such a sword to wield. He was full of the boyish confidence I had counted on to best my brother and set my love and me on the high throne in Camelot.

I told you I leave as little to chance as possible. Now that Accolon had the finest sword in Britain, I wanted Arthur to have an inferior blade for the upcoming fight. So I had a sword fashioned for him in the very image of Excalibur. Except this counterfeit weapon was made of base metal rather than of the finest blends of metals. And likewise, my workmen fashioned a counterfeit scabbard, spear, and dagger for him.

My sweet boy would be fighting with the very best and my brother with the very shabbiest. I was not interested in a fair fight.

When Arthur was suited up in Damas' armor for the combat, one of Nimue's acolytes approached him.

"Your Highness," she said on bended knee. "I come on behalf of your loving sister Morgan. She became aware of your plight here in the wilds of Dyfneint. Be of good cheer. She sends these arms which have hitherto made you invulnerable. May you get what you deserve."

Arthur thanked the maiden and mounted his charger with great assurance in his weapons and agility.

The two combatants rode onto the field to the excited shouts of a crowd of spectators. Trumpets blasted, flags waved, and bells rang. It was a spectacle indeed.

Neither combatant recognized the other. The helmets covered their facial features and the armor was such that neither had ever seen on the other. The only spectators who knew the true identity of the gladiators were Nimue and her attendant acolytes.

Accolon had youth on his side. Arthur had maturity and years of practice. Accolon had worthy weapons. Arthur had an assemblage of weapons that were inferior in every way. The two men were not aware that the combat had been rigged in favor of the younger. They were not intended to know.

The mounted champions entered the field and commenced the battle with jousting. At the first encounter both combatants were knocked off their mounts and clattered to the ground. They drew their swords and Arthur was immediately aware that both their weapons were identical in appearance. But while his blows inflicted no noticeable effect, his opponent's sword was often quite damaging. This stirred him to renewed effort, which threw Accolon into a state of disequilibrium. Then the younger man saw that his enemy was bleeding and that he himself was without a single cut.

Accolon perceived his clear advantage. Arthur, weakened by loss of blood, asked leave to pause to take a breath. But Accolon pursued him with increased vigor and struck Arthur a sturdy blow on the helmet. This enraged Arthur, who struck back with such force that his shoddy sword shattered.

"Yield, pitiful swordsman, or suffer death," Accolon shouted.

"No, fool," Arthur replied. "I fight to the death or not at all. Prepare for a fresh assault."

Accolon struck him again on the helmet and Arthur rebounded by pressing his opponent with his shield. The impact was so sudden and so violent that Accolon reeled backward three steps and stumbled. As he stumbled, Excalibur dropped from his hand. Arthur scooped it up. As Accolon staggered back onto his feet Arthur struck a blow which pierced his opponent clean through. Accolon dropped to the ground, blood spurting from both sides of his body.

Arthur bent over his dying opponent and snatched his helmet off.

"Accolon! My companion in arms. What in the world are you doing in a place like this?"

Arthur removed his own helmet, confronting the dying Accolon with the face of his liege.

"How came you by my sword, Accolon?" Arthur asked.

"My mistress, your sister Morgan, gave it to me that I might slay my opponent. Believe me, Lord, I knew not it was you I was pitted against."

The silly goose. There was no reason for him to reveal to Arthur that I had been involved in this sordid matter. But that's what I get for trusting an eighteen-year-old.

Arthur swore vengeance on me at that moment. We were now openly sworn enemies. It would be more difficult for me now to destroy him and achieve mastery of the kingdom. Oh, that fool child of an Accolon!

Arthur revealed his identity to Damas, Ontzlak, and the assembled crowd as Nimue and her lovely acolytes disappeared from the scene.

The prisoners were released. Ontzlak was restored as master of Castle Drogo and Damas was shorn of hair, beard and clothing and was turned naked into the forest to deal with the wilds as best he could.

My loverboy lay dead of his wounds on the field of honor. Oh, well. He was eighteen years old, I thought. And he was already growing too old for my tastes. I must have had a mad moment even considering him for my consort.

Leaving my old fool of a husband behind in Camelot, I flew off to the land of Cambo on the other side of the Wall. Avalon might have offered a safe haven from Arthur's wrath but the Lady of the Lake favored him, and things might have become awkward.

No, the only safe place was among the Fay where I was always accepted and where I would always be safe. I remained in Pixiland for a long time, plotting what mischief I could against Arthur. I could not forget the slights I had endured from him.

I advise you, Folks: Never irritate a priestess of the Goddess.

CHAPTER TWELVE

Pelleas and Ettarde

GWALCHMAI SPEAKS:

Arthur, Urien, and Accolon went hunting together. Urien came back first and was very uncommunicative about where they had been. Accolon never did return to Camelot. And when Arthur returned, he was in a foul mood and extremely angry at his sister Morgan. She had flown away while Arthur was off hunting.

I say she flew away. She always claimed she could fly, but I never knew anyone who ever saw her do so. I always wondered about that.

Arthur wanted to find his sister and punish her for some reason or other he never would explain. Myrddin sent out his spies to attempt to track her down. No luck at all. The longer he had to wait, the more peevish Arthur became. He just had to live with his seething anger and he was most unpleasant to be around during that time.

Camelot reflected the king's doleful mood. The place simply was not much fun any more. I told Arthur so to his face.

"If you don't like it here, get out!" Arthur shouted at me.

Shit! That from a companion I had known from the old days of Palomides' warband. So, get out I did. I would rather be out seeking adventure than walking around on tiptoe at Camelot with the king constantly pissing and moaning.

I rode north many a day without encountering any adventure worth relating. At last I came to the river the Romans called Tamensis. It was there that I found myself in deep dark woods called Ddinas. I spied a castle in the forest and rode up to its portcullis. Young ladies of ravishing beauty were busy at the gate, near which hung a shield. And each time one of the lovelies passed the shield, she spat on it. The sight was disconcerting, for in all my life I had never ever seen a female spit. And here, there was a veritable pool of spit oozing on the face of the shield. And each glob of spit had issued from lips so kissable that I was quite disturbed.

I approached one of the gorgeous hussies.

"What ho, Maid!" I hailed. "Wherefore do you profane yon shield with spit that would better be passed from mouth of maid to that of mounted warrior?"

"Sir," replied the little charmer, hawking up a massive globule to her cherry lips and lobbing it onto the slimy shield. "The shield belongs to a man named Pelleas. There is not a maid in Ddinas who can abide him. He is in love with Lady Ettarde and allows himself to be debased by her. Who can stand a fool in love who cannot accept 'no' for an answer?"

And with that she spit on the shield a globule so full of green phlegm that my stomach came close to churning.

"Behold," she said. "Here comes that foolish warrior, Pelleas, to approach his shield. As he does so, watch what happens. But do not interfere with the ensuing skirmish. You must see the comedy through to believe it."

The damsel sure had *that* right. For a rather scrawny, frail, armored warrior did indeed ride towards the portcullis and picked up his slimy shield. And when he began to ride off with the shield, ten opponents appeared on the scene, brandishing lance, spear, sword, and dagger.

Pelleas was also well armed and used sword and pike with skill, thwarting the blows of his opponents with his spit-bespotted shield.

Amazingly, the frail appearing Pelleas overcame all his adversaries. He was a brave, feisty gladiator and it pleased me to cheer him on. The lady with whom I was conversing yawned at the proceedings.

After vanquishing all ten opponents, but killing none, the young man seemed to wilt and allowed himself to be tied and got his sorry ass tossed back onto his horse. The ten losing combatants led him away thus trussed to his horse and the entire party disappeared into the forest.

I shook my head in disbelief and asked the sweet young thing who stood passively at my side the meaning of the spectacle we had just observed.

"That idiot of a Pelleas is hopelessly in love with Lady Ettarde," she declared. "He has vowed that if he cannot bed her, he will surely die. She will have none of him and scorns his very presence. Every day she sends forth her champions to challenge him, praying that he will be killed and she will be rid of the annoyance. Every day, Pelleas defeats his assailants, but allows them to bind him and haul him to her castle so he can set his lovelorn eyes upon her once again. Ettarde scoffs at the wretch and sends him on his way.

"Pelleas is a great fighter but a greater fool."

At this she spat in the direction of the shield which had been placed back in its former location. This time the spittle missed its mark. But overall, I had to admit to myself that her aim was better than many a warrior I knew. She could certainly win out over Cai in a spitting contest.

"Where does this Pelleas dwell?" I asked.

"There is a hermitage down yonder path some fifteen leagues away" the chick told me. "The hermit there gives refuge to the lovesick wretch. When Ettarde drives him away again today, he will hie thither."

I was quite interested in meeting this Pelleas. If I do say so myself, I am quite the lady's man. I'm taller than most. Blonder than most. Stronger than most. And better looking than any. My fucking average is unmatched by any male on the Island. As a lover, I am legendary.

Llenlleawc (Lancelot) may have scored more conquests than me. But that is because he practices his seductions not only on the fair sex, but on boys, girls, men, trees, and beasts of the field as well. My own interests are restricted to girls and women. I welcome the fair sex of any age from puberty on. But unlike Llenlleawc's lovers, mine has to be female and human.

Since I am so accomplished, I felt that I would be able to counsel this Pelleas on how to get into the drawers of the cold-hearted lady.

I reached the hermitage in the early afternoon before Pelleas' return. The hermit invited me to join him in a dish of thin gruel for which I thanked him and dropped a contribution in the alms box. If this gruel was what Pelleas was living on, no wonder he was so scrawny.

At long last the despondent looking Pelleas appeared in the clearing in front of the hermitage. The hermit offered him a bowl of the gruel which the young man refused with a doleful shake of his head.

I greeted him and informed him of the contest I had seen him in earlier in the day. He told me the story of his one-sided love affair and the despair he was feeling. The story was the same as the one the chick had told me. No embellishments. Just the woeful tale I already knew.

"But why do you persist if the answer is always the same?" I asked

"I hope that my constancy will win her heart," the doleful lover replied.

"Well," I said. "If you'll excuse my saying so, it looks to me as though your approach isn't going anywhere. I've never heard of a lady getting fucked through a stratagem of a would-be lover getting himself trussed up and delivered like a sack of shit."

"What would you suggest?" the sad-assed youth asked despondently.

"As a man of considerable and varied experience in scoring amorous successes with the fair sex, I'm sure I can come up with something," I advised him.

"And you are…who?" he asked.

"Gwalchmai, a member of the warband of Camelot and liegeman to

Arthur the Pen-Dragwn. Scores of willing ladies are trophies of my prowess with my prick."

"I will accept your succor, Gwalchmai Varchog. I am Pelleas, Lord of Star Castle in the Fair Isles. I have never screwed a woman before. You see before you a male virgin"

My heart overflowed with pity for the pathetic asshole.

"Tell me," Pelleas continued. "What must I do to win the heart of my beloved Ettarde? I've just got to screw her or go nuts."

I had a splendid idea which I related to him.

"What we have to do, Pelleas, is exchange armor. I will ride up to Lady Ettarde's castle and tell her I have killed you and have donned your armor. Then, since no woman can resist me, I will win her heart. At that point, you come riding into her castle in my armor as though resurrected from the dead. She will then undoubtedly shower her love on you, and I will ride off into the forest leaving her to be roundly fucked by you."

Lacking experience in affairs of the heart, Pelleas readily agreed to my plan. The first impediment involved my fitting into his armor. Fortunately, the good hermit had been an armorer before becoming a holy man and for a hefty contribution agreed to adjust Pelleas' armor to my gorgeous physique and mine to fit his scrawny-ass frame.

Accoutered in my new guise I rode boldly into Ettarde's castle.

As I entered the central courtyard of the castle, Lady Ettarde looked down from her balcony. It was clear that she was not deceived by my disguise.

"Wait right there, Varchog," the damsel cooed. "I descend to extend the hospitality of my castle to your astounding presence."

I dismounted as she entered the courtyard.

"Remove your helmet and hauberk that I might see your face and chest," she ordered imperiously.

I, of course, complied.

When she caught sight of my manly beauty, she sighed. I well recognized the sigh. I have this effect on the ladies you know.

She invited me into the inner precincts of the castle and ordered a feast to be placed before me.

"How came you by the armor of that asshole Pelleas?" she asked sweetly.

"I met him in combat and dispatched his scrawny ass to the hereafter," I replied.

She seemed delighted at the news.

"And how did you ever fit that brawny, magnificent physique into his mini-armor?"

"A master armorer refit it to my dimensions," I replied. "It does fit me well, doesn't it?"

"Tell me then, good varchog. Who might you be?"

"I might be Pelleas, but I'm not," I replied with my ready wit.

She was wildly amused by my skill at repartee.

I then went on to say: "I am Gwalchmai, one of the most valiant and worthy varchogs of the high king of Britain, Arthur Pen-Dragwn."

She was duly impressed, as I knew she would be.

I sipped from a cup that was filled with a wine I recognized as coming from Gawl. A noble vintage it was.

I then passed the cup to her, that she might sip from my vessel. Our lips met. Her eyes fluttered, and I never had the chance to finish the feast for she dragged me by the hand to her chambers where we fucked up a storm in her bed as soon as we were able to remove each other's clothes.

The lady was very skilled in the arts of love. And, as the world can attest, I was magnificent.

We spent the entire rest of the evening and all the ensuing night fucking away like hares.

I felt very virtuous about all this since I was only doing it all to help poor Pelleas.

It was time to build Pelleas up in Ettarde's regard. So I asked her:

"Why is it that you have rejected Pelleas so forcefully?"

"In the first place," she replied, "it's his breath. When he opens his mouth, I all but gag."

"That is true," I had to admit. "Whereas my own breath has often been likened to the sweet scent of garlands of mayflowers. But, surely that is not enough to reject the creature so heartlessly."

"In addition," she continued. "His body stinks like a pile of shit. He walks into a room and I have to open the windows."

"I have noticed the same about my good friend and companion. I admit it is a pity," I acquiesced. "Whereas my own body exudes an exciting musk odor that causes the female heart to palpitate. But, still, I'm sure he must have his redeeming qualities."

"Have you taken a good look at his fucking face?" she asked. "It's covered with pimples, pustules, and rashes. There is scarcely a spot thereon that does not make him appear to be in the throes of some dreadful disease."

"It's too bad. But you sure got that right," I hated to have to admit. "Whereas my skin is smooth and caressable. Every damsel has told me so."

She summed up her case.

"Altogether, the man is completely loathsome. I cannot bear to be within sight or smell of him. I am afraid he is a completely lost cause."

I had to agree with her. I decided to put off trying to help my good friend Pelleas until another day or time.

Have I told you that all this happened in the merry, merry month of May? The weather being most enticing, Ettarde had three pavilions set up on the grounds of her domain. One was for three of her warriors to guard the safety of the outside area. One was for four of her maids, who were available to serve us fine wines, viands, and eggs. And the third pavilion was for her and me, that we might fuck, suck and feel each other up in the open air of Britain's finest season.

For three days and three nights, we were encompassed by naught but love. We made love in every way imaginable, taking time out only to refresh ourselves with many an egg and with sips of fine wine. I fear that we scarcely had time for the viands.

On the third night, as dawn was approaching, who should appear in our tent but Pelleas himself. And what is more, he was accompanied by a nymph. On closer scrutiny I saw that it was Nimue who had led him to our love nest. It happened that Nimue had encountered Pelleas back near the hermitage, and he had told her his tear-stained story.

She suggested to him that they seek us out to see how his suit was being forwarded by me.

They scarcely needed Nimue's skills as a sorceress to find us. Ettarde had filled the surrounding countryside with ecstatic moans and groans that could be followed by a deaf brachet.

I say the two appeared at our tent. But, engaged as we were in our fucking, they must have stood there observing us in amazement for well over an hour. At last, Pelleas coughed discreetly and Nimue giggled.

Pelleas spoke first.

"So, false varchog. This is how you forward my cause with the one who is the love of my life. Beware, dastard. I shall return to the hermitage and bring back my sword to cut your false throat."

"No," Nimue interrupted. "Do not do this thing you swear, Pelleas. I can cast a spell on these two that will be better punishment than anything you could possibly devise."

I was sore amazed. I knew Nimue had a wickedly mischievous streak and I would have preferred that Pelleas come at me with a sword than suffer from one of Nimue's spells. But, compromised as I was, I had no voice in the matter.

Nimue gathered up herbs and plants from the area close by as Ettarde and I clothed ourselves. We could hardly appear dignified with her tits and my dong hanging out in the breeze. The young sorceress set up a small bonfire at the pavilion entrance, enhancing the flame with the magic incense of the plants she had gathered.

She first invoked a spell on Ettarde.

"Lady Ettarde. Henceforth you will have but one love in your life. And that love will be for Pelleas. And the curse that goes with this spell is that your love will be unrequited by him as his has been by you."

Ettarde looked at Pelleas and the lovelight shone from her eyes. The spell had taken.

"Pelleas," Nimue intoned. "Henceforth you shall have but one love in your life. And that love will be for Gwalchmai Varchog."

Pelleas looked at me and the lovelight shone bright in his eyes. Never had a male other than Llenlleawc looked at me thus. But Llenlleawc's passions were always short lived. I feared such would not be the case with Pelleas.

"And Gwalchmai," she continued. "You have been unfaithful to a friend. For this, you will be amorously pursued by Pelleas for as long as he lives."

Nimue turned heel and disappeared into the forest.

Ettarde hurled herself at Pelleas. Pelleas repulsed her and tried to grab my ass.

I ran out the door of the pavilion with Pelleas on my heels and Ettarde on his.

I headed for the stables where my trusty horse Kincaled fortunately was saddled and ready to go.

Off I rode into the woods with Pelleas crying after me, "Come back. Come back my love" while Ettarde was attempting to embrace him fervently.

I didn't like having to kill that pest Pelleas.

But I just don't swing that way.

CHAPTER THIRTEEN

War and Peace

BEDWYR SPEAKS:

Soon after we won the war against Lot and the Pixies at Arderydd Ford and had cremated Lot in Caerlleon we returned to the castle at Camelot. The place had become Arthur's main seat of power. In those first months after Arderydd Ford an uneasy peace hung over Britain. The English settlements on our eastern shore were restless. We knew the English meant to take over Britain if they could. As high king, one of Arthur's chief trusts was keeping the English on their reservations.

Gwledigs Ban and Bors from the Continent remained with us after the Pixie War to have their troops here ready for the real wars we knew we would eventually wage against those English dogs on our eastern shores. Gwledig Ban brought his sons Llenlleawc (Lancelot in English) and Accolon to Britain. But Accolon had somehow mysteriously disappeared from sight.

The battle with Lot's forces was in Feabhra, 518. Two months later, in An t-Aibrean, Walda Cerdic led his English troops out of the reservation and headed inland up the valley of the River Glein.

Cerdic was very likely counting on the tribes beyond the Wall joining him in anger against us for our victory over Lot. But the Pixies had concerns of their own. They had no interest at the time in joining with the English. It is doubtful they trusted the English any more than we did. As they marched up the Glein Valley the English laid waste every British village and settlement along the way. The devastation was brutal and enormous.

Arthur immediately marshaled our troops, accompanied by those of Ban and Bors, and we set out for the North. By the time we encountered the enemy they had reached Caer Pedryvan.

They had misjudged in two ways. They assumed the Pixies would join them and they underestimated the size of our forces. We inflicted great damage, killing nearly a third of their warriors before they retreated back to their reservation in the East.

Within a month Cerdic marched the remnant of his troops down past Deira and joined forces with Osric, the walda of that region. With their joint forces the two waldas marched west with the intention of devastating Britain. Our forces met them at Uffern on the river Dubga. Our vanguard threw the English into a panic. When the rest of us arrived, the English were in total disarray and had retreated back to their reservation.

We had to contend with Cerdic twice more before he gave up his incursions into Britain. He amassed a larger force than before and made a wild attempt to break into our territory at River Bassus. It was our cavalry that completely crushed his forces. The English did not really have any cavalry to speak of. And none of their horses had footstraps. We had many excellent horsemen trained in Roman cavalry tactics. Arthur's foster-father Ector had served with distinction in the Roman cavalry and trained Arthur's forces when his foster son became king. The tactics Arthur and Ector devised worked particularly well at fords. That is why Arthur chose fords for so many of his military engagements. At the Battle of River Bassus it was the enemy dead that, as usual, fed the ravens.

These battles consistently won against the English showed the British that their eighteen year old king was an able general capable of taming the wild English host howling at our gates. The few doubts about the "boy general" were dispelled. Britain was firmly behind its king.

Cerdic cringed back in the English settlements licking his wounds. We did not encounter him again for more than a year and a half.

It was Walda Oesc who pestered us next. He had led his English troops up past the Wall. Myrddin and Arthur determined that it was bad business to have the English up in Pixiland. They had to be driven back to their settlements.

Oesc had led his troops way up north past the River Clyde to Loch Lomond. He clearly hoped to assemble Vikings, Irish, Pixies, and any other possible enemies of Britain while far enough from Arthur to be safe. That was a serious mistake on his part. Our forces marched up past the Wall, across Pixiland, and met Oesc's forces at Cat Coit Celidon. Oesc hadn't counted on Myrddin's ubiquitous spies and thought he could hide away and quietly assemble a force capable of meeting the army which, he knew now, was not composed of Arthur's troops alone but of those of Bors and Ban as well.

I had never been to those far reaches of our Island before and was astounded at the beauty of the Loch Lomond region. But I was not blinded by it enough to restrain my sword arm from bloodying the glens and braes with English blood. We engaged the enemy and drove them to retreat to the Firth of Clyde. The English had brought a number of their keels there and sailed across the waters to the Green Island. Apparently Oesc had managed to form some kind of alliance with the Irish king Fergus mac Finn. The English keels were joined by Irish curraughs and a hearty wind brought the combined English and Irish troops down to Southwest Britain before our troops were able to get there. Myrddin's spies had no inkling of the maneuver. So when we arrived at Gwynedd it was an unhappy surprise to learn that the enemy had arrived at Guinnion, had sacked it, murdered all the men, raped the women, and enslaved the children.

Arthur addressed the troops:

"Men of British blood, I exhort you. The English dogs, assisted by the Irish swine, have landed on our sacred shores and desecrated our land. Our women shriek out for us to avenge the rape of their bodies, the murder of their men, and the enslavement of their children. You have fought well, men. But until now we have fought simply to protect the land our gods have entrusted to us. Now we will fight with vengeance in our hearts. Let us go forth with hatred behind every sword thrust and with contempt behind every arrow. Forward to battle, my brothers."

I stood before the host and shouted, "Alator, Arthur, and Britain."

A thousand voices echoed my cry. Vengeance was to be ours.

We were in country where every hill, dale, stream and river was known to us. Familiarity with the land was on our side. But our intense anger was an even more decisive factor in the victory we enjoyed when we marched into Guinnion. Oesc's forces met us at the Dee, and with wild ferocity we decimated the English and the few Irish we encountered.

Oesc retreated to Caerlleon, one hundred Roman miles to the south, and Arthur's military capital. We were right on his tail the whole way. We managed to collect over one hundred heads of English stragglers as we marched forward. We carried those heads with us to taunt the invaders when we finally caught up with their cowardly retreat.

At Caerlleon, our cavalry, which was first to arrive, provided English flesh as feast for the ravens before our men on foot were able to join the killing spree. Oesc and the remnant of his forces managed to escape on keels that were waiting for them in the harbor. We were not able to catch up with the rag-tag forces that remained with him. We were to see him and that devil from Annwfn, Cerdic, again within six months.

In the year 519, Cerdic and Oesc joined forces leading their troops up the valley of the River Tribuit, some forty Roman miles from the Wall. I'll give the English this. They were persistent. Like a bad itch.

Again we marched and rode north for days to arrive at the Tribuit. We met the English forces some thirty miles south of the waterfalls, engaged them in battle, and drove them north to Mount Agned.

We had an ally in the area, Gogyrvan Gawr, who joined forces with us. His troops were defending their homeland and fought the enemy as fiercely as we did. The English were roundly defeated. But we did not capture their leaders, Cerdic or Oesc. As before, they managed to save their own hides while hundreds of their solders were left behind to manure the fields or serve as slaves.

Two weeks after Lughnasadh we finally put an end to the vile incursions of the English dogs. The English made one last enormous attempt to convert our Britain into an England. Since Cerdic and Oesc had fared so poorly in their battles with Arthur, Bors, and Ban, the foe needed a new leader to carry the war against us. They chose Walda Aelle who was reputed to be a great strategist and who had a thousand warriors of his own under his command. Cerdic's and Oesc's troops were reportedly rather demoralized from their defeats at our hands. But Aelle's English infantry was said to be anxious to shed our blood.

By now Arthur was twenty-one years old and the most popular person in all Britain. He led troops that were undefeated and devotedly loyal. Aelle was reputedly over forty years old. He and Oesc were the lead waldas when Arthur's father was slain at the Battle of Camlann on Ambrys Plain in 515. If we could defeat the combined forces of Aelle, Cerdic, and Oesc, Myrddin and Arthur felt that our troubles with the English would be at an end.

The English massed their troops in Aelle's bailiwick of Cawnyt. We allowed them to march across the width of the Island while small warbands of Britons sniped at their heels. The units we set on them were similar to the warband that Arthur, Gwalchmai, and I were members of back when Uthyr was king. The lightning attacks by small mounted groups were devastating to the English. Aelle's troops were more and more demoralized as they crossed the land and found themselves pecked at by our bands.

By the time they arrived at Caer Badon our troops were waiting for them. Arthur's forces were confident and fighting for the glory of their homeland. Aelle's troops were weary, harassed, and far from their home base. We were ready.

On that day, a glorious day for Britain, Arthur's cavalry slew nine hundred sixty English. Caer Badon was scarlet with the blood of the accursed dogs. Aelle, Cerdic, and Oesc were captured and Myrddin ordained that they be emasculated in the sight of those English who still lived after the slaughter. Not one English soldier escaped back to the settlements on the eastern shores. Every soldier who had followed the three waldas was either slain or made a prisoner/slave to serve British masters for the remainder of his days.

This was the final victory of the fatherland, of Britain. Following that great slaughter the English remained peacefully on their reservations virtually without leaders. And the Arthurian Peace reigned on our Island for twenty-one years.

At long last, we were a land at peace.

In the midst of the wars against the English, when we were fighting Cerdic and Oesc at Mount Agned, Arthur's headquarters were at Castle

Agned. The Gwledig of Agned had never broken fealty to Arthur from the very beginning. His name was Gogyrvan Gawr. When his bailiwick was besieged by the English he welcomed the aid Arthur brought to his lands.

Gogyrvan Gawr had a daughter named Gwenhwyvar (Guinevere). I have known a number of very beautiful women in my time. But I must say that Gwenhwyvar was the fairest of them all. She was certainly the loveliest damsel in all Britain. During our stay at Agned it was not Arthur who seduced Gwenhwyvar but she who seduced him. Not that it was difficult to lure Arthur to bed, ever. But the lady, in this case, was decidedly the aggressor. Arthur commented on this to us several times. Gogyrvan Gawr's daughter made a definite impression on our king.

When the so-called Pax Arthuriana settled on our land and all our battles were behind us, Myrddin suggested that Arthur take a wife. The Pen-Dragwn lineage needed to be established and required an heir. Arthur was not adverse to the idea and he decided that Gwenhwyvar would be just right for him. Myrddin liked the idea because it would seal Arthur's right to suzerainty in the North. But he had one reservation that he shared with Arthur.

"Arthur. I am delighted with the political aspects of your choice of a queen. But I must warn you that I foresee that Gwenhwyvar will love not only you but other men as well. She is a woman who cannot be satisfied with the attentions of one man alone."

Arthur was unfazed.

"Right you are, Myrddin. Exactly what I want. If my queen is fucking other men outside the matrimonial structure she won't be nagging at me for fucking other women. I could never be true to one woman. You know that. So that's simply one more reason why Gwenhwyvar is the very woman I must wed."

It was determined that the wedding would be held at Camelot and would be the most sumptuous feast the kingdom had ever witnessed. Camelot was the glory of Britain. From all over the Island the people flocked to Camelot for the event. Arthur's nephews Agravain and Gaheris came all the way from Skara Brae for the festivities. The king was a handsome hero to his people. And the queen was absolutely radiantly beautiful. The kingdom took the young couple to its heart.

And with the royal wedding, a period of peace, prosperity, tranquility, and national pride enveloped Britain as never before. It was the best of times our people had ever known.

Arthur was the greatest general Britain ever had or ever will have. I believe he stopped the incursions of the English on our lands forever. As a consequence, I feel in my heart that there will always be a Britain. There will never be an England.

CHAPTER FOURTEEN

The Prince of Love

LLENLLEAWC SPEAKS:

Everyone wants to hear the wonderful stories of my adventures.

That must be because I am the Prince of Love and the most handsome varchog in the Kingdom of Britain. I am known to be the greatest lover in the land. Queen Gwenhwyvar herself will tell you, I am sure, that my prowess on the couch exceeds that of any of her lovers, including my very good friend and boon companion, her husband the king. And, as the world knows, I am the most valiant warrior ever to grace a battlefield.

Where should I begin? Every aspect of my life has been so splendid it is difficult to choose which tale to relate first.

All right. I will begin with our wars against the English. I came to this big Island from the Continent with my father, Ban of Bawn. He knew we would be fighting the accursed English to save Arthur's kingdom for him. Papa knew that with my military skills at his disposal we would be invincible.

Oh, yes. My brother Accolon tagged along, too.

During the Agned campaign the lovely Gwenhwyvar fell under the sway of my charms and bedded me as often as we could find the time between battles (and between the sheets).

When the wars were over and Papa and Uncle Bors went back home to confront the Franks and Burgunds I remained in Britain. Arthur married Gwenhwyvar. She was now living at Camelot. And it would have broken her heart if I had left the country with my relatives.

After a few months of peace I grew restless. I had taken every nubile creature in Camelot to my bed by then. And I had serviced the queen with such regularity that I was growing jaded with the experience. I began to long for new experiences.

So, in the month of March, when the blood begins to quicken, the prick keeps pointing upward, and adventure calls, I took my leave of Camelot and rode west towards Killiwic.

I was riding aimlessly, seeking romance, challenges, swordfights, or whatever might amuse me along the way. Nothing noteworthy occurred for the first few days. On the fourth day, as I was riding through a heavily wooded section, dusk was approaching. I hadn't passed any inns, hermitages, or castles for hours. I had nowhere to spend the night and needed shelter.

Then, in a clearing, what ho! I spied a bright red silk pavilion. I approached it, dismounted, and poked around a bit. As nearly as I could tell it was deserted. It was very comfortably appointed and quite welcoming. What a piece of luck, I thought. I would make use of it for the night and leave a bezant or two behind when I parted in thanks for the shelter. What I did not know at the time was that the owner of the pavilion had set it up as a trysting place where he planned to meet his paramour.

I had provisions in my saddlebags and prepared a simple repast for myself before repairing to the pavilion. After a simple meal, I divested myself of armor and other clothing and slipped naked under the linen sheets that awaited me inside the tented refuge. I was fast asleep in moments.

While I was asleep the owner of the pavilion arrived. He peeked inside the pavilion, and seeing me there, assumed I was his lady love awaiting him. He quickly shed all his clothing and climbed under the sheets with me. He took me in his arms and began caressing me. I awoke with a start wondering what was going on. But I certainly had no thought of complaining.

Still thinking I was his paramour, he made wild, passionate love to me.

His well-oiled prick slipped up my ass and his hand slipped around to my front and gave my dong a slow, smooth jacking off. He was a great lover and I was enjoying every minute of our intimacy. The man had wonderful technique and muttered pleasing, romantic nothings in my ear.

When he had finished his lovemaking we reversed directions and I repaid him in kind. Again, he made no objection to my actions. Instead, he made cooing sounds of enjoyment. We both apparently were having a wonderful time. Just as I was finishing him off, who should pop into the pavilion but his lady love.

She feigned shock. But before long she had divested herself of her clothing and was under the sheets with us engaged in a threesome that I remember with relish to this day.

All three of us had worthy stamina. I got very little sleep that night. I fucked and got fucked. I sucked and got sucked. I felt and got felt. I never regretted that loss of sleep one whit. It was a night to remember.

My host had brought breakfast provisions with him. So next morning, when we emerged from the pavilion, hungry from our night's exertions, he fetched the food he had brought with him. As we breakfasted we introduced ourselves.

"Llenlleawc, a varchog from King Arthur's court. I am delighted to have made your acquaintance," I announced.

I was eating a piece of honey-bread and wiped the honey away from my lips.

The young lady curtsied and the gentleman introduced himself as Belleus, a squire of the demesne. He then introduced our companion from the previous evening, Tegan. By morning light we all three presented a lovely picture. All of us were striking looking Britons who had enjoyed good sport together. He, in particular, was a fine broth of a man. Of the two of them, he was the more exciting. But I had the good manners not to point that out.

I knew at once that these two would make a fine addition to the Camelot crowd. So I invited them to come to Camelot on the feast of Alban Eilir. I assured Belleus that I would see to it that the king dub him a varchog and make him a member of the Table Round. The couple agreed that they would be there.

After breakfast I left the couple and headed on west in search of new adventure. By noon I was hungry and thirsty, and consequently sought refreshment. On the outskirts of a settlement I came upon a well-kept house. I approached, dismounted, and knocked on the door.

A goodwife answered. And after looking me over from head to toe she invited me in. I asked if I might have a bit of victuals, drink, and repose.

"Indeed you may," replied the goodwife. "I have been hoping someone like you might drop by. But you exceed my expectations."

Her larder was well provided. And before long I had before me a fine roast capon, a loaf of fresh-baked bread, and a horn of mead. When I had eaten and drunk to satiety I thanked the lady for taking care of my needs and asked her if she had any needs of her own that I might take care of.

"I am just a poor widow-woman," she answered. "My husband was a simple soldier in good King Arthur's forces and he was killed by the English dogs at the Battle of Mount Badon. Since then, I have been very lonely."

I answered politely and valiantly as befits a varchog of his majesty.

"Be lonely no more, widow-woman," I assured her. "I have known many a widow before and anticipate your needs. Let us repair to your upper chambers and see if we cannot find a way to assuage your loneliness."

For the rest of the afternoon we took care of each other's longings. She was in sore need of a good fucking.

With my exertions of the previous evening it was all I could do to continue at it until dinnertime. But I did persist. The goodwife was very happy.

After an extended fuck-fest we returned to the first floor for some mutton stew and ale. I became very sleepy and told her I needed to go upstairs and get some rest. She accompanied me up there, undressed me, and laid me down on the bed.

She played with my dick to her heart's content. But I was incapable of relieving any more of her loneliness at the time and dropped off into deep slumber.

I do not know how long I had been asleep when I heard a frantic knocking on the downstairs door of the cottage. Night had fallen and it was difficult to make out who was pounding on the door directly below my window. I could see a horse tethered nearby so knew it had to be a horseman. I could also make out that the horseman was a real fat-ass. Hmm! Fat-assed horseman. I strained my eyes a bit into the murky distance and perceived that three men were approaching. It was obvious that the three had been pursuing the fat-ass with malicious intent and would soon catch up with him if no aid was immediately forthcoming.

Now the man at the door was beating at it with both fists and head. The urgency of his situation was obvious. A cloud that had been hiding the moon slipped past and the moonlight revealed who the horseman was. It was the king's foster brother, the seneschal of Camelot, Cai ap Ector.

I truly detest that man. But he is the king's brother. And if he were harmed while I was in the area I would never be forgiven. So I tore the sheets from the bed, rent them into strips, and tied them together. Then I grabbed my sword and stark naked slid down the rope I had made of the sheets and called to Cai.

"Psst! Cai!! Step over this way into the shadows. I am here to rescue you."

I don't believe he recognized me. It became rather dark as a new cloud covered the moon. And Cai had never before seen me stark naked.

The ruffians who had been chasing him hove into view. They were expecting Cai's feeble defense. Instead, they met with a naked madman wielding a sizzling sword. I ran the leader through the belly and the other two spun their horses around and hightailed it back down the path in the opposite direction from the village.

Cai was mightily relieved but was shaking like a dog that has suddenly had water thrown on him. The goodwife had heard Cai's knocking and the following the tumult as I dispatched the one pursuer and sent the others on their way. She opened the door and was astonished to see me standing there, sword in hand and bare-assed as when she had left me in the upstairs bedroom. Then she saw Cai and invited him in.

She welcomed Cai very politely and asked him if he wanted anything to eat.

"No, thank you, Goodwife," he said. "I have had a rather harrowing evening and need nothing so much as a bit of rest. I am very, very tired."

"Well, then," she answered. "Why don't you just go upstairs to the bedroom and you can sleep with the varchog up there. Do you happen to know him?"

"Yes, I do. We are companions of the Table Round in Camelot," Cai replied. "We help each other out whenever we can, you know. But isn't there somewhere else I can sleep? I wouldn't want to inconvenience my boon companion."

"I'm afraid not," the goodwife told him. "And I know the varchog will not mind sharing the bed with you, Sir. Now you just run along upstairs and get some well-deserved rest."

She retired to another room to fetch additional blankets. While she was out of hearing Cai addressed me.

"Look, Llenlleawc," he said. "Don't think I don't appreciate what you just did for me. Quite sporting and all. But appreciative as I am, I'm not inclined to sleep with you. Particularly garbed, or should I say ungarbed as you are. I'll just stretch out on the couch here in the front room and settle in for the night. Would you care terribly?"

I do not know why Cai was shy about sleeping in the same bed with me. But since he's not my type I shrugged my shoulders. The goodwife stepped back into the front room with some covers in hand. She handed the covers to Cai and was content for him to sleep on the downstairs couch. Then she and I locked arms and went upstairs together to put some finishing touches on the encounter we had enjoyed previous to my going to sleep.

It seems my pecker had by then arisen to the occasion.

The next morning I stole downstairs and fit myself into Cai's armor. He was snoring away and was totally unaware of my presence. I bid goodbye to the goodwife and in Cai's armor I hopped on my trusty steed and set out towards Camelot

I had left my own armor behind for Cai. I knew that if he wore it back to Camelot people would see my armor on him, think it was I, and no one would dare accost him. It was important for me to keep on Arthur's good side so I had to protect that braggart Cai.

I rode through a beautiful countryside of lush meadows, gurgling springs, and lazily flowing rivers. It was an uneventful ride until I came upon a group of Arthur's varchogs taking their ease beside one of the many springs that are in that country. Who would the varchogs be but Gwalchmai, Gaheris, and Sagremor. I rode by pretending to ignore them.

"Oh, ho," said that dumb-ass Gwalchmai. "Look who's riding by with his nose in the air. It is the cowardly seneschal of Camelot, Cai the Ungainly. Let's have some sport with him."

It was sport they wanted? I would show them some sport. But hardly what they expected.

It was Sagremor who left the rat pack first. He trotted up behind me intending to slap the rump of my horse with his sword. I spun my charger around, knocked the sword out of his fucking hand, and then knocked him off his horse. He looked up at me with a very surprised expression on his ugly Byzantine face.

I rode on unconcernedly as though the attack on me was absolutely unimportant.

Gaheris was the next one to try his luck with me. He was ordinarily a reasonable sort of bloke but was in the bad company of his brother and Sagremor. I looked over my shoulder to see him charging at me with his lance, intending to knock me off my horse. Again, I spun my mount around and with a quick upward flick of my own lance I unseated him.

He immediately found himself sprawled on the ground and laughing at his ridiculous position. I had to chuckle myself.

Gwalchmai saw which way things were tending and simply let me pass on without attempting to play any tricks on me. He must have suspected that I was not Cai. Though he probably did not guess who was in the suit of armor.

My wanderings about the countryside continued with many an adventure which I will be happy to relate to you at some more convenient time. But for now I want to tell you about my return to Camelot for the festivities of Alban Eilir, the date when day and night are of equal length and Arthur's court welcomes new varchogs into the fellowship of the Table Round.

Cai of course was there as he had to be as seneschal and a varchog of the Table Round. He had heard of how Gwalchmai, Gaheris, and Sagremor had been outmatched in the West Country. He, braggart that he is, claimed it was he himself who had bested them. Since none of the three was absolutely sure that such was not the case, they did not contest his bragging. For my part I let the matter ride. I preferred for the three errant varchogs to think that perhaps they were inferior combatants to that asshole Cai.

At noon on Alban Eilir my companions of the red silk pavilion arrived at Camelot as I had requested. I recommended to Arthur that Belleus be dubbed a varchog, citing extraordinary feats for him that had never happened. Yet I knew him to be extraordinary in the feats I have told you about.

After Belleus had been accepted as a member of the Table Round, his paramour Tegan took me aside and whispered that she would like to show her appreciation for what I had one for her lover. She suggested that I come to their sleeping quarters that night after the feast.

The feast, I must say, was one of the best. Arthur was a wonderful host. The food was superb and the liquors were even better. When I saw that Belleus and Tegan had gone to their quarters I excused myself from the table.

I found Tegan waiting for me outside the door of their room.

"Psst! Llenlleawc. I have stepped outside, giving Belleus an excuse. There is a bed chamber next door which is empty. What Belleus doesn't know won't hurt him."

"Tegan," I said. "I am deeply touched. Please go into that bed chamber and close the door. I am going into the room you just left and make love to the person you left behind."

Heartbroken, she did as I asked.

She was nothing exceptional in bed. But Belleus...

CHAPTER FIFTEEN

Family Reunion

MORGAN SPEAKS:

After that little episode with Accolon I decided that I would never again attempt to create a king. That particular business had turned out a bit sordid. And though I was still quite peeved at Arthur for his disinterest in me, for preferring Myrddin's advice to mine, and for fucking my sister rather than me, I decided we were probably all better off with him alive than dead. Arthur was doing a splendid job of keeping the English in their place. And the Irish, Vikings, and Franks seemed to be intimidated enough by him to leave our shores relatively unmolested.

So I decided it would be best to allow Arthur to live. But I would continue to create little annoyances for him. I do not easily shed my pique. So my plan was simply to make life miserable for him whenever I could. Yet without leading to anything fatal.

However I miscalculated. One of my little pestering pranks turned out badly for Arthur and consequently for our beloved Britain.

I worked out what I then thought to be a delicious plan to aggravate Arthur. Something that would rub his nose in that squalid little interlude he had with our sister.

Years ago, Morgawse returned from Caerlleon to Skara Brae with an interesting wee royal gift planted within her womb. Arthur had filled it to overflowing with his seed and her fertile womb had been very receptive to it.

That vile wizard Myrddin's spies sniffed out the truth of that situation. Myrddin passed the word on to Arthur.

"Arthur. I have disturbing news for you," Myrddin said.

"Really, Myrddin. Is it something you can take care of and not bother me with?"

"I am afraid that you will probably have to take action on it yourself, Arthur."

"Well, out with it old man," Arthur replied gruffly. "Don't be tedious with me."

"You're going to be a father," Myrddin informed him.

"You mean I've sprung another bastard? Gods, man. I have bastards all over Britain and even a few outside my realm if I'm not mistaken. See that the bitch receives bezants enough to take care of the little bastard and keep her out of my way. I can't stand these women whining about their burdens. Is that all you have in the way of disturbing news?"

"It is not quite as easy as that, Arthur," Myrddin insisted. "This particular bastard carries more import for your rule than the other ones. You see, you are not only the child's father but its uncle as well."

Arthur was not slow of wit. He understood at once.

"Great Lleu," he exclaimed. "You mean I knocked Morgawse up?"

"You have fathomed the situation, Your Highness. Your sister carries your child. If the creature turns out to be male he will be in a position to lay claim to the throne as your heir. Since the child will be born of incest, controversy concerning his lineage could cause complications, including civil war. I'm afraid we have a problem on our hands."

Arthur issued his famous edict. Myrddin calculated the expected date for the inconvenient birth and Arthur declared that all children born within two weeks of Beltane were to be put to death. The midwives of Britain could be relied on to carry out the wishes of the high king. The matter appeared to be settled.

But Myrddin's spies were no more alert than my own. I probably knew about Morgawse's pregnancy before the wily wizard did. The eyes of the Pixies are ubiquitous. And my band of Fay-folk are the most inquisitive of all Pixies. I knew not only that Morgawse was pregnant with our brother's child. I knew exactly how Arthur would deal with the matter once Myrddin told him. And I was absolutely aware of how Morgawse's husband Lot would respond. Between Arthur's political decision and Lot's personal annoyance, the child, male or female, was destined to be placed in a wicker basket and sent to sea, as Gwalchmai had been. And I knew what to do about that.

When the child was born my Pixie spies knew it as soon as Lot did. When Lot took the boy to the frigid waters of the North Sea and set him adrift, that could have been the end of the story.

But I saw to it that my Pixie folk would guide that tiny wicker boat and keep it afloat. And that it would wash ashore at Duncasby Cliffs, a Viking settlement on our shores that was independent of any British gwledig. The Norse people dwelling there were not warriors but simple fishing folk who lived in peace with the surrounding Pixie communities. It was the perfect place for the little lad named Medrawd to grow up.

I made it a point to become acquainted with the foster parents of my little nephew. I told them that I was the child's mother, and that the boy was the illegitimate son of a gwledig who was very violent and meant to do his bastard son harm. There was an element of truth in the story and it aroused the compassion of the simple Norse folk who were raising him.

When Medrawd was of an age when he could understand, I visited him often and informed him of the true nature of his begetting. I laid the full blame of his attempted murder on the high king, Arthur, his father. I wanted the lad to learn to hate Arthur. That was part of the plan.

When Medrawd was thirteen I went to Duncasby to take the boy away to encounter his destiny. I explained to the foster parents that the gwledig who was his father had relented and would welcome his son back. I paid them well for the care they had taken of him and they were content that their foster son was heading for a life filled with fine opportunities.

An on that note, I took Medrawd to Camelot.

Arthur did not trust me. And with good reason. So I had to approach Camelot in disguise. I assumed the role of an Irish princess who had escaped from the Green Isle. My story was that my husband, the King of Ballynahinch, had been overthrown and killed by an uncle who usurped the throne. I had escaped with my son and was seeking asylum for young Prince Medrawd in the court of Good King Arthur. The varchog I chose to tell my tearful story to was Llenlleawc.

When I told Llenlleawc I had to leave the adolescent boy at Camelot with a strong protector so I could return to the Green Isle to help organize an overthrow of the wicked uncle, the lascivious varchog's eyes lit up. Medrawd was a very attractive young man. After all, he came from handsome stock. And I knew very well that Llenlleawc took a very special interest in attractive young men. He immediately agreed to take Medrawd as a protégé.

Medrawd knew that he was now at the court of the man who was his father and who had attempted to murder him when he was an infant. He also knew what kind of man Llenlleawc was and was not adverse to bearing up against the kind of attentions that bisexual varchog would bestow on him. I withdrew from the scene but was kept aware of what was happening to my nephew in Camelot as Llenlleawc's ward.

When Medrawd turned sixteen Llenlleawc prevailed on Arthur to dub the lad a varchog of the Table Round. Medrawd was a good candidate for the distinction. He had learned the manly arts of swordplay, equitation, jousting, and seduction. The young ladies of Camelot were won by his good looks and his charm. He kept in Llenlleawc's good graces by always being an apparent willing partner. Among Medrawd's libidinous conquests was Queen Gwenhwyvar herself. But that was not too surprising. The queen had as voracious a sexual appetite for boys as Medrawd had for all womankind.

Medrawd was still not a problem to his father-uncle. Arthur was fond of the lad. And after he had made him a varchog he included him in the royal hunting parties, jousting matches, and the grand festivities of the castle. It was then time for me to make my next move.

Arthur organized a great boar hunt for the Sunday after Lughnasadh in the year 533. Medrawd had turned sixteen years of age the prior Beltane and under Llenlleawc's tutelage had learned to be a very skillful hunter. He had his own brace of hounds and sat to horse with elegance and skill. At dawn the hunting party set out for a forest where a particularly ferocious boar had been spotted the previous week.

Medrawd was in wild pursuit of the hounds with the other youthful hunters. And Arthur, Gwalchmai, Bedwyr, and Llenlleawc were riding at a more leisurely pace.

I had anticipated their trail and placed myself up in a majestic oak that was at the edge of a clearing. The pyrotechnic skills that are part of the working accouterments of the sorceress trade were employed for the illusion I desired. As the four men came into the clearing, I created a fog around me. I then illuminated what appeared to be a circle of fire and appeared within this frame. The riders brought their horses to a fast stop. Their hounds went slinking off to the edge of the clearing.

From within the branches of the tree I addressed my brother:

"Hail, Arthur, King of the Britons. It is I – Priestess of the Goddess and Queen of the Fay."

Arthur never did know what my exact relationship was to the Fayfolk. Queen I was not. But who among the people who dwell below the Wall would know?

Arthur had to strain his eyes to make out the figure in the mists surrounded by fire. But he soon had me spotted.

"Hail Sister. Are you here to bring torments to your brother, or are you truly here on the Goddess' business?"

"I come in peace and to fulfill the will of the Goddess," I answered.

Gwalchmai, Bedwyr, and Llenlleawc still looked bewildered. They did not seem to know quite what to make of the apparition before them. They weren't meant to.

Arthur answered, "If you truly have come without malice, Sister, I welcome your appearance."

I answered him: "The Goddess would have it known, Arthur, that your royal son rides with you to the hounds this day."

"The Goddess is all-knowing and wise above the wisdom of men," Arthur replied. "However, I know of no royal son, neither riding with me today, nor at any other time."

"Sixteen years ago, Majestic Brother, you lay with our sister. By the advice of your evil sorcerer Myrddin, word went out from you concerning all children born close to the day of the expected arrival of your heir."

"I know whereof you speak, Morgan," Arthur admitted. "The remembrance haunts me yet."

A lie and I knew it. Arthur was incapable of feeling remorse about such a matter. But I let that pass.

I informed him further: "The blue gwledig of Skara Brae sent the child born of your royal union to visit the court of Llyr. The Goddess saw fit to protect that child and guided the wicker craft to shore where he was fostered by kindly fisherfolk."

Gwalchmai said in a hushed whisper, "A miracle." He was not to know yet that he had survived exactly such an ordeal. Had he known, it would certainly occur to him that Arthur was his uncle and Medrawd his brother. I smiled at the thought.

"If this be so, what would the Goddess have me do?" Arthur asked.

"It is the will of the Goddess that the child born of the royal house of Britain, through co-mingling of blood of the Gwledigs of Dyfneint and the Pen-Dragwns of Britain, should be recognized and magnified."

"Tell me the name of the man," Arthur asked.

"Gwalchmai and Bedwyr," I commanded. "Think hard. Remember the way Arthur appeared to you when he was riding with you in Palomides' warband. Who have you seen at Court who is an exact image of that early comrade of yours?"

Both men knew that Arthur had fucked and knocked up Morgawse many years before. And they had been aware that Medrawd reminded them of someone. But that someone was from a far past and had not fit into the picture of the current figures at Camelot. However, upon my prompting, they blurted out with one voice, "Medrawd."

It was apparent that both Arthur and Llenlleawc were dazed when they heard their companions' exclamation.

"Is this so, Morgan?" Arthur asked.

"Just so," I answered.

"Medrawd, then, is brother to Gaheris and Agravain," Gwalchmai blurted out.

"And brother, then, to you as well," I informed him.

It was just one more bit of mischief on my part.

I left Gwalchmai wondering whether he was Morgawse's son. I could see so on his face.

Having scattered enough discord for one day, I disappeared from their sight. It is no great feat of conjuration to fade into the foliage of an oak tree.

That was the extent of my retaliation for the insults Arthur had visited upon me. I had left Arthur with a problem. His closest companions were aware of the problem. I had exacted enough revenge. I was well on my way to forgiving my brother for his near rejection of me, his sister and a priestess of the Goddess. I never meant the retaliation to have the tragic repercussions that followed on Ambrys Plain on the Field of Camlann.

Arthur did acknowledge Medrawd as his son. He embroidered the tale with Llenlleawc's assistance by claiming that Medrawd was his son by Branwen, Queen of Ballynahinch, and thus of double royal blood. He welcomed the lad to sit at table with him on festive occasions.

Medrawd now became one of the king's favorites. But hatred for Arthur continued to burn in Medrawd's heart.

Forgive me, dear Britain, for what came to pass as the result.

CHAPTER SIXTEEN

The List

MEDRAWD SPEAKS:

My friends. This year, 540, I plan to collect debts owed me. Everyone here at Camelot knows I am Arthur's bastard. Da tries to treat me nice but I can never forget that he sent out an edict to have me killed when I was a newborn. He owes me for that and I intend to collect soon.

But he's not the only one on my list. How about Mum, who let Lot send me out to sea? Or my brothers who scorn me as bastard?

Even Gwalchmai, who is as much a bastard as I am, looks down on me.

None of them will escape my vengeance. And they all seem to think I am just the sweet young man I pretend to be.

I have made myself a list. An elimination list. I plan to rid the earth of Da, Mum, and my brothers. That would be just about my whole accursed family, leaving just me to rule.

Wait! I hadn't yet put Aunt Morgan on the list. Surely she shouldn't escape. No, wipe them all out. Auntie too. I alone will remain. And I will be king.

Oh, yes. Nicest irony of all. I want that hot twat bitch Gwenhwyvar to be my queen when I wear Arthur's crown. How I relish my plans. They crowd my mind day and night. You see, I just want to have fun.

You all know what a whore Mum is, don't you? She has a consuming sexual appetite. Even stronger than Da's. Even stronger than Llenlleawc's. And that says a lot. I doubt there is a male living in the Skara Brae islands who has not fucked Mum at least three-times over. I know it. My brothers know it. My father knows it. The world knows it.

The first step toward the elimination of my cursed family recently fell into my hands. A Viking by the name of Lamorak was sent to Skara Brae by the Norse on a peaceful trade mission. Our northern islands were seeking peace with our fierce Norse neighbors, so Lamorak was welcomed at the Skara Brae court. And he was welcomed especially by Mum, who seems to have a thing for the blond giants of Ultima Thule. Brother Gwalchmai is ample evidence of that, isn't he?

Having successfully completed the trade treaty, Lamorak rode down to Camelot to discuss a similar treaty with Da. With the English now under control, Da was looking for a way to avoid Viking invasions of our Island, so welcomed Lamorak enthusiastically.

Lamorak was quite open about his relationship with Mum. I don't doubt that she was as good a fuck as he said. But my brothers took umbrage at how public the Norseman was about spreading the details.

"Yes," Lamorak would say. "Castle Baledur is the greatest little love nest on your islands, Boys. The queen dowager up there among those little blue painted folk is a robust, redheaded ball of fire. When she takes you between her legs she has a special squeeze that practically sucks your brains right out of your head."

That was among the milder accolades he spread all over Camelot about Mum's extraordinary amorous abilities. Naturally that amused me. But it bothered Gwalchmai, Gaheris, Agravain, and Gareth to the point of near madness. Since Lamorak was an honored guest of the king there was nothing they could do about it but seethe.

In honor of the Norse diplomat, Arthur called a jousting tournament. Naturally, my brothers joined in. They knew that Lamorak would be in the lists and they hoped to take revenge on him in the course of the sport. One by one my brothers challenged the Viking to a bout. And one by one he unhorsed them. But barbarian that he was, when they were lying on the ground in defeat he scoffed at them openly.

Now everyone in Camelot knew that the man who bragged about fucking our mother also had humiliated four of her sons in the jousting matches. I had no intention of jousting with the man. But I could see that the situation was playing right into my hands. Lamorak's presence at Camelot might just help me eliminate a few family members whom I would like to see dispatched to Annwfn.

After the tournament, while my brothers were tending to their bruises, I suggested that someone go to Da and ask him to invite Mum down to Camelot. The idea was to provoke Lamorak to act in such a way when she was present that we would be justified in taking revenge. My foolish brothers thought that was a fine idea, and Gwalchmai approached Da.

The king was not too pleased with the idea of inviting his sister to visit. Both of his sisters were troublesome for him. But with his four nephews pleading to see their dear mother what could he do? He sent for her. She knew her Norse lover was down in the South with us and readily accepted the invitation.

When she arrived Arthur threw a fine feast for Mum. And all Camelot smirked when they saw the looks exchanged between Mum and Lamorak.

Da set her up at Castle Caerrys, the closest royal residence in the area, where she ruled with the total freedom she was accustomed to at Castle Baledur.

I made sure that my brothers were constantly on the alert for any hint of a tryst between Mum and the Viking. So we watched and waited. There was not a moment when Lamorak was not under the surveillance of one of my brothers. We watched as Mum and Lamorak exchanged whispered messages. It was clear enough what the import was of those exchanges. A tryst was being arranged. A fuck-fest that my brothers were determined to interrupt.

Mum had only been in the neighborhood for a few days when matters ripened. One evening Lamorak mounted his steed and rode toward Castle Caerrys. Brother Gaheris followed at a discrete distance. It was clear that Lamorak was not expecting to be followed because he gave not a single glance behind. When he arrived at the castle the guards let him right in.

Gaharis rode up to the gate, saluted the guards, and with two deft strokes decapitated them. He then entered the castle as though he had been invited. He had previously been at the castle helping Mum settle in when she arrived so he knew the layout well. He was able to proceed directly to her chamber.

By the time Gaharis got to the room, Lamorak and Mum were undressed and in bed and fucking away with abandon. They were so involved in their lovemaking that they did not hear Gaharis open the door.

Everything was working out so well for me. I couldn't have planned the whole business any better. Once in the room, Gaheris searched around for Lamorak's sword and threw it out the window. Then my brother brandished his sword and swooped down on the bed. Mum looked up, recognized her son, saw the sword in his hand, and screamed. Lamorak jumped out of bed seeking his sword. But it wasn't there.

He came back to the bed to fight Gaheris.

But Gaheris had grabbed Mum by the hair, pulled back her head, and chopped it right off. Blood was spurting all over the room, covering Gaheris and Lamorak, and drenching the sheets. Lamorak cringed in revulsion. Then, in order to avoid being dispatched by my brother's word, the Viking made a lunge and landed on his paramour's bleeding headless corpse.

Gaharis said, "I have done what I came to do. You, knave and coward, may get dressed and leave the castle unharmed."

Lamorak was stunned.

"I do not understand you, madman. You have killed your mother. You

153

might have killed me as well."

Gaharis answered the Norseman in such a foolish fashion I chuckle just recalling it.

When Gaheris told us his answer to the Viking's statement I thought Gwalchmai would choke with anger. I had a hard time suppressing a giggle. It was the silliest thing I ever heard. But I guess it was about what I'd expect from the weakest flame in the family's candelabra.

What Gaheris said was, "Your offense is natural to man, so you are not considered as culpable as my mother. She can shame us no longer. But even if your crime is not as foul as hers, I could not kill you now since you are naked and without arms. But take note, foul Norseman. When I next see you clothed and armed I will dispatch you to your Viking Annwfn."

Have you ever heard anything so ridiculous in all your life? No wonder I planned to kill of my whole family. Such people do not deserve to live in the same world with us sane folks.

The whole sordid story got out immediately. Da was shocked. He had no particular warm feelings left for his randy sister. Yet, matricide?

"A crime against all that is decent."

Those were his words, not mine.

The king immediately banished Gaheris from the kingdom below the Wall. I suppose he thought that was a rather lenient sentence for the crime. Or perhaps Myrddin told him what the exile could expect from the Pixies when he fled north of the wall and they discovered that he had murdered their queen dowager.

From my own sources, I heard how the subjects of Skara Brae dealt with the matricide. I am happy to report that Gaheris met the slowest death of any member of our family. The details are delicious. But I shan't burden you with them at present for I must get on with my tale.

Lamorak remained at Camelot after Mum's demise. He had no fear of man or beast as far as I could tell. For Gwalchmai and Agravain, he was a target for any kind of revenge that might present itself.

Gareth was revolted by the deed his brother had committed. He would not associate with his two brothers who approved of the matricide. I played a double-edged game. With Gwalchmai and Agravain, I pretended to agree that Lamorak had to die and that I was willing to be part of his murder. With Gareth, I pretended to agree that our mother's death was a heinous crime. I had plans for all three of them and needed to play the double role very carefully.

Gareth's wife, Dwynwen, was pregnant with her first child. Gareth was, naturally, delighted. He was also somewhat gullible. My plan for him did not require great subtlety.

That braggart womanizer Llenlleawc had little sense when it came to discretion. He may or may not have had his way with Dwynwen. It made no difference to me. He could not bear to have it thought that any woman could spurn his charms. I asked him if there was any chance that Dwynwen's pregnancy was any of his doing. He considered for a moment and answered that it was very possible and then laughed that sly laugh of his.

I spread word around Camelot that Llenlleawc was bragging that he had fathered the child in Dwynwen's belly. The varchogs asked Llenlleawc if such was the case. He would never, ever, deny such a possibility. I reported the gossip to my brother Gareth, who asked the other varchogs about it. All the varchogs agreed that Llenlleawc was claiming paternity.

At Camelot there was no way of challenging Llenlleawc. He was a favorite of both the king and the queen. And Gareth could no longer bear to be around his brothers who were responsible for the murder of our mother. Needing to disassociate himself both from his brothers and from the varchog favorite, he left Camelot under cover of night and disappeared into the countryside. But I knew we would see him again.

Everything came to a head at Surluse. Arthur had called a tournament at Castle Surluse. All Camelot went there for the jousting festival.

At that tournament, as usual, Llenlleawc challenged any and all comers. No varchog in the land accepted because Llenlleawc truly was an unbeatable champion. But at Surluse, a challenger to Llenlleawc did appear. A varchog incognito in white armor and white shield. He challenged Llenlleawc. There was a stir of excitement among the spectators. Many had never seen Llenlleawc actually defend himself since it had been a long time since anyone had accepted his challenge. No one seemed to know who the varchog incognito was. I knew, though. It could only be one person. A very foolhardy person indeed. But one burning with revenge in his breast.

The contestants entered the lists and charged. The varchog incognito, who, as you have guessed, was Gareth, was sorely mismatched. He was a very good horseman and wielded his weapons way above average. But he was no match for the finest jouster in all Britain. Gareth's fierceness was astounding. He fought like a wild man. Neither combatant seemed able to knock the other off his horse.

I don't believe Llenlleawc actually meant to kill his opponent. But after repeated clashes, Gareth was not fast enough in using his shield to deflect his adversary's blow and Llenlleawc's lance went right into the young man's heart. When Llenlleawc removed Gareth's helmet and saw who he had killed, he wept. How touching, I'm sure.

I giggled. But no one was aware of my reaction. Everyone was too involved with what they perceived as a tragedy.

There was no tournament the next day. The day was devoted to mourning for Arthur's stricken nephew Gareth. You can imagine how deeply moved I was. One more family member had bitten the dust. Things were coming along splendidly.

The next day, though, the tournament was reconvened. After all, deaths were not all that unusual in jousts. It was known that Lamorak would challenge all comers at the tournament. Gwalchmai saw this as the opportunity to avenge himself on our mother's lover. But he wouldn't fight Lamorak openly. Lamorak was clearly a better jouster than any of us. Llenlleawc would not be jousting after the tragedy of Gareth's death. So the Norseman was very likely the next greatest gladiator in the land. Gwalchmai's plan was to meet Lamorak when he was leaving the tournament and while everyone was watching the next match.

Lamorak did, indeed, enter the contest. And I assume he fought well. I was not there to witness the jousts. I was with my brothers just outside the walls. When Lamorak left the lists he was riding all alone outside the walls. Gwalchmai stepped in front of him and drove a lance into Lamorak's horse, felling it immediately.

Lamorak hurled himself off the falling horse and unsheathed his sword while in the air. An astounding feat. This was a warrior to admire. I held back while Gwalchmai and Agravain attacked him with their swords. While he was thus engaged, I stepped up from behind and drove my sword through his back. He was dead immediately. My two brothers and I quickly ran around the fence, entered the tournament stands, and watched the proceedings as though we had been there all the time. When the crowd filed out of the tournament field, they came across the bodies of the horse and the Viking. We were all astounded. Who could have done the filthy deed? No one knew. Well, three of us knew. But we weren't telling.

My list was getting smaller and smaller. Crossed off now were Mum, Gaheris, and Gareth. I still had Da, Gwalchmai, Agravain, and Aunt Morgan.

Then word came from the Continent. Ban and Bors both had died since the Battle of Mount Badon. Their sons, Hoel and Dysgyfdawd, sent word that they needed help against the barbarian Franks and Burgunds. Years before, Arthur had promised assistance. Our continental cousins were calling for us to repay them for their help in our time of need.

Da promised our continental relatives he would lead an army to their assistance.

I knew he would be out of the country with his most powerful varchogs. I needed to make sure he would appoint me as regent in his absence. With him out of the way, and with the power of the throne turned over to me, I knew I would be able to continue to fuck my stepmother (who was, incidentally, also my aunt by marriage). And if I could work out a treaty with the barbarians on the Continent I could defeat my father and my remaining brothers on the battlefield and assume supreme power in the land.

Da became convinced that he needed to leave a blood relative behind as regent while he was out of the country. Who was left? Little me.

Everything seems to be coming my way. The king leaves tomorrow evening to bring assistance to our cousins in Lesser Britain and in Bawn.

The rest is up to fate.

CHAPTER SEVENTEEN

The End of Camelot

BEDWYR SPEAKS:

Peace! That's what we had in Britain. Peace. From our victory over the English at Mount Badon in 521 until the Battle of Camlann in 542, we had what the people who speak Latin call the *Pax Arthuriana*.

And I hated it.

Twenty-one years of boring peace. Not that we didn't have skirmishes now and then. Even during the Roman occupation there had been skirmishes with Pixies, Irish, Vikings, and, of course, English. The Pixies were not a problem for us during the Arthurian Peace. After we defeated them at Arderydd Ford back in 518, they were nominally our allies. Not allies you could trust. But still, they kept behind the Wall. But the Irish would make raids from time to time, pulling ashore in their curraghs. Our forces met and destroyed them with ease. And despite the death of the Viking diplomat, Lamorak, we still had a treaty with the Norsemen. And it protected us from them. The English kept to themselves after Mount Badon, except for an occasional raiding party when they got hungry. But while Arthur was king we had that enormous lull – peace.

Not so across the Sleeve on the Continent. The Vandals, Visigoths and Franks were running wild all over Gawl. Their target was the riches of Rome. They didn't bother with us because we could defend ourselves. The Roman Legions, however, could not hold the barbarians back in their trek through Gawl.

When Arthur had called on his uncles in Nanteos and Bawn to help us fight off the English back in 518, they had responded by leading their troops to our defense. Arthur, at the time, promised to help them if they should ever need our assistance. While Clovis the Frank was busy fighting the Northern Gawls, Gwledigs Ban and Bors were not being attacked by the Franks or Burgunds and were free to help us. Now, Clovis' son Childeric was threatening the demesnes of our allies on the continent. Both Bors and Ban had since been laid to rest and their spirits ferried to Annwfn. Their successors, Hoel of Nanteos and Dysgyfdawd of Bawn, were relatives of Arthur. Dysgyfdawd was reported to be Llenlleawc's step-brother and apparently was in some kind of adversarial relationship with him. Whatever the case, Arthur was beholden to the two allies we had on the Continent. Childeric the Frank was threatening Nanteos and Cynric the Burgund was making hostile demands on Bawn. So our allies called for help. Arthur asked me to take Gwalchmai across the water to discuss with our Gawlic brethren what we might be able to do to assist them.

Gwalchmai and I were ferried across the Sleeve to Lesser Britain, landing at Plwbyln. We ordinarily would have been able to ride to Nanteos easily in three days if we had no trouble at the river crossings. As it turned out, it took us a week to get to Hoel's court on the Lwyr River.

We were riding along, enjoying the fair countryside but not loitering, when we arrived at the banks of the Wlyn. We were challenged by three Frankish horsemen. I knew them to be Franks by the emblems on their shields.

"Whence come you, Strangers?" asked the more surly of the three.

"From the court of good King Arthur in Camelot," Gwalchmai answered.

"You may turn about and return to 'Good King Arthur in Camelot' if you wish to continue breathing," the ugly Frank announced.

"You may bend down and kiss my ass or I may have to chop off your fucking head and plant your lips smack dab on my asshole," Gwalchmai answered.

There was always a quip on my companion's lips. This particular quip seemed to displease the Frank particularly.

The bad-ass Frank dressed his shield and leveled his lance by way of intimidation. His companions openly scoffed at us. Gwalchmai unsheathed his sword, spurred his horse, and headed in what appeared to be directly at the challenging horseman. The look of surprise on this opponent's face caused me to burst out laughing, for I knew exactly what my companion was doing. Causing his horse to deftly sidestep the pointed lance, with a sudden upstroke of the sword, Gwalchmai cut the lance in half and simultaneously unhorsed the Frank.

His two companions' scoffs tuned into sudden expressions of surprise. As they looked on, stunned, I rode between the two of them and with two strokes of my sword cut off their gods damned heads. As the first Frank looked up from the ground in amazement, Gwalchmai rode his horse over him and spit. The fallen guard arose groggily, only to meet Gwalchmai's sword piercing his heart.

So much for the enemy threatening our allies.

When we arrived at Hoel's court in the Nanteos of Lesser Britain we told him of our encounter with his Frankish enemies. Hoel had a laugh that resounded throughout the great hall of his castle. He said that if Arthur could send him a hundred varchogs of our caliber we could defeat the entire armies of the Franks and the Burgunds. We told him Arthur meant to honor the promise he had made back in Year 518 to come to the aid of Lesser Britain when needed. We assured him we had authority to promise him the entire army at Arthur's disposal, but that it would have to be split into two equal sections once we reached the Continent, half coming to Nanteos and half to Bawn. Hoel embraced us, feasted us, provide us with wine and wenches for the next two days, and bid us gods' speed on our way to Bawn.

We met no opposition of any kind between Nanteos and Bawn.

Varchog Dysgyfdawd greeted us when we arrived at Bawn. He warily asked about the health of his step-brother Llenlleawc. And when assured that he was well Dysgyfdawd seemed not particularly pleased. However, he welcomed the help Arthur had authorized us to offer.

And again, it was feasting, wine, and fucking for several days before we set out to return to Camelot to tell Arthur of our adventures.

When we told him how we had disposed of the three Franks at the river ford Arthur's laugh was nearly as exuberant as that of his cousin on the banks of the Lwyr.

"Aye, Lads," he said. "Just as you disposed of those three scoundrels, so shall we decimate the cowardly forces of the Franks and Burgunds. Do you look forward to some fine battles after all these years of peace?"

"Yes, Arthur. Our spears and swords have been too long idle. They crave the blood of barbarians," Gwalchmai answered.

I added my hearty agreement to his words. It was to be war. Sweet war. It seemed there would not be blood-letting on our shores, thus maintaining the Arthurian Peace. But on the Continent, an honorable set of battles against people of the same race as the hated English was in store for us. I anticipated a great deal of joy in the coming months.

So, in 541, Arthur led his troops to the Continent. The younger men in our army had never experienced real battle, only skirmishes with sporadic stealth attacks. These young warriors were as anxious to meet the enemy as those of us who were battle seasoned.

Arthur had left Medrawd in charge of the kingdom as viceroy until his return. Llenlleawc did not accompany us on the campaign since he felt his presence would not be welcomed by his step-brother, the Gwledig of Bawn. I believe that there was more to it than that. I wasn't at all sure that Arthur felt Medrawd had the maturity yet to rule as viceroy without the counsel of a great warrior. Arthur considered Llenlleawc such a warrior.

The Sleeve crossing was difficult this time. A storm beat the waves to such an extent that several of our boats nearly capsized. When we landed at Plwbyln half our troops were sick and wobbly. It was stormy ashore as well. So we were a sick, bedraggled looking crew. We marched south in such condition as we were in.

When we got to the Lwyr River we were met by Hoel and his army of well over a thousand men. We felt sure that with his forces and ours we could send Franks, Burgunds, and whatever other barbarians we might meet in the lands of Gawl, running back to their black forests nursing their wounds.

We moved east as a combined army, following the north bank of the Lwyr. The plan was to keep the force intact as we moved in the general direction of Bawn. If we should meet any of Childeric's army we would encounter it full force. If our scouts found any Frankish forces to the north, half of our troops would head in that direction to meet them and the rest would proceed on to Bawn.

As we proceeded, our scouts sought out the army of the Franks. Day after day they came back to report that there was no sign of the barbarians as far north as the Seyn. This was very strange indeed. For by all reports, the Franks and Burgunds were swarming all over the countryside. We did not know what to make of the situation.

Then, on the fourteenth day of Nolag, one of our varchogs came riding through a rainstorm into camp at full speed. To our great surprise it was Llenlleawc. I knew at once that he could not be bringing good news.

Arthur, Hoel, Gwalchmai, Llenlleawc, and I repaired to a hastily prepared pavilion. Llenlleawc spoke:

"Arthur, My Lords. I am a bearer of evil tidings. The gods forgive me for being the carrier of news of such events as will shock your ears and astound your hearts.

"A few days after your embarkation to this continent with your troops, the viceroy Medrawd betrayed you in myriad ways. He robbed the royal treasury, removed your crown, and declared that all your ships had sunk in the Sleeve and that you and all your men had drowned. Myrddin came to me and told me that the announcement was false. That you had landed safely and had joined forces with Hoel.

"Medrawd also announced that your queen, Gwenhwyvar, had agreed to be his consort and that they would be crowned high king and queen by a High Druid. Myrddin, again, told me that it was true that Medrawd and Gwenhwyvar were cohabiting and apparently smothered in mutual bliss, but that no high druid in the land would marry them, much less officiate at any kind of coronation.

"But worst news of all for Britain, My Pen-Dragwn, is that the traitor Medrawd had been negotiating with Childeric the Frank as soon as he knew you would be leaving our land with the troops. While you are seeking Childeric's army here in Gawl, the Frank is leading his troops across the Sleeve to stand against you on your return. In exchange, the Franks are promised the land of Reged as their fiefdom."

It was betrayal. Absolute betrayal. The Franks had been promised large portions of our Britain in return for supporting Arthur's bastard son in his usurpation of his father's crown. I have wept few times in my life. But on that occasion, tears swarmed down my cheeks. I could see that it was the same with Gwalchmai. Arthur turned ashen, sat sullenly on a camp bench, sunk his head into his hands, and physically shook until I thought he might tremble to death.

Gwenhwyvar's infidelity did not surprise me in the least. Unlike the sick ideas of the Christians about the inferiority of women, a Celtic queen can take on lovers. Gwenhwyvar had an insatiable sexual appetite. I can't fault her for that. I have always valued sexuality above everything except warfare. She had fucked every male in Camelot except me. I may have fucked every female in the court except her. But she was Arthur's wife and off-limits as far as I was concerned. I had seen, long before now, that she and Medrawd had been fucking away like there was no tomorrow. Good Lleu! Arthur's son. I'm no prude but that sickened me.

What did surprise me was Medrawd's duplicity. I thought we knew the young man. That he would betray Britain by inviting in the foreign host was truly shocking. It was greater treachery than that of Vortigern. The greatest duplicity in the history of our nation. It was not to be borne.

When Arthur seemingly got hold of himself, he spoke to us.

"My companions. This is the result of a very great wrong I committed many years ago. The gods are punishing me for a carnal act held foul by gods and goddesses."

What rot! I had known Arthur for nearly thirty years, and had never heard him whimper before. I felt like slapping some sense into him. I was disgusted with Medrawd. I was disgusted with Gwenhwyvar. And now I was disgusted with Arthur. That kind of unmanly talk from a great warrior was most unbecoming. I strode out of the pavilion saddened by the miserable turn the world had taken.

I wandered about camp for nearly an hour, the drizzling rain depressing my mood even further. At length I felt that perhaps Arthur would have stopped sniveling and I returned to his pavilion. When I got to the tent Hoel and Llenlleawc were not there.

Arthur and Gwalchmai were drinking a horn of wine when I entered. Whether Gwalchmai had shaken our old companion out of his silly talk of retribution by the gods, or whether Arthur's good sense had simply returned, I never knew. But here my companions were, talking about how we had to get our troops moved back across the Sleeve to wipe out that little bastard who had dared to sully Britain by inviting in the Frankish dogs. I called for a horn of wine myself, and the three of us were downing the good Gawl wine when Hoel and Llenlleawc returned.

"I have met with my counselors," Hoel said. "We will join you back to Britain where we will fight at your side against our common enemy, the Franks."

Llenlleawc chimed in. "I have spread word to the troops, Arthur. They now know of Medrawd's betrayal and are vowing 'Death to the traitor.'"

We were all, now, flush with the fire of vengeance. When Arthur went out to address the troops, even the weather seemed to join in our spirit, for the drizzle that had accompanied us ever since we had started out for the Continent faded, and a bit of Gawlic sunshine peeped through.

Our ferrying back across the Sleeve to Britain was accompanied by much more friendly seas than our crossing to the Continent. With Hoel's troops accompanying us, we were nearly twice the size of the force that had departed from the homeland. We landed at Llongborth without opposition from the enemy. Medrawd certainly had received intelligence that we had arrived because our own spies informed us that he was leading his troops south onto Ambrys Plain. We learned that his forces included many British troops belonging to gwledigs who had not pledged to join the expedition to Lesser Britain. Medrawd had secured their loyalty. In addition to the Britons there was the much larger force of the Franks, led towards the fray by their own king, Childeric. I smelled blood. And the odor was pleasing.

It was two days before Medrawd's forces and ours met in battle position at Camlann Field. Each side spent a day in preparation for the battle. We had learned that Gwenhwyvar had accompanied her new lover, Medrawd, south to the battlefield. It was just like her. She was there to see her new paramour defeat her rejected husband.

Myrddin's secret stealth-force was able to infiltrate the enemy camp and kidnap the duplicitous queen and carry her back to our encampment. Arthur, Gwalchmai, Hoel, and I were consulting a detailed map of the Camlann area when Myrddin entered the pavilion unannounced.

"Arthur," he smiled. "My agents have brought us a package. Pray step outside and see what we have."

Intrigued, we hurried out. There, wrapped tight in homespun cloth and gagged with the same material, lay a female figure with long blonde hair. Defiance and outrage blazed from those deep blue eyes. When Arthur realized who it was, rage was the only expression on his face. I was sorry Llenlleawc was not present. He had been Gwenhwyvar's most consistent lover other than Arthur for many years. It would have been interesting to see his response. But unfortunately he was elsewhere in the camp at the time.

"Well, well, well," said Arthur. "Look what we have here. A prisoner known to consort with the enemy of Britain. Tell me, Myrddin. What do the gods suggest for a traitor such as this?"

"It has been written in the Annals of the Wise Ones, Arthur, that the rending by stallions is the only offering the gods will receive in propitiation for such defiling of the sacred earth of Britain."

"Just so," said Arthur.

I didn't have the slightest idea what the fuck they were talking about. And I doubt that any of the others did either. So I just waited and watched to see what would happen.

Arthur ordered that four battle coursers be brought to the scene. Then he ordered Gwalchmai and me to unbind the wrappings holding the queen, including the gag. Then we were told to strip the lady naked.

Four husky guards were then called to tether each of Gwenhwyvar's limbs to a stallion.

It was clear that Gwenhwyvar knew what was happening to her. To her credit she did not plead with Arthur nor did she whimper. She glared defiance at each of us. This was the first time since I knew her that I respected the lady. This could have been a Celtic warrior queen. She was a free soul to the end.

At a sign from Arthur the four stallions were sent moving in directions away from the lady tied to them. The sound of her body being rent into pieces was unlike anything I had ever heard on any battlefield. It was a death of deepest vengeance. The ropes were cut when Gwenhwyvar had been reduced to bits of meat, bone and offal spread out the field before us.

Myrddin called the kennelmen to bring forth the hounds of battle.

The hounds sniffed at the pieces that were left of our former queen and reduced them to dogs' dinner. Arthur watched until there was little left of the woman he had been married to for most of his life. Then we followed him back into his pavilion to partake of a horn of mead.

At dawn the next day our troops met the enemy in direct battle on Camlann Field. The troops were well matched and victory was not clear for either side the entire morning. With the scent of battle, all my senses were heightened, as they always were in war.

I managed to trample, run through, decapitate and wound warrior after warrior. I could see that it was so, as well, with Gwalchmai, Llenlleawc, Agravain, and Hoel. Arthur himself was in the thick of the battle. He had never been the kind of general who sits behind the fray and keeps his hands unbloodied.

All afternoon the fight raged. Our troops were beginning to get the upper hand. The enemy was wearying. Our troops were convinced we had right on our side. Arthur was the king chosen by the gods.

Medrawd was the bastard who had usurped the crown. The Franks were invading dogs as filthy as the English. Conviction carried our side with a force not available to the enemy.

Many a companion lost his life that day as his blood seeped into the soil of Britain. My lifetime companion Gwalchmai lay dead of a wound through that brave heart of his. Agravain, another of Arthur's nephews, was trampled to death during the battle. Llenlleawc was victim of a Frankish lance. Death finally visited the greatest varchogs of Britain.

Late that afternoon Arthur encountered Medrawd on the banks of the Avawn River. The two leaders met face to face. Word spread to all the warriors. By all civilized rules of war, when the commanders engage in personal battle, hostilities on the field cease. The engagement is settled by hand-to-hand combat of the leaders.

The two dismounted and faced each other on the ground. They looked each other in the eye. Father to son. Legitimate king to usurper. Hero to traitor. Each attempted to reach the other with the weapons he had in hand. Each was equipped with sword and shield. Medrawd was younger, lither, faster, and probably stronger. But Arthur had a lifetime of practice with his sword.

The battlefield was hushed. The slaughter had been great. Of the two large forces, a remnant of less than half remained alive or unwounded.

The battle of the soldiers was over. The decision rested with the outcome of a contest unto death of two chiefs.

The clang of iron on iron rang out over the silence of the stilled battleground. Arthur would feint to the right. Medrawd's shield would deflect. Medrawd followed with an attempted blow to Arthur's helmet. I had seen Arthur fight ever since I knew him. He was the best swordsman in Britain. But his son must have inherited his father's adeptness. There was no cheering on the part of the on-lookers. Just marvel at the expertise of the protagonists.

Just as the sun set, Arthur lunged and managed to swing his sword below Medrawd's shield and penetrate the area of the kidneys. As he extricated his sword it pulled Medrawd towards him. Medrawd, with his last ounce of strength, brandished his sword with both hands, striking Arthur on the head. The sword cut through the helmet, cutting into the king's skull. Arthur pulled the sword out of his son and Medrawd fell dead at his feet. Arthur fell then upon his son, mortally wounded. The remaining troops were left in great confusion.

One of Medrawd's lieutenants approached and hauled away the corpse of his leader. Eerily, all the remaining live troops withdrew from the battlefield leaving only one of our captains, a man named Lucan, and me to care for our leader.

Lucan was badly wounded himself. Nonetheless, he and I attempted to lift Arthur. With the exertion of doing so, Lucan's intestines burst through his abdominal wound and he expired before us. We dropped Arthur as Lucan's grasp loosened. This revived Arthur enough that he could view the battlefield. The grim view he had was of camp followers robbing the dead and killing the wounded. Arthur sighed, not from his physical pain, but at the view of the evil that lurks in the heart of the human race.

Arthur, who had been the mightiest monarch our nation had ever known, was left there on the banks of the Avawn by all but me. There were none to mourn for the stricken hero but the son of a churl who had risen to prominence by knowing the son of a king.

Arthur revived enough to be able to speak to me.

"Bedwyr, old companion. Take my sword to the river and cast it as far out as you can."

"Yes, Arthur," I assented. "If that is what you really want me to do."

As I stood on the banks of the Avawn I looked at this sword, Excalibur, that had carried British troops to victory upon victory. Whether today's fight had resulted in victory or defeat, I did not know. No one knew. But the sword was a symbol to our people. I hesitated to toss it into the brink. Yet if such was Arthur's dying wish, I would do it.

With all my strength I hurled the mighty sword into the Avawn. And as I did so I was overcome by a hallucination. For what I thought I saw was a lady's arm reach out of the waters, catch Excalibur, brandish it, and pull it into the flowing stream of the beautiful river.

I returned to inform Arthur that I had done his bidding and mentioned the vision of the arm from the water. His lips formed a word I could not decipher and he died in my arms.

To my surprise, at that moment a woman appeared at my side. She seemed to manifest herself out of thin air. On closer inspection I realized it was Arthur's sister, Morgan. She said not a word. She motioned towards the river where I saw a barge moving upstream in our direction. I knew what I was to do. I assisted Morgan in carrying the body of my king and companion to the edge of the river. The barge pulled to shore and Morgan and I placed the king's body on the barge.

Then, without a word, the gold colored barge pushed out into the river's flow again, carrying the companion of my youth off…where?

The last I saw of Arthur was his body laid out on the barge attended by Morgan, her acolyte Nimue, and a priestess I believe might have been the Lady of the Lake.

CHAPTER EIGHTEEN

The Heart of Britain

MORGAN SPEAKS:

Gone. All gone. Within the last year they have all left our earth and are now in Annwfn. Of our whole family, only I remain alive. My brother Arthur. My sister Morgawse. My nephews Gwalchmai, Gaheris, Agravain, Gareth, and Medrawd. All gone.

Morgawse was murdered by Gaheris. Gaheris was put to death by the Pixies for matricide. Gareth was killed by Llenlleawc while jousting. Gwalchmai, Agravain and Medrawd died on the Battlefield of Camlann. And Arthur, hero of Britain, was slain by his bastard son in deadly battle.

Many years ago I forgave my brother Arthur for the wrongs he had committed against the Goddess and me. Over the years I had exacted enough vengeance to satisfy both me and the Goddess. Now Arthur was dead and my heart was heavy laden with sorrow. Despite his grievous faults, he had protected the holy soil of Britain against the scum that would assail us from all sides. I knew the Goddess would welcome his soul and send it well cleansed to Annwfn.

So we bore his corpse to Avalon on the Golden Barge. Once on the Holy Isle, the rites of Wycha were performed over his body. His heart was removed and incinerated on the Goddess Stone. The ashes of that brave heart were then buried beneath the stone itself.

So long as Avalon endured and the Goddess was worshiped on our shores, we knew that Arthur's heart, the Heart of Britain, would protect us from such filth as the English, Irish, Vikings, or other outsiders.

After the rites were duly performed, we invited Myrddin to Avalon. I still did not like or trust the man. But he was the only one available to undertake the next necessary step.

Myrddin took the king's body, minus its heart, across the waters of Lake Avalloc to the abbey of the Christian monks. Those monks celebrated their lugubrious rites over the body that had lived and died a devotee of the Goddess, Cerunnos, Lleu, Llyr, and all the gods who had watched over Britain since our Island was brought forth from the sea.

Arthur was buried at the Abbey of Saint Joseph of Arimathea, not far from the thorn bush the monks believe to be holy to their religion. If they would but listen, we could tell them that bush was placed there by Dagda, the god of the earth, long before their religion was born. That religion based on some kind of evil god who must regularly drink his son's blood. Well, their religion got our king's body. We retained his heart.

Arthur was buried in the abbey cemetery, not with his shield, but with a leaden cross. And on the cross were inscribed words in the hated language of the people who occupied our Island for four hundred years:

HIC IACET SEPULTUS INCLITUS REX ARTURIUS IN INSULA AVALONIA.

The monks were deceived by the person who inscribed those words on the cross. They did not know that the writing referred to Arthur's heart, which was, indeed, buried on the Island of Avalon and will remain there to protect Britain forever.

ABOUT THE AUTHOR

Tim Desmondes

Tim Desmondes has written five works of fiction.

He lives with his wife in a Southern California beach community.

They sit of an evening on their balcony, sipping sundowners, and observing the sun descend into the Pacific.

How sweet it is.

Tim Desmondes is also the author of:

- » *Sex and Loathing in Hollywood*
- » *Sexual Diversity and Perversity in California*
- » *Dracula Sucks Hollywood Dudes*
- » *Venus Does Adonis While Apollo Shags a Tree*

These books and more are available at Amazon.com, TheNazcaPlainsCorp.com, or your local bookstore.